The Wonderful World of Marceline

By

Diane Manley

First Electronic Edition: August 2021
First Print Edition: October 2021

Book Design, Formatting and Publishing by
D. D. Scott's
LetLoveGlow Author Services

Indianapolis, Indiana
www.LetLoveGlow.com

PRAISE FOR

THE WONDERFUL WORLD OF MARCELINE:

"Such an incredible debut book by an author I can't wait to read more of! And the absolute best hero written that I've read for a long while! This romantic comedy has it all – the laughs, the warm hearts, and a magical story!"

~~ **D. D. Scott**, International Bestselling Author

*Dedicated to Jean and Carolyn
and all those who share favorite books
with the ones they love.*

Laughter is timeless,
imagination has no age,
dreams are forever.

~~ Walt Disney

PART I
The Project

CHAPTER 1

Recently, while looking for a gift in a local novelty shop, I ran across a print of a poem entitled *Things My Mother Taught Me.* The author must have been eavesdropping during my childhood as there was simply no other way that "Anonymous" could have penned every bit of the nonsensical wisdom my mother passed onto me over the years.

Standing alone in the store, laughing aloud (which I admit drew a few quizzical stares from the other customers), I realized I could quote each of the hyperboles listed on the framed print, verbatim. If they were part of a new gameshow called *"Name That Expression"*, I would have gotten every one of them right in under three words.

But that day, two of my mother's infamous bits of advice stood out from the others.

The first was:

If I told you once, I've told you a million times, never exaggerate!

I should have followed that one.

Her second morsel of wisdom was this one:
Never ruin a good story with the facts!
I should never have obeyed that one. And that was how I ended up in my current predicament.

I have to admit, every now and again, I might be inclined to stretch the truth and send out signals which aren't exactly what I mean. It's definitely gotten me into trouble from time to time, and that is how I wound up being sent to a small town in rural Missouri – which is where my story begins, although I should probably clue you in on how I got there.

My name is Jessica James. And yes, my parents clearly had a sick sense of humor. All of my friends, colleagues, pretty much everybody except my Granny, call me Jess (NEVER Jessie, for obvious reasons). To Granny, I'm better known as Jessica Dear. "How have you been, Jessica Dear?" "When am I going to see you, Jessica Dear?" "When are you going to make me a Great-Grandmother, Jessica Dear?" That last question, by the way, I refuse to answer!

I was born in Los Angeles (more specifically, Sherman Oaks) and, like so many of my friends, I followed a career in television after graduating Summa Cum Laude from UCLA. I got a fabulous job with one of the major networks and am on the fast track to an illustrious career.

Ok, the truth versus the exaggerated version is that I graduated with an average GPA from Pacific Union College, and I now work for a small, relatively unknown, cable channel – *LeisureTV*, who wants to become a combination of *HGTV*, *The Food Network*, and *ABC Family*. Actually, *Disney+* should be added to the list because recently our executive producers pitched a new show with Disney roots … but I'm getting ahead of myself.

I live with Mona, my very large Monstera house plant, in an otherwise minimalistic studio apartment, furnished in what I like to call "tasteful tacky" (meaning it's full of great garage sale finds and flea market treasures). It's a perfect location. Only fifteen minutes from work and thirty minutes, without traffic, to my parents' house.

You would think living so close to work I would never be late, or could even be early some days, but that's just not in my DNA. I'm usually running out the door in a panic and barely making it to my cubical by 9 o'clock (and fifty-nine seconds).

Take the day that changed my life, for example...

Waking up to the brilliant California sunshine pouring through my bedroom window, I wondered how a day starting so spectacularly could be anything less than perfect. And it was even a Friday!

Full of energy, I jumped in and out of the shower, threw on my new floral sundress and favorite, strappy black sandals, all in record time. I styled my naturally highlighted blond hair and artfully applied designer cosmetics to enhance my flawless complexion.

I wish!

Truth: I did shower and choose the sundress and sandals, but as for the rest, I pulled my brown hair into a haphazard bun at the top of my head, added some mascara to lengthen what few lashes I have around my dark eyes and applied a touch of my favorite drug-store-brand lip gloss – Rebel Rose.

Realizing that I was ready for work early – a miracle in itself – I decided to straighten the mess in my apartment before heading out the door. I was in such a good mood, singing at the top of my lungs as I began to clean, that I half expected to see little woodland animals dancing around, helping me.

Living alone with no one to badger me about the mess in my apartment, I usually waited until I had lost something important before setting out on a massive cleaning marathon. But with extra time that morning, I decided to trash the junk mail lying on the entry bench, move a few dishes into the kitchen and straighten the magazines scattered on the coffee table.

Picking up the latest *Cosmo*, a headline caught my eye – #JOB*GOALS* - *Do What You Love, Get A Fat Paycheck*. I already liked what I did, but who couldn't use a fatter paycheck?

Sitting down to scan the article, I became completely engrossed in reading about taking risks and challenging oneself, and I devoured the tips presented that could help me move ahead in my career. Eventually glancing up from the magazine, I spotted the clock on the wall.

Oh NO! I should have left five minutes ago!

Being late was definitely not on *Cosmo's* list of tips to improve one's career.

Grabbing my bag, I flew out the door, fumbled a few seconds with the lock and sprinted down the steps towards my car. *Can someone please explain to me why I always think I have time to do one more thing before I leave my apartment?*

As I reached the bottom landing, I ran smack into another tenant carrying a bag of groceries up to his unit.

"Sorry," I murmured and offered a meek smile.

I don't remember him – he's pretty cute.

'Cute guy' gave me a look as if to say, "Watch where you are going, lady" and continued to trudge up the stairs.

I changed my mind. He wasn't so cute, after all.

Aside from Mrs. Jackson, I didn't really know any of the residents in my building. It seemed everyone was always coming and going in a rush as if they were headed off to save the world. Me? I was just in a hurry because I was going to be late for work, again!

My route to the office was always timed perfectly, but that morning, after getting lost in the *Cosmo* article, my timing was a bit off. I missed the stoplights I normally made, didn't secure my usual parking space and, by the time I raced off the elevator, the clock in the reception area read 9:10. Of all days to arrive a teeny bit late! It's the morning of our weekly staff meeting, which started promptly at – you guessed it – 9:00.

I scurried into the conference room. My eleven colleagues from the production team, seated around the oval, black lacquer table, all looked up at the same time. Not one of them appeared to be shocked that I was tardy. *Luckily, I have a great boss, Cassandra, and I love my co-workers, even though they harass me mercilessly over what they call my 'Jessisms'.*

"Nice of you to join us, Jess," Cassandra quipped, straightening the stack of paper in front of her.

Cassandra is in her mid-forties, goes to the gym regularly, gets manicures and highlights routinely, and rocks a perfectly cut suit and stilettos, every day. It wouldn't surprise me if she even dressed for bed in tailored flannels and high-heeled bunny slippers. Everyone's first impression of her is that she is completely unapproachable and downright scary, but that couldn't be further from the truth. She is actually a great listener, understanding, and open to the staff's ideas. Although, she can also be quite stubborn. And when she has made up her mind, there is absolutely no chance of changing it!

Lucy, a team member from our Marketing Department, was powering up her tablet, so evidently she had just taken her seat, which made me feel somewhat better. Apparently, I wasn't the only one who missed the 9:00 start time.

"Did another random stray cat race into your apartment, Jess?" Trevor asked and chuckled.

Trevor is this gorgeous, 6'1", sun-bleached blond, crystal blue-eyed, single guy, whose cubical was next to mine. A near perfect specimen, he's smart, funny, and completely out of my league! Even though his desk was just over the partition, having never worked directly on a project together, he, for the most part, had remained an enigma. So far, the only downside to him was his willingness to repeat a private conversation he overheard me having at my desk about a mishap I had a few months ago with a stray tabby cat. Although I must say, he not only had the entire staff in hysterics, at my expense, but he had me laughing at myself as well.

I read somewhere (probably *Cosmo*, since a half-page article is about the limit of my attention span) that 'laughing at oneself is good for a person's health', which is why I didn't feel too bad about the junk food I purchased from the vending machine later that day to soothe my ego.

Trevor was still trying to figure out how a couple of months ago a tabby cat, about the size of a small lion, snuck between my feet and ran into my apartment as I was leaving for work. He must have been listening in as I described in dramatic fashion to my best friend, Mollie, how the cat practically knocked me over and started jumping from one piece of furniture to another, causing complete havoc. After what seemed like an hour of chasing the cat/lion around my apartment, I was able to finally shoo it out the front door and down the steps to the first floor where a very relieved Mrs. Jackson was extremely happy that I found her Cuddles and had brought him back home to her. I wound up not only being late for work, but also had several unsightly bruises on my body that lasted for months – okay, maybe a few days – but they were a really ugly shade of greenish purple that clashed with every outfit in my closet. The upshot was that Mrs. Jackson felt so indebted to me she brought me a plate of homemade chocolate chip cookies every couple of weeks as a thank you. And who doesn't love a plate of warm, chocolate chip cookies?!

After blushing at the reference to an incident I would rather forget, I slouched I my chair trying not to draw any additional attention to my tardiness. I decided to listen to the already-in-progress conversation until I could find an opening where I would be able to prove my worth, since I had already disproved my punctuality adeptness.

"So that's a brief description of the new, exciting project we've been handed. Thanks to the success of our last two shows, we've been given this opportunity that can move us into the same class as the other cable networks. We're going to need a team of four, preferably with some background knowledge in restoration," Cassandra explained.

Background in restoration is perfect for me!

Growing up, there were always repairs being done around our house. I can't tell you the number of times I helped my dad fix a faucet, painted a room the newest 'dramatic color' my mom needed on the walls, or redesigned the landscaping. I even spent two weeks one summer building a house with Habitat for Humanity. *If I volunteer my expertise for this project, that should make up for coming late to the staff meeting, shouldn't it?*

I was also anxious to start a new project. In our office, we all had different strengths, which is what made us click. Some were good at pitching creative ideas for new shows, but I was one of the hands-on people who loved working directly on a show's production.

"I would love to be part of this project," I said. "I spent every summer as a teen building houses with Habitat for Humanity, I do repair projects around my apartment and I have redecorating experience, helping clients with color and décor selections for their homes. Being an integral part of *LeisureTV*'s last two successful projects, this seems like a perfect fit for me!"

Okay, in the interest of truth, it was one summer, I knew what a flange was and how to stop my toilet from running nonstop, and I had helped my mom choose her most recent kitchen paint color – Warm Sunshine.

"Anyone else up for the challenge?" Cassandra asked.

Looking around the conference table, I noticed that everyone had their heads down, averting eye contact with our boss. *I can't believe they aren't all jumping at the chance to start this new project!* Not one of them was volunteering. What was going on?! Usually, we fought over who got to be on the forefront of a new assignment.

"I've already put a great deal of thought into who would make up the best team for our new show, *Main Street*, but I wanted to see if any of you had a special interest in this genre," explained Cassandra. "Remember it has only been picked up as a three-episode Pilot, but if all goes well, we're planning on turning it into a regular series. We will reevaluate at six months to see who stays with the show and what direction it will take."

"Trevor, I'm going to put you as lead for this production," Cassandra continued. "Your last show had our highest ratings to date, and the studio is investing a great deal of money in this project, so we need to make it a success. Andre, I've selected you to be chief coordinator for the local trades we will be employing at the sites – carpenters, electricians, pipefitters, etc. Lucy, you will be directing our promotions and media relations, and Jess, I want you to organize the interior decorating of these buildings. I've seen some of your creative ideas, and they fit seamlessly with our endeavor. You will be working with a local designer to help keep the feel of the area. I believe this is an excellent opportunity for us. Several of the larger studios bid for this project, but being as it's a small town, they are more interested in a smaller production company with a limited staff. The rest of the team will be working behind the scenes here in the California studio. It is imperative we start immediately. An enormous amount of planning needs to transpire before the four of you leave next month for Marceline, Missouri."

CHAPTER 2

Wait a minute, leave for Marceline, Missouri?
What is Cassandra talking about?!
I was now in full panic mode.

"I want to meet with the four of you, Trevor, Andre, Lucy, and Jess, in an hour to go over the details," Cassandra said. "Meeting adjourned!"

We all rose from the table and headed to our individual cubicles. I was in a fog. I had no idea what was going on. One minute, I was volunteering for a new renovation show and, the next minute, I was told I would be moving to ... where did she say? Somewhere in Missouri. For the next six months! I wasn't even sure which one of the Midwest states Missouri was. *Is it the one with the boot heel?*

What had I gotten myself into? I didn't want to move. I was a California girl. The only boot heel I was interested in was on the black, knee-high pair of boots I had bought the previous week from Rag and Bone (on clearance, of course). I loved the beach, the sun, the shopping, the nightlife, and all the amenities a big city had to offer. I couldn't even picture me in some backwoods, slow-paced, nowhere town. And why would we want to do a show in a place like that anyway? I had to get out of it. And one hour was all I had to figure out a story as to why I couldn't leave L.A. *Think, think, think!*

Doing what I always did in a crisis, I called Mollie. Texting was totally out of the question for such an emergency as I needed to hear her voice and level-headed advice.

She answered immediately without even saying hello, just a "Jess, I can't talk right now. I'm headed out to a meeting. I know you are probably in some desperate dilemma, but I have to go. How about drinks at Tucker's Bar and Grill, say 8:00? Good, see you then, bye."

Click!

My lone fallback, and she couldn't help.

Staring at my phone in exasperation, I realized I was down to forty-five minutes to concoct a story as to why I was an unfit candidate for the front lines of our new show.

I know, I mumbled to myself, Granny recently returned from a trip to South America ... she contracted a virus from a Capuchin monkey in the jungle ... might have infected the family ... and was gravely ill. *Wait a minute. Does South America have Capuchin monkeys?* I'd have to look that up. But overall, it was a good excuse, right? (Granny had more energy than me or any member of my family, so why couldn't she have just flown back from South America? It was worth a try. Cassandra had never met Granny, which meant she wouldn't know whether she'd taken that trip or not or whether or not she was ill and needed me. Thankfully, she wasn't, but anyway, it sounded believable. At least I hoped it did.)

I could hear Trevor on the other side of our thin work divider pecking away as usual on his computer as if his life hadn't been completely turned upside down by Cassandra's announcement. *How do guys do that?*

I made one last call to try to garner moral support before heading off to the disastrous meeting awaiting me. I needed the unconditional empathy that one can only receive from who else but their mom.

"Hi, Mom. I can't talk long, just needed an ear so I can rant about my new assignment."

I filled her in on the few details I had learned while she inserted a few 'really' and 'my goodness' responses in all the right spots.

Realizing the meeting was set to begin in a few minutes, I said, "Gotta run, Mom. See you at The Villa this weekend. We'll pop open that bottle of Screaming Eagle Sauvignon Blanc to celebrate the great news."

My mom chuckled at my sarcastic reference to our family joke. My parents had won a free weekend at NAPA's exclusive wine country, with its unimaginable $5000-a-bottle wines. After the trip, we started planning our get-togethers in NAPA code. The truth? I was looking forward to joining her and Dad on Saturday for a glass of Franzia Crisp White, right out of the box that resided in their refrigerator.

● ● ●

At the appointed time, the four of us slowly converged on Cassandra's office.

Although we were a small production company, no expense had been sacrificed for Cassandra's corner suite. Great views of the city gleamed out every window. Sleek and modern, her uncluttered executive desk was used for one-on-one meetings. For larger groups, like now, there was what Cassandra called the 'Brainstorming Table' to the right of her desk.

Each of us took a seat in one of the white, shell task chairs at the table.

Ashen looks of disbelief were etched on Trevor, Andre, and Lucy's faces. Evidently, they were experiencing the same trepidation I was feeling over our Missouri assignment.

"Before we begin," started Cassandra, "I need to emphasize that this is a mere six-month assignment. It is an amazing opportunity and a chance to highlight your individual expertise. You were hand selected because I believe you are the top people for this project. I wasn't sure who on the team had the best skills as the interior design lead, but with your background, Jess, you are a perfect fit. I appreciate your enthusiasm, and the way you eagerly volunteered for the position. And don't worry, you will all be well-compensated for the inconvenience of briefly transferring to another city to work on location."

Me and my big mouth. Ugh!

"Now, I don't want to hear any excuses as to why you can't relocate for six months – pets who will be traumatized by a move, apartments that will be lost, or made-up illnesses of family members."

Cassandra gave me the stink-eye when she said that last bit. You didn't have to be an Italian mother to give that look, you could also be an Italian boss. *Did I mention Cassandra's last name is Vitelli?* How that woman has such insight into the pulse of the company and the thoughts and actions of her staff is beyond me.

"I listen to each of you talk in the office and know that you are currently available and expect you to take this opportunity and make it into something special, not only for *LeisureTV*, but for yourselves … as a way to grow personally and professionally."

She listens to us? What? I could tell by the looks on their faces that my coworkers were wondering the same thing.

"Before we begin to hammer out the details of the project, I need to explain the focus of our show. I also want to give you a little background on the city of Marceline, Missouri, which should help you understand why this special city is the perfect location for our new show, *Main Street*."

I figured I had better pay attention, as it didn't appear as if I would be getting out of my adventure in the boot-heel state.

"All across the nation there are towns that were once vibrant and thriving, but today, they are full of boarded-up buildings and streets that are frankly, depressing. These areas were often referred to as Main Street USA. The plan, with the help of our syndicated show, is to take one of these areas, revitalize it back to its glory days, but for residents of the 21st century, and encourage other small towns to combine their past with their present and bring their Main Streets back to life."

"Now you're probably wondering, why Marceline, Missouri?" Cassandra continued. "There are three main reasons. I'll try not to bore you with too much history, but you need to know some background to make this project a success."

Staying awake through history classes in high school and college was difficult enough, but based on what Cassandra was saying, I felt as if I was about to be dropped into one of those Old West museum dioramas. *Tell me that I'm right back in History 101, that I have fallen asleep, as usual, and am experiencing a nightmare that I will be waking up from any minute – please!*

"First," Cassandra said, "a major fulfillment center is being built by USAMade on vacant land located less than two miles southwest of the Marceline town center. As USAMade continues to grow, their plans are to erect multiple centers across the country to help meet their shipping demands in a more timely and cost effective manner. Since USAMade only handles products made in this country, these fulfillment hubs are scheduled for construction throughout rural areas where many of the factories producing their products are located.

"One reason this location was chosen by the company for its first regional fulfillment center is that an active rail line currently runs from Chicago to Kansas City and beyond, directly past the property. USAMade has worked a deal with the Santa Fe Railroad to reestablish a stop in Marceline, Missouri. Together, they are partnering to debut the use of hi-speed rail for shipping cargo across the country. A second reason for deciding to build in this location is that Missouri is perfectly positioned in the middle of the country, making it easier to ship in any direction … be it to the north, south or either coast."

Cassandra continued, "So what does that have to do with us?" She read my mind!

"Since this is USAMade's first major fulfillment center, they are moving some high-paying executive positions to the area to oversee the construction process. The facility will also employ over three hundred workers, once the center opens. Here is where we come in. With people moving to the area for these jobs, Marceline's City Council wants to revitalize its Main Street. They are creating a joint venture between themselves, the local Chamber of Commerce, USAMade, and area business owners to chronicle the revival of America's Main Street. Using our production skills and equipment, combined with local construction and design teams, we have been contracted to film and air the renovation of Main Street, one building at a time."

She paused, took a deep breath and continued, "The third reason for creating a new series based on the renovation of Main Street in Marceline, Missouri is that we are being requested to incorporate into our theme the legacy of the town … Walt Disney."

"What do you mean Walt Disney? Like Tinker Bell and Winnie the Pooh?" Andre asked.

"I can see it now," Trevor said with a smirky grin, "a fairy princess castle in the middle of town. This is crazy! I thought we were selected for a great opportunity, not an amusement park."

I hate to admit it, but that whole Disney thing was the first part of what I heard that day that piqued my interest. Since my colleagues weren't too happy about it, though, I wasn't going to say anything out loud, but it almost sounded fun – if it were in California, that is!

"Here me out," Cassandra carried on. "Walt Disney lived in Marceline, Missouri from age four to nine. He is quoted as saying the time he spent in that small town was some of the happiest days of his life and where he formed the basis for his future projects. Main Street in Disneyland and Disney World are based on Main Street in Marceline. Our projects will combine the past Main Street into a present Main Street where people want to shop and go for entertainment. Not entertainment the way it was back in Disney's time, but exciting venues that people today will want to attend and places where they can relax and have a good time. The bones are there. We want to take what Marceline has and make it into the envy of every small town in America.

"Our first of three renovation projects along Marceline's Main Street will be the Uptown Theater. It has been closed since 2014. We want to reinvent the main floor as a performing arts center with an auditorium, educational facilities, practice rooms, and a large multi-purpose room. A courtyard and empty building currently sit to the north of the theatre. We will be adding these spaces to the square footage of the original theater, which will allow for new opportunities within the existing historical structure.

"As I stated earlier, Andre, you will be working with a local construction crew to handle demolition and remodel. You will share camera time with Jess, bantering about the reno, discussing pitfalls as they come along, and showing the progress being made. Jess, with a multitude of antique stores in the area, I believe you should be able to locate some charming finds. Kansas City is only about an hour away so, with a pretty healthy budget, you should easily be able to mix some new with the old and create an inviting, classic style. Remember we are in Disneyland (no pun intended), so we need to keep that theme in mind. The people of Marceline are proud that their town was Walt Disney's boyhood home. We can't forget that, but at the same time, we are not designing a fairy princess castle, as you so eloquently stated, Trevor.

"Lucy, Uptown Theater is our first project on Main Street, so the grand opening needs to be well-promoted and include some star power. I'm assigning Maddie as your assistant. She can handle things from this end. USAMade is backing the project and will be our main corporate sponsor, but we need to get our current advertisers on board, as well as pitch our show to new clients.

"Lastly, Trevor, as head of the production, your main duties consist of working with the camera crew, general production staff, editing team and, most importantly, keeping the project on schedule. I know it's the toughest job, with the least accolades, but when we pull this off, it will be because of your leadership.

"We start production at the beginning of May, so that gives you approximately four weeks to ready yourselves for the move. Some newly renovated *Airbnb*s are available in Marceline, which will allow each of you to have your own place in town, conveniently located to the shoot. We have already secured the two apartments directly above the theatre, but we will get into more of the specifics as we draw closer to our start date. Any questions?"

We all sat there shell-shocked, wondering how it was possible that the day had started as a normal Friday, with the usual, somewhat boring, weekly staff meeting, and had ended with the four of us heading off to a city we had never heard of, with a population of probably about 50 people, in the middle of the country, far, far away from California.

"If there are no questions, I'm due to meet with Bob, up in Finance, to wrap-up some details for the project. We will meet on Monday at 1:00 to take a look at our first renovation and start the initial planning. Four weeks sounds like a long time, I know, but it will be here sooner than we think. I want the four of you to begin by researching Marceline, the town itself, as well as the Uptown Theater. You are welcome to stay in my office and brainstorm before heading back to your desks. I should be back in about a half an hour," Cassandra said and then hurried out the door.

No one spoke.

As I looked around the table, I noticed Lucy twisting a strand of her long, jet black hair around her purple-tipped index finger. Perspiration was beading up on Andre's forehead as he stared, deep in thought, out the wall of windows lining Cassandra's office, and Trevor was frantically texting on his iPhone.

The silence was killing me, so I decided to break it. "Got any ideas how we can get out of this?"

"What are you worried about? You volunteered," Lucy chided. "I can't believe she expects us to uproot for six months. I was planning on taking a Sommelier course this summer and start my certification as a wine connoisseur."

"I didn't realize she meant an out-of-town project when I volunteered. Believe me, I'm as unhappy as you are about this. I also had a ton of plans this summer."

I was absolutely not going to share with Lucy, or the rest of the group, that my big plans were actually eating, sleeping, going to work, maybe hitting the beach a few weekends, and spending time with Mollie and my family. So, yeah, basically, nothing out of the ordinary. For all Lucy knew, my plans could have included climbing the East Canyon Trail, learning to kiteboard, or attending a weekend retreat in the Art of Female Domination. She didn't need to know I lived a pathetically boring life.

"Hey, listen," Trevor interrupted, "it looks like we need to make the best of this. She did say we will be well-compensated. I don't know about the rest of you, but I can use the money. How about we all head over to The Roofstop after work and drown our sorrows about being 'hand-selected' for this – how did she say it – 'new and exciting project'?"

"Sorry, dude, can't. I've got my weekly tee time at 6:30," Andre said. "Better play tonight since it looks like I'm going to have to give up my spot for a while."

"I've already promised my friend Kiely I'd meet her for a mani/pedi," Lucy countered.

How did everyone, and I mean everyone, have a more exciting life than me, I wondered.

"I'm free," I squeaked, soft enough I hoped no one really heard me.

"Well, Jess, it looks like it's just you and me. Want to meet in the lobby at 5:30, and we'll walk over to the bar together?"

"Sounds great," I said with more confidence than I felt.

What a day it was turning out to be.

CHAPTER 3

It's just two colleagues going for a drink after work. You can do this, I told myself, as I rode the elevator down to the lobby. So why were my hands sweaty and my heart pounding in my chest? Surely, Trevor didn't know the way I fantasized about him outside work. It was kind of pathetic. I didn't even know him that well. But he seemed so self-assured and all-together and ... *OMG! There he is waiting for me.*

I spotted him, dressed in tight jeans and a fitted, gray T-shirt, leaning against a wall near the exit to our building. As he scanned the lobby, he noticed me walking toward him and greeted me with a gleaming white smile peeking from behind his scruffy, short beard. As I approached, he opened the door.

"After you, my lady," he said and followed me into the sunshine.

"I hope you don't mind walking. Parking around here is such a pain, and The Roofstop is only a few blocks away," he added.

"No, walking is good. I love to walk. I walk whenever I can," I rambled as I pushed through the crowded sidewalk.

What I really meant was that I loved to walk in tennis shoes, not sandals that were made for aesthetics over function.

Apparently, Trevor and I weren't the only people going out for drinks after a long workweek. We waited in uncomfortable silence at the crosswalk with several other groups in high spirits, chatting nonstop like best friends who had been apart for the last twenty years.

This was rapidly turning into a very awkward afternoon. One drink and I was sure Trevor would be out of there, wishing he'd never made the suggestion.

The signal finally flashed 'Walk' and the mass of humanity surrounding us rushed forward as if there were only minutes before the bars announced, 'Last Call'.

Trevor and I advanced with the rest of the group. Even though he was only about a head taller than me, his stride had to be twice the length of mine. I needed to walk/run in order to keep up with him. As we crossed the street, he didn't realize that he was leaving me behind.

Upon reaching the opposite side of the intersection, the crowd began to thin, people heading to various destinations. Feeling like I could actually see and breathe again, no longer enclosed in a sea of chests and swinging arms, I caught a glimpse of my favorite consignment shop's display window. There I spied an amazing, vintage, red jacket that I impulsively knew I must own. Paying more attention to the to-die-for jacket, rather than to where I was going, I failed to notice the uneven sidewalk and splat!

Next thing I knew, my face and the sidewalk became one. *Please let me get up fast enough that Trevor doesn't see me face-planted on the ground.* This was not the sort of impression I was hoping to make on him.

I struggled to my feet as people on the sidewalk politely moved around me. Pushing forward, I notice my right sandal was now flopping off to the side of my foot with one strap completely detached from its sole. I couldn't believe it. Those were my favorite sandals!

Trevor turned to speak to me, and realizing I wasn't next to him, began to scan the crowd. When he finally found me, I could tell by the surprised expression on his face that I must look a mess. He rushed back to where I was standing, appearing to be completely mortified.

"Are you alright?! What happened? I thought you were right behind me," he sputtered.

To be honest, for just having become one with the sidewalk, I wasn't hurt too bad. I saw a small scrape on my knee, as if I was some eight-year-old. My palm stung from bracing myself for the fall, and when I moved my mouth, my cheek ached.

"Just tripped on the sidewalk back there, no big deal," I said as whimsically as possible, trying to explain why I was standing still in the middle of the sidewalk, one shoe half off, brushing dirt from my dress with a dazed look on my face.

"Are you hurt?" he asked.

"No, I'm fine," I lied, trying to hide my utter humiliation.

Not more than a hundred yards ahead was the red awning over the entrance to The Roofstop. I stuffed the strap of my sandal back into the tiny hole where it used to fit securely.

"We're almost there now, so let's just head up for a drink," I said as I began to limp forward with my broken sandal and battered body.

Entering The Roofstop can lift anyone's spirits. The best word to describe the atmosphere is – cheerful. Colorful chairs and tables are scattered around the perimeter of the bar, giving off a relaxed vibe, while striped couches in matching reds, blues and yellows are positioned in the center to allow for more intimate group conversations. The music being pumped through the speakers makes you want to move, but it isn't so loud you can't talk to the person next to you. I guess that's why it's one of the most popular hangouts for the area's young professionals.

Luckily, we found a table near the railing with an amazing view of the city. Excusing myself to go to the restroom, I headed off to inspect the damage from my graceful swan dive.

Talk about embarrassing. I cleaned the scrapes on my knee and palm and examined in the mirror the large bruise forming on my cheek surrounding a cut with drying blood in the center. It looked like I just finished a boxing match and had undoubtedly lost.

Grabbing make-up out of my bag, I applied some emergency repair cover-up. Smearing foundation over the damage, I looked at my reflection again and realized I now had a big brown splotch on my face, tinged in purple, still with a major cut down the center. It looked even worse than it did before I 'fixed' it! People were going to think I was about to grow a horn out the side of my face.

Trevor had never given me a second look at the office, but I bet he wouldn't be able to take his eyes off me tonight – in horror!

Immediately upon my return, our waitress, Shellie – according to her name badge – arrived to take our drink order. Seeing my face, she did a double take, but quickly tried to hide her shock.

"What can I get you to drink?" she asked.

"I'll have a Stella," I said.

"Make it two," Trevor added, giving me a quizzical look.

"Any appetizers?" she asked.

"Add some of your house-made tortilla chips and fresh guacamole, if that's alright with you?"

Trevor looked my way, and I nodded.

Shellie headed off towards the bar to place our order.

"A beer girl … I'm surprised. I would have pegged you as a *Sex in The City*, foo-foo drink, sort of person."

"No. My parents never drank much alcohol, and I couldn't afford to buy anything too expensive in college, so I wound up acquiring a taste for beer, and now it's what I prefer. Although, at least I've moved up from Natty Lite to Stella Artois."

"Definitely an improvement. I'm pretty sure they would call security and have us removed if you ordered a Natty Lite at this place."

"So, what do you think of the new project?" Trevor asked, moving right into shoptalk.

So much for the casual conversation I was beginning to enjoy.

"I guess the project itself sounds interesting, I'm just not too excited about being on location for six months in the middle of nowhere. I did an online search for the city of Marceline, like Cassandra suggested, and read about its history and demographics. They only have a population of around 2000 people and, aside from a Main Street, it seems pretty rural."

"I'm guessing you didn't read about any rooftop bars where we can hang out after a long shoot?"

"No, but I did see a corner café that raves about its homemade pies."

I paused as Shellie dropped off our drinks and appetizer.

"You didn't seem too excited when Cassandra dropped the bombshell on us," I continued, "so what are your feelings regarding the show?"

"I've had some time to mull it over and although I could do without the Walt Disney, cutesy, aspect of the show, overall, I believe it has some real potential. I can see why Cassandra picked you as lead designer, though. I'd bet the price of admission to Disneyland that you think the best part of this project is the Disney theme."

I must say that had crossed my mind. But why did he think that? *Do I look like Disneyland was my favorite place to go as a kid and that I was a different Disney princess every year for Halloween until I was about ten?*

To be honest, the princesses are pretty awesome, right? Not only do they wear great clothes, but they're also kind of badasses, in their own way. Look at Mulan, a warrior. Belle, standing her ground against a ghastly beast. Or Jasmine, refusing to follow long standing traditions. I could learn a thing or two from these ladies.

I was contemplating what my strength would be if I were a princess when I realized that Trevor was still talking.

"I'm ready for a new challenge. I recently ended a toxic relationship, so maybe the timing of leaving town for a few months isn't so bad."

"Same for me," I said, trying to appear as if I had been listening rather than zoning out in the land of make believe.

"My boyfriend just left for Cambodia with the Peace Corps and felt it would be better to break things off since he was leaving the country," I blurted out.

Why did I say that? I had not even been on a date in a month, much less have a boyfriend. I had to stop watching Nat Geo documentaries (the previous night's - *A Towering Task: The Story of the Peace Corps*) while by myself on the couch, eating a dinner of leftover takeout.

"Wow, that's impressive! Did the two of you do a lot of volunteer work around here too?"

Volunteering was on my list of things to do this summer, but to be perfectly honest, it's on my summer to-do-list every year. Time slips and I never seem to get around to it – bad me!

"Oh yeah! We loved to help with the beach clean-up each spring and other stuff," I answered as vaguely as possible.

Truth: I did pick up a discarded plastic bottle and throw it in one of the recycle bins when Mollie and I went to the beach. I thought that should count.

We talked easily for the next hour as we munched on the chips and ordered another drink.

Trevor has one brother who lives in Denver with his family. He's already making plans, once in Marceline, to set aside a three-day weekend for a quick road trip through Kansas to visit his adored niece and nephew.

Conversely, I told him about growing up as an only child of two, very doting parents. And I tried not to over-exaggerate as I described my family. I explained that I had lacked for nothing during my youth, but in a streak of independence, I changed my mind about attending UCLA with my best friend and decided to prove to both me and my parents that I was capable of making it on my own. So instead of UCLA, I put myself through Pacific Union College, without their financial assistance. I stated that my goal, now, was to prove myself an invaluable asset to *LeisureTV*.

"I've never wanted people to assume I had things handed to me. Being self-sufficient has actually made my parents really proud," I said.

Before I realized it, the sun was setting, and it was time for me to leave if I was going to still meet Mollie.

As I drained the last of my beer, Trevor asked if I would like to continue our conversation over dinner.

I nearly spit my drink all over the table, coughed a bit, and sputtered that I couldn't because I was meeting up with a friend. The guy of my dreams had just invited me to dinner, and I came across as making excuses not to be around him, that I was meeting a 'friend'. *What is wrong with me?!*

"I mean, it sounds like fun, but I really have to get going," I said.

Once again, that did not come out the way I meant it.

"Maybe some other time," I muttered. *Keep digging the hole deeper, Jess.*

"No problem," he said and shrugged. "How about I run back to my car and pick you up at the front door? I can give you a lift back to your car, so you won't have to walk on that broken shoe."

It occurred to me that he had managed not to stare in horror at my swollen face the whole time we'd been at the bar. Between not staring and giving me a ride to my car, he had earned himself major good guy points!

Forgetting I'd been running late and had to squeeze into a different spot that morning, we wound up circling the entire parking structure two times before locating my Honda Civic, which looked like a Matchbox car, wedged between a Ford Expedition and a Cadillac Escalade.

I thanked Trevor profusely for the ride and reluctantly exited his vehicle.

Once in my own car, I luckily found a different pair of shoes under a pile of clothes in the backseat. I had just enough time to make it to Tucker's and not be too late. (Thankfully, Mollie was used to my lack of timeliness).

Pulling up to the garage kiosk, I began to search for my access card, but couldn't find it, anywhere. I frantically rummaged through my bag. Why was it not in the place I usually kept it, I wondered, which, to be honest, was at the very bottom, under receipts, my brush, make-up case, wallet, a used napkin (*Yuck!*), and other unidentifiable objects?

As I scrounged though my purse, a horn beeped, letting me know I had used the allotted time – determined by Mr. Black Escalade – for exiting the garage. Since this was my third day this month to be without my mandatory access card, I was required to pay CASH in order for the red and white-striped mechanical arm to rise and let me out of the garage.

So now, I was scrounging for change, also at the bottom of my bag.

I almost had enough and prayed that there were some loose coins in my console because if this took much longer, I was fairly certain I'd end up as an SUV hood ornament. Luckily, I found enough change to escape the garage and head west towards Tucker's.

• • •

As I entered the retro-themed bar, I saw Mollie's dark red curls at a high-top table near the back. She had a beer waiting for me. She was on-time and well-organized, two words never used to describe me. Clearly, she was my polar opposite.

Mollie had been my best friend since middle school. We met when the world's strictest bus driver assigned us as seatmates. I'm pretty certain that perfect Mollie MacInerney and I would have never sat next to each other had we not been pushed together by Mr. Crabby Pants (a name only middle school kids could think is funny, but somehow still made us giggle). As it turned out, we became inseparable all the way through high school and even planned to room together in college, but we decided to attend different schools at the last minute, her UCLA – really – and me Pacific Union.

Now that we were back in the same city, we tried to meet in person as often as possible, although we text and/or talked daily. We used to go to the bars every weekend, until Mollie met Justin, then it changed to one weekend night for him and one weekend night for me. Now that they were engaged and cohabitating, we typically only met for dinner every couple of weeks. I like Justin, but I missed Mollie. Justin was out of town for the week, so I got Mollie for a rare weekend night – like old times.

"So, what's the big crisis?" Mollie asked as she glanced up from her phone. "Oh wow! What happened to your face?!"

Did she have to shriek? I did mention that aside from being on-time and well-organized, she was also brutally honest, didn't I? If not, now you know. Most of the time, I love that about her. Okay, sometimes, I love that. Well, really, only when it's what I want to hear.

"I have had the worst day of my life!" I began.

Once I started speaking, the words came rushing out. It's like I yelled *FIRE* in my brain and each of the day's events were trying to escape all at the same time.

"I was late for work because I wanted to earn a fat paycheck, so I walked into the staff meeting that had already started and told everyone how I'm great at restoration ..."

I took a shallow breath before continuing my rant.

"Now, I'm being sent to Missouri with Lucy, Andre, and Trevor for six months. Then, I was the only one who could meet Trevor for drinks, and he was walking too fast so, when I spotted that great jacket in Reformation's window, I tripped on the sidewalk, broke my sandal, and royally messed up my face."

I made another feeble attempt to breathe.

"I told him 'no' when he invited me to dinner in a way that sounded like I wouldn't be remotely interested in spending more time with him, which you know is completely untrue. We couldn't find my car in the parking garage, and on the way here, I discovered I'd lost my exit pass again, and I can't park in the garage until I buy a new one with extra money I don't have right now."

I sighed, basically because I was out of oxygen.

Mollie just stared at me and then all at once, she burst out laughing.

I sat there thinking I couldn't believe she found all of this funny. Then, as always happens when I'm with Mollie, her contagious giggling gets to me and before I knew it, I was giggling with her.

"Stop it! This isn't funny. I'm going to have to pack up and move out of town for six months and then who will you have to laugh at?"

"Oh, Jess, it's only six months, not forever. Maybe you should look at it differently. Perhaps today wasn't as horrible as you imagine ... even though I'm not sure I completely follow your ramblings of everything that happened. First, you complain all the time of being bored. ALL your friends are busy, and you spend EVERY weekend alone. Just quoting you, by the way. So, this is a new opportunity."

"When I said I was bored on weekends, that didn't mean I wanted to move to the middle of boring nowhere and with none of my friends so I could still be bored on my days off!"

Ignoring my comment, Mollie trudged on, "You just had a drink with the guy in your office that you constantly drool over."

"After I fell down in front of him, made a complete fool of myself and then blew him off when he asked me to dinner," I countered.

"And now you are moving to small town America with said hunk. Personally, I see major opportunity, but that's just me."

CHAPTER 4

After our night at Tucker's, Mollie had me thinking that maybe opportunities are what you make of them. So, with a more positive attitude, I began to focus on the possibilities in front of me and dig into the Main Street project with new vigor.

A jumble of ideas for designing the interior of the theater and adjacent building bounced around inside my head, but I was unable to execute much until I arrived in Marceline and met up with my local designing partner.

Between planning frameworks for the show, designing the theater renovations and preparing the move of staff to the on-site location, work flew by in a blur.

A truck had been secured to transport the filming equipment, and we would each been given a small space to ship something that might not fit in our own cars – like bikes, golf clubs, or, in Trevor's case, a motorcycle. (Too bad he wasn't driving that the night he gave me a ride back to my car.)

For me, I couldn't imagine going on this adventure without Mona, my faithful houseplant, and since she was over five feet and still growing, putting her in my little Honda was totally out of the question. That said, I was pretty nervous about her traveling in a truck, but I bought a tree box from the local nursery (who knew there was such a thing) and should be able to give her enough water to last the entire trip.

Mona and I had been inseparable since I brought her home from the Green Living Festival Mollie dragged me to during her 'Friends of the Earth' phase. It was completely out of the question that I could live in Missouri without her by my side and besides, no one I know was willing to babysit a giant houseplant for six months.

Time was moving forward so swiftly it made my head spin. It was just a week before we packed up and left, and I was still finding it difficult to believe this was truly happening. I also kept hoping Trevor would ask me to dinner again, but so far, he had not. I almost began to believe that I had heard him wrong and that all of this – the show, the move, the drinks with him – were some bizarre dream.

The entire staff had been working extra-long hours so that when we got to Marceline we were ready to begin shooting on Day One. Today, had been exceptionally strenuous, ending with Trevor and me finalizing some details for the educational wing of the theater. We had finally decided to call it a night.

"Want to get a drink and a bite to eat back at The Roofstop?" he asked.

"That would be great! Are Lucy and Andre joining us?"

"Didn't invite them," he added with a playful grin.

I was so tired, I didn't even have the energy to get nervous about going for a drink with him. Although, I wasn't so exhausted that I had forgotten about the sidewalk Olympics I performed last time we went to The Roofstop.

"I think I'll drive tonight. There should be plenty of parking this late on a Thursday, and it would probably be best if I didn't try and walk in the dark since I obviously don't do it very well in daylight," I said and laughed.

"Good idea," he chuckled. "I've got a few things to finish up. How about I meet you there in say, half an hour?"

"Perfect." I headed back to my desk, answered a few emails, and shut down my computer.

As I walked toward the parking garage, I began to feel a rumble of nerves churn through my stomach.

• • •

It was another beautiful California evening. A full moon was peeking above the outline of the downtown buildings with their twinkling lights acting as stars. A gentle breeze cooled the warm spring air, making it feel like summer was just around the corner.

Surprisingly, our same table was open, as if it had been waiting patiently for Trevor's and my return. I took that as a positive sign and quickly sat down before someone else snagged it. I read somewhere (probably *Cosmo*, where I seem to gain my wealth of trivial information) that when coincidence happens, it's not chance, but good luck.

Trevor arrived about five minutes after me. Walking up to the table with a confident swagger, he had more than one pair of female eyes following him.

"Wow, the same table – that's lucky," he remarked.

Now I know we were meant for each other! Talk about a sign!

"I don't know about you, but this schedule is wearing me out," he said as he plopped down into the chair opposite me.

"Can I bring you something to drink?" I hear a voice from behind ask.

Turning around, I see Shellie, our waitress from a few weeks ago. Okay, this was a bit too much, but hey, I'll take all the good luck I can get.

We ordered our drinks and some food and for a few minutes stared in companionable silence at the city lights.

"The city really is pretty at night," I said. "The lights look like stars. Did you know, if you make a wish when you see a light go on in a building, your wish will come true?"

"You made that up," he said, his tone one of disbelief.

"No, it's true. Oh, I just saw one go on!"

I closed my eyes and wished that the night turned into more than two colleagues out together because they worked too late and missed their regular dinners.

"What did you wish for?"

"You know I can't tell you or it won't come true."

"So, you really believe in that stuff?" he asked.

"It can't hurt to dream, can it?"

I began to relax as we bantered back and forth on subjects from superstitions and taste in movies, to how we spend our free time and of course, because we work together, a little office talk.

The night had turned into such an amazingly, pleasant evening that I didn't want it to end, but the next day was another workday, and it was getting late. I got the feeling Trevor was in no hurry to leave either, even as he stifled a yawn for the second time.

"Tonight, has really been nice, thanks for inviting me," I said.

"I've enjoyed it, too. Maybe we can do it again soon, even try a new restaurant!"

I never do this, but decided to go for it – it was my lucky night, right?

"My best friend, Mollie, and her fiancé, Justin, are having a small get-together tomorrow night with some of our friends. It is officially called a *Not Goodbye but See You in Six Months* party. Care to join me?"

"Sounds like a possibility. I'm leaving before dawn on Saturday for an end of the season ski weekend at Bear Mountain.

Not to sound like a total bore, but I really don't want to stay out late. If you don't mind going separately, I could join you for a little while."

I couldn't believe it – my wish had come true!

• • •

I decided to surprise Mollie and not mention that Trevor was joining me for the party. And I couldn't wait for her reaction when she opened the door. The look on her face should be priceless.

Looking forward to the party had made work feel as if it were moving in slow motion. I was having a hard time concentrating on my research of the Uptown Theater.

I had recently learned that the second project we were filming would be the total renovation of the old Allen Hotel, so I began to research that property as well.

I had a feeling we may need to tread lightly with some of the local business owners. They seemed to be wary of the show coming to their town, although there were those who did appear pleased to be acquiring much-needed upgrades in exchange for showcasing their properties.

We'd been instructed, as a group, to lay low and try to blend in.

My head had been in my computer all day, and therefore, I had seen very little of Trevor. As the longest day of my career wound down, I heard some movement in the cubical next to mine. Popping my head over the partition, I found Trevor looking over some figures. He saw me and immediately minimized his screen.

"Still on for tonight?" I asked.

"Sure, what time do you want to meet?"

The Wonderful World of Marceline

With Trevor having never met Mollie or Justin, we decided, for obvious reasons, to arrive together. I gave him Mollie's address, and we planned to meet at 8:00. He would need his car to leave early, but since the party was for me, I planned on staying until the last guest had headed home. I would probably stay the night at Mollie and Justin's place, anyway. It wouldn't be the first time.

• • •

I saw Trevor, already parked on Mollie and Justin's palm tree-lined lane, by the time I drove up. He was in his signature tight jeans, T-shirt and leather jacket, perched atop a green and black Kawasaki Ninja motorcycle.

He looked like he belonged on a billboard, I thought, as I timidly slunk out of my very practical, white, Honda Civic fondly named Betty after my favorite Golden Girl.

"Nice bike," I said.

He glanced my way. "Thanks. Wow, you look great … a lot different than at work."

Unsure whether to take that as an insult or a compliment, I decided on the latter.

Typically, I don't wear my twist-back black top, skinny jeans and black knee-high boots to the office, but I didn't think I go to work looking that bad (except maybe when I wake up really late and still try to slide into my cubical on time).

We strolled down the sidewalk toward Mollie and Justin's building. They had only lived there for three months but had fallen in love with the place. Finding the right flat took them a while, but with some serious real estate searching and a little bit of luck, Mollie snagged this great unit within walking distance to the Sunset Strip. Located on a cul de sac, their apartment sat at the rear of an attractive, yellow stucco property, over the building's arched car ports. This meant they had no one above, below, or next to them and a sense of privacy unheard of for a residence in the area.

As we headed up the staircase leading to their teal front door, I informed Trevor that I hadn't gotten a chance to talk to Mollie today, so she didn't know I was bringing him.

"Are you sure it's okay that I'm here?" he asked.

"Oh definitely! She loves crowds and surprises. When it comes to parties, for Mollie, the bigger the better! It will be great!"

Just as I was reassuring Trevor that no, he was not crashing the party, Mollie opened the front door. She looked like Mollie with her long, dark red curls flying around her face, but why was she wearing a floor-length blue dress with a quiver slung over her back and carrying a bow and arrow?

"Surprise," she exclaimed.

Standing in the doorway, I stared at her without moving.

"You should see the look on your face, it's priceless. Don't you know who I'm supposed to be? Merida, you know, from Disney's *Brave*."

Justin appeared at her side, usually impeccably dressed, but he was wearing a green tunic and matching felt hat. He was also sporting a quiver across his back with bow and arrow in hand.

"Let me guess, Robin Hood?" I presumed, shaking my head.

"Correct. Come on in."

Before I could introduce Justin, I saw a Mickey and Minnie sitting on the couch, Moana, Aladdin and Jasmin gathered around the food table, Rapunzel with the guy from *Tangled* (don't know his name) talking in the corner, and Captain Hook coming from the kitchen.

"Was I supposed to dress up?" I questioned, mortified.

"No, we wanted to give you inspiration and get you in the mood for your new assignment. Everybody thought it would be fun to be a different Disney movie character. What do you think?"

I didn't know what to say. I had brought Trevor, who had made it clear he was not into the whole Walt Disney scene, to a Disney-themed costume party. Could this get any worse?

"By the way, this is Trevor," I introduced him to the group that had gathered at the door. "He's our lead producer and will be heading off with me to Marceline, Missouri next week."

Everyone greeted him as we got pulled inside the apartment.

I looked around and couldn't believe all the effort Mollie had put into my *Not Goodbye but See You in Six Months* party. I thought it was supposed to be a small gathering of our friends, but she had Disney-themed decorations everywhere.

I steered Trevor over to the table to grab a drink and some food. Amazingly, all of the appetizers were Mickey ears-shaped – a cheese ball with sausage and crackers, twisted pretzels and dip, the veggie platter, even the sushi.

This was not what I had in mind when I invited Trevor to join me. I pictured a small, intimate gathering of friends, quiet mood music, and intellectual conversation. I should have presumed with Mollie as the party planner, there would be loud laughing, a festive atmosphere, and a roomful of people (some I wasn't sure I even knew). Although, in my wildest dreams, I could have never guessed she'd have them all in costumes.

"How did you come up with all of this?" I asked her.

"You know I love Pinterest. It was fun!"

We mingled and I introduced Trevor around to the group. There were so many people, I didn't have any chance to be alone with him all evening. Unlike work earlier that day, the time flew so quickly that it seemed we had just arrived when Trevor told me he had to get going.

I walked him to the door and, together, we descended the staircase into the chilly, night air.

"I'm so sorry about all of this tonight," I said as I waved my hand toward the party going on in the apartment above me. "I had no idea Mollie was making it into such a big deal. This one was over-the-top, even for her."

"You said she loves parties and surprises," he said and laughed.

"Well, I was definitely surprised. Thanks for being such a good sport. I know it wasn't exactly the small get-together I described."

"It was fine," he said reassuringly.

We stood for a few seconds in awkward silence, when suddenly, he leaned over and kissed my cheek, then promptly turned, and strolled down the sidewalk to his waiting motorcycle.

"Thanks again," he said while looking over his shoulder.

"Enjoy your ski weekend," I responded, electricity moving through the cheek he kissed to my entire body as I climbed, weak-kneed, up the stairs and back to Disneyland.

The party went strong late into the night, or early morning, depending on your point of view.

After everyone finally left and we began moving dirty plates, glasses and leftover food into the kitchen, I quizzed Mollie on what she thought of Trevor. Justin had just headed down the hall towards their bedroom. He learned a long time ago to leave when it was just the two of us, so he didn't get pulled into our 'girl talk', which he avoided, at all costs.

"I don't know, he seemed okay," she said vaguely.

Have I mentioned that Mollie is brutally honest? I love and hate that about her.

"You don't like him," I pouted.

"I didn't say that. Don't go putting words in my mouth, Jessica James. To be fair, I didn't get much of a chance to talk to him since he left so early. By the way, who is he going skiing with this weekend?"

"I don't know, he never said. And don't change the subject, Miss Mollie MacInerney (since we're having the serious, full-name kind of discussion). Tell me one thing that is wrong with him."

"I'm not sure. I can't put my finger on it, but he doesn't seem … authentic."

"What do you mean?" I stuttered, needing clarification.

How was it Mollie couldn't see, aside from being gorgeous, that Trevor was also thoughtful, easy-going, and a gentleman? I mean, who still kisses someone goodnight on the cheek – seriously?

"Oh, I don't know. It's late, I'm tired and I'm not thinking clearly right now. You like him and that's all that matters."

She threw me some blankets and a pillow to make up my usual bed on the couch and headed off down the hall to her Prince Charming.

CHAPTER 5

It was almost time. The next morning, we were leaving at sunrise for the more than twenty-four-hour drive from Los Angeles, California to Marceline, Missouri.

Andre, Lucy, Trevor and I were caravanning for our three-day marathon, cross-country road trip. I had pretty much packed all my necessities, so it was just a matter of stuffing them into my car, gassing up, and heading off for Middle America.

For my last night in L.A., though, I was scheduled for dinner and hockey with Mom, Dad, and Granny. Mom was making my favorite – lasagna, with wedge salad and garlic bread. (As you can tell, I wasn't raised to be your typical, ultra-thin, tofu-eating, California girl.)

Usually full of opinions, my family had been uncharacteristically quiet about my temporary move, making it hard to gauge their true feelings.

Pulling into the driveway of what my mother affectionately called 'The Villa' (a haphazard mid-century ranch, with a bright orange front door, funky yard art sculptures, and landscaping that includes weeds as part of the aesthetics), I realized how much I was going to miss visiting my parents' home for our weekly family dinners.

I was greeted at the door by my dad. A quiet man, uneasy with outward displays of affection, he immediately pulled me into a tight bear hug.

"Glad you could make it tonight, sweetheart," he said.

Even though it had been years since I lived with my parents, I got the feeling, judging by the emotion in Dad's voice, my moving nearly two thousand miles away, even if it was for only six months, was going to be difficult for them.

"Of course I made it," I said and laughed, trying to lighten the mood. "When have I ever missed lasagna night?"

"I think I'll see if Mom needs any help," I said, making my way toward the smell of pasta and garlic, as Dad and his rare show of emotion was making me extremely uncomfortable.

No one had ever accused my mom of being the world's best housekeeper, but upon entering her bright yellow kitchen, even I was taken aback. Contents from the cabinets were strewn everywhere. Mom, oblivious to the mess, was adding some final garnishes to four salads sitting atop her newly-installed, quartz countertop.

She turned around, flashing me her wide, infectious smile. "Did you come in here to help me or did your dad get all sentimental on you and you're running away from him?"

"A little of both," I confessed. "I love the countertops … what I can see of them."

"Thanks! I'm really happy with them, too, but now I need a new color on the walls. I'm leaning toward Graphic Charcoal," she said, pulling a paint sample out of a drawer and handing it to me. "What do you think?"

"I think Dad's not going to be too happy about painting again, is what I think."

"Oh, your dad needs projects to keep him busy or he becomes restless."

"Where are you, Jessica Dear?"

"Granny's here," I said and chuckled as I helped move the food to the table.

"We're in here, Granny," I called out. "And bring Dad with you. We're ready to eat."

Dinner was delicious, as always. We talked on top of each other throughout the meal, as was our norm, about nothing of major importance, just happy chatter. By the end of our meal, I had to unclasp the top button of my pants just so I could breathe, which was typical after devouring one of Mom's culinary masterpieces.

We all pitched in to clear the table.

Mom had made tiramisu for dessert, but none of us had room for even one more bite of food. We were full and ready for the game.

Moving into the living room, we each headed for our lucky seats.

The living room was the only neutral-colored room in the entire house – a rare argument won by my dad. A brown leather couch and loveseat sat perpendicular to one another with a large, flat-screen television, flanked by a pair of cluttered bookshelves, mounted on the opposite wall. The main feature of the room, though, was the collection of "artwork" scattered about. Framed pictures of my life's progression dot the walls, sit on end and sofa tables and rest in bookshelf nooks. Favorite school photos, vacation highlights and significant events, ranging from baby pictures to college graduation, greet friends and family as they enter my parents' home. Yes, I am the sole subject of my parents' "collection".

I stared at a grouping of pictures from our last vacation together to Seattle, remembering the fun we had, as I waited patiently for puck drop. Coincidently, the Kings were facing off against the St. Louis Blues.

"You better NEVER become a Blues fan," Dad scowled, breaking me away from my reverie.

"Not a chance. They stole Gretzky. They're the sworn enemy … forever!"

"That's my girl," Dad said as he sat back in his recliner with a broad grin on his face.

After sixty minutes of grueling play and Granny yelling "SHOOT!" at any forward touching the puck, we squeaked out a 2 – 1 victory.

"I can stay for a quick slice of dessert and then I need to get home. We're leaving early in the morning," I announced.

We trudged back to the messy kitchen. The spirited mood from the King's victory had suddenly subsided. The fact that I was leaving was quickly turning into a reality.

Mom cut the dessert and passed a piece to each of us. Unlike dinner, we ate in virtual silence.

After all the crumbs had been cleaned off our plates (My mom makes a mean Tiramisu!), my parents got up from the table and retrieved something out of the same drawer the paint swatch came from earlier in the evening. They walked to my chair and handed me a small, square box.

"Jess, we don't tell you often enough how very proud we are of you," Dad began. "You are a bright, creative, independent, and caring young woman. We will miss your frequent drop-ins and weekly dinners, terribly. Your mother and I know that we'll talk and text often over the next few months, but not seeing you in person, well, it won't be the same. We want you to know that even though you're halfway across the country, you are close in our hearts."

With glistening eyes, Mom continued, "We want you to have this little present, so you know we are always near you, honey, even when you are miles away."

I sat staring at the box. This was so unlike my parents. I don't remember ever receiving a gift from them unless it was my birthday or Christmas.

I slowly removed the lid of the box. Sitting on an ivory satin pillow was the most beautiful, gold and diamond infinity bracelet, inscribed with the words, *"Forever in our Hearts"*.

My heart squeezed. I knew they would miss me, but I had no idea how much. Even though they still had Granny nearby, I felt more conflicted than ever about leaving on my journey to, what felt like, the middle of nowhere.

CHAPTER 6

The chirping of the alarm on my phone sounded in my ear, but I couldn't figure out why since the clock read 5 a.m.

Rolling over, I hid my head deep in my pillows and tried to slip back into my dream – bedazzled in jewels, a designer bikini and a floppy straw hat. I was sailing on a luxury yacht, headed for the shores of my private island and seaside mansion. And I wished the noisy birds circling high above the yacht would fly away.

I faded in and out of my dream. Vaguely aware of reality, I decided I must have set the alarm wrong last night when I got home from my parents' house.

There had been a tearful good-bye. *I remember now. I'm leaving this morning.*

Why did early mornings hold so many surprises for me?

I had to get a move on. I could not be late. I was supposed to meet up with the others at 6 a.m. in the parking lot adjacent to our office. *I can do this!*

Throwing on the comfy, driving clothes I had laid out (at least I had thought ahead on that one), I pulled my hair into a ponytail, gathered my last few items to throw in Betty's trunk, snagged a banana muffin and energy drink (the only items left in the pantry) and locked my apartment door for the last time for six months.

As I was driving away from my apartment (I couldn't look back or I would start getting nervous), I spied the beautiful bracelet I received adorning my wrist. I vowed to my parents that I wouldn't take it off until I returned home and, if I ever felt in doubt or uncertainty while in Marceline, I'd know they were right by my side (actually on my wrist, but that's not how the saying goes).

As I joined Andre and Lucy, I couldn't ignore my jitters of anticipation. After so much preparation, I suspected we were all anxious to reach Missouri and get started.

Trevor whipped into the parking lot a few minutes behind me, making our group complete.

Imagine Jess James not being the last to arrive at a meeting spot. Maybe I would make that my goal while we were gone, sort of like a New Year's Resolution, only I could call it my Marceline Mantra! *Yeah! I like it!*

"So, Dude, what happened to that dirt you had on your face?" Andre teased Trevor as he got out of his car and joined our trio.

"I decided to shave off the beard. You know … new location, new look. You like it?" he asked, winking at Andre.

"Get back in your car, you lunatic," Andre said as he pushed Trevor back to his open car door in a good-natured, guy kind of way.

We vowed, amid Trevor's protest, to drive no more than ten miles over the speed limit once we were out of the city so we didn't get too far apart. Climbing into our vehicles, Andre led the way out of the parking lot. We followed him toward the I-10 and were officially on our way!

Traffic was light, for Los Angeles. We were actually making great time. I could see Andre and Lucy ahead of me, and in my rearview mirror, respectively, but Trevor was nowhere in sight.

Other cars were flying by us like rockets, so it had also become impossible to keep our speed limit pact.

We quickly moved from palm trees and buildings packed on top of one another to less congestion and a view of mountains dotted with green foliage.

Having never road-tripped far from the coast, I was excited to watch the changing topography as we headed east. I was particularly anxious to reach the Cajon Pass and enter the desert. I had recently read The Mojave Desert described as *"magnificent, an ever-changing kaleidoscope of shape and color."* And I love kaleidoscopes!

Once there, though, I looked around me and decided I must surely be driving through a different desert. All I saw was brown sand, dried up tumbleweeds, prickly cacti, mountain buttes which appeared as random, large rocks growing out of piles of dirt, and flat, endless barren land.

Averting my eyes from the scenery, I saw a message, from Trevor to our Group Chat, pop up on my dash screen.

"Meet at HOTTA's on Dean Martin Drive for lunch," Betty read the text aloud. "Best steak sandwich ever!"

Plugging the restaurant into the navigation system, Betty told me that we were a mere twenty-two minutes away from the Las Vegas restaurant. *Perfect!* I needed to stretch my legs, plus the muffin I had for breakfast had worn off about an hour ago.

We easily found the restaurant. Miraculously, Andre, Lucy and I had managed to stay together. Trevor, looking anxious for our arrival, was sitting in a booth with menus ready.

The restaurant's laidback vibe had something for all the senses. Painted on reclaimed wood were large, colorful murals covering the walls, upbeat music pulsed throughout the seating area, and the aroma from the grill made my mouth water for what they described as "heathy items with incredible flavor".

"What took you so long? Didn't you know the unofficial speed limit on the Mojave Highway is 90? And if I remember correctly, we even decided to push it a big ten miles an hour over that," Trevor stated.

"You're welcome to take one for the team. I know a dude whose ticket cost over $1000 driving through here. I'll pass, thank you," Andre said.

We mull over the lunch choices, and I learned that HOTTA stands for Healthy Options That Taste Amazing, even though the menu items appeared anything but healthy. Not sure when French fries ever became good for you, but they promised HOTTA's preparations had made them that way. I definitely planned on finding out.

I must have been starving because everything looked so delicious that it was hard to make a decision.

Our waitress arrived, and we placed our orders. Trevor was the only one getting "the best steak sandwich ever".

I collected and handed our menus to the waitress.

"That's a pretty bracelet," she commented while taking the menus.

"Thanks," I said as she headed off to get our drinks.

"I noticed your bracelet this morning, too. I really like it. It's elegant but casual," Lucy said.

"Trevor, don't you feel the same way about my Apple Watch ... elegant but casual?" Andre mimicked, brandishing his wrist so Trevor could mock admire his expensive timepiece.

Ignoring them, I answered Lucy. "I agree, and it goes with everything. My parents gave it to me last night as a going away present. My mom's got a great sense of style. I wish I would have gotten that gene."

"I wish I would have gotten your parents," Lucy said and chuckled. "Your mom has exquisite taste."

"Thanks," I replied.

Trevor's approving gaze moved from my wrist slowly up my arm and locked seductively on my eyes. After a few long seconds, I broke his stare, feeling red-hot heat creep into my cheeks. *What was that all about?* Suddenly, I wished our food would arrive and soon!

Stuffed after eating HOTTA's generous portions, we needed to hit the road. This was our shortest drive day, but we still had to maneuver some mountain passes, plus we had lost an hour changing time zones.

"Great pick for lunch," Andre complimented Trevor.

"I found it when a group of us stayed at Mandalay Bay. As a matter of fact, I'm heading over now for a few hands of Blackjack. I'll meet you at the hotel in St. George, unless anybody wants to join me," Trevor offered.

"No thanks," we all murmured.

"Are you sure nobody wants to try their luck at some cards or slots before we leave Vegas? There's even a little chapel next door. Hey, Jess, how about you and me get hitched?" Trevor said and chuckled.

I shook my head, blushing for the second time, which might have been a record – twice in one hour.

"I think I'll pass today, maybe on the way home," I joked, attempting to brush off his flirtation by playing along.

Lucy and Andre gave me quizzical looks.

"Have it your way," he shrugged. "Here's my first wager. Even with a head start, I bet I wind up passing you slowpokes on the interstate and beating you to St. George. Any takers?"

We moved to our individual cars, ignoring his offer and proceeded to Utah.

● ● ●

Arriving at our hotel approximately the same time our colleagues were leaving the office back in California, we decided to shower, change, and relax for a bit before meeting for dinner. I probably needed to hit the hotel gym since the only activity I had all day was sitting in a car or restaurant, but as I've never been a gym kind of girl, I quickly shook off that thought and decided on a nap, instead.

Choosing The Cliffside as our dinner destination – highly recommended by the hotel lobby clerk – the three of us finalized our evening plans and headed off to our rooms.

Trevor was about an hour behind us, he said, which for him would probably be more like forty-five minutes. *I should have taken his bet.*

Once refreshed, Andre, Lucy, Trevor and I congregated in the bar for a drink before being seated at a round table on The Cliffside's patio. Overlooking the St. George Valley and surrounding mountains, the view was stunning. Luckily, we arrived in time to watch the entirety of nature's twilight spectacular.

The pageant began as the sinking sun illuminated the mountains in vivid scarlets and burnt oranges, as if the desolate mesas were a ring of fire around the town below. The flames gradually faded to a lavender hue while night descended over the valley wishing the inhabitants a peaceful slumber.

If it sounded like I was quoting a brochure, I promise you, I wasn't. That sunset was literally the most breathtaking scene I had ever observed, one which would be etched forever in my mind's eye. And I finally understood. I had just witnessed the magic kaleidoscope of the Mojave Desert.

As evening settled around us, we began to relax in each other's company. Although we had been colleagues for several years, we had never really socialized as a group. A few Happy Hours here and there, but not anything on a real personal level.

Maybe it was time for us to get better acquainted. We would be a team for the next half year.

"I recently read an article entitled *You Are What You Eat*. It claims you can determine someone's personality by what they order from a menu," I said, pulling out my phone and opening my online subscription to *Cosmo*. "Here it is. What did you order, Lucy?"

"The Vegetarian Risotto."

"This is what it says about your personality if you eat vegetarian food … *Vegetarians are compassionate, empathetic, and extremely generous with both time and money. They should never be underestimated because a tremendous yet very quiet strength and resolve lives inside their hearts and souls. They are social creatures who do not like to be the center of attention but blossom when their considerable creative and artistic endeavors are noticed and praised. They have naturally sophisticated and discriminating taste. As peacekeepers, they will do anything to avoid conflict. Good fortune will land at their feet.*"

"What do you think, Lucy, is that you?" I asked.

"I can't believe it! I don't usually believe in this stuff, but that was spot on. And I'm counting on good fortune landing at my feet during the next six months. Do Andre's."

"What did you order, Andre?"

"I had the Roasted Baby Back Ribs."

"Let me see what I can find. Alright, this is your personality based on bar-b-que … *Lovers of smoked meats are the most committed to peacemaking of all personality types, but don't be fooled into thinking this means weakness. Physically they are extremely strong, possessing great courage and stamina. Because of their loyalty and trustworthiness, they are sought after and considered revered friends. Honest to a fault, snarky and quick tempered they are not easily pushed around, but always find a way to calmly resolve conflict. They will be successful in their endeavors."*

"Well, Andre, how close does that fit you?"

"I'm with Lucy. I usually consider this stuff to be a bunch of bull, but I have to say, overall, that's pretty much me. It's kind of scary."

"Okay, Trevor, you're next. What did you order tonight?" I inquired.

"This is pointless. I don't want to do it."

"Oh, come on," Lucy begged. "What can it hurt? He had the New York Strip."

"Steak ... here it is ... *The steak eater is usually very social and can emit a charming personality –* "

"Sounds good, now it's your turn, Jess," Trevor said.

"Not yet, there's a lot more in your category," I said and continued, ignoring his reluctance to play along. *"They are extremely athletic and love a good race or sports challenge. Always moving at a rapid pace, they learn new skills at an accelerated rate but continually change their minds and strategies. Vanity and volatile tempers cause them to throw titanic tantrums. They have a heightened sense of awareness of danger making it easy for them to escape harm in business and relationships. They are excellent in keeping secrets and have no qualms about using other's weaknesses to their own advantage. Lovers of all things monetary, they are extremely greedy. Success will come when they live on the edge."*

We all looked in Trevor's direction, but no one said a word.

"I told you this was meaningless," he grumbled as our checks arrived and broke up the conversation, or lack thereof.

I recognized Trevor was probably right about there being no connection between what you eat and your personality, but I still couldn't help but take a peek at my own before I went to bed. I fell asleep with one quote from the article on my mind ... *Once they begin a relationship or project, they will persevere for however long it takes to see the situation through, whatever the conclusion may be.*

CHAPTER 7

Leaving for Colorado the next morning, Andre, Lucy, and I planned on sticking close together for Day Two of our trip. Trevor got an early start so he could spend time with his brother's family in Denver, but he planned on hanging with us the following day, for the last part of our journey.

It was a sunny May morning as we began our trek across the Rocky Mountains.

Just before entering Colorado, the landscape began to change from the barren rocky mesas of Utah to the higher elevations and evergreen forests of Colorado. I was nervous about the sheer drop offs and uphill grades of the mountain passes but was relieved that the drive remained easy on the wide interstate.

Breathtaking beauty surrounded us on all sides as we wound beneath the steep mountains with their snowcapped peaks. Tall pine trees stood erect along the highway like soldiers guarding our path, suddenly breaking away to crystal clear lakes, rapidly flowing rivers and fields of wildflowers displaying colorful spring blooms.

Even with the required slowdowns for traffic to squeeze through small canyons, travel inside florescent-lit tunnels, or navigating over passes as high as 10,000-feet (according to the elevation sign on the side of the road), we were able to stay on schedule.

As we neared Denver, I began to feel as if we'd traveled back to Los Angeles, except the noticeable difference in greenery – no palm tree-lined streets, instead blossoms bursting from cherry, crabapple, and ash trees native to the area.

A growing metropolis, the lofty pines of the Rockies were substituted for construction cranes, and as we drove deeper into the city, skyscrapers replaced the mountain peaks. As the landscape moved from Mother Nature's masterpieces to man-made structures, the highway shifted from light traffic to city congestion.

Night had begun to fall, and the Denver skyline was alight with the twinkle of building lights. I thought of the evening on The Roofstop with Trevor and hoped we might be able to have a few more of those once we were settled in Marceline.

But tonight, tired from a long day of driving, I settled instead for a hot shower, room service, and a comfy bed.

• • •

Finally, morning dawned on the last leg of our journey. Unfortunately, though, as we packed ourselves back into our cars, it was apparent we wouldn't be experiencing the same sunny weather we had the past two days. Heavy clouds hung overhead, but at least the forecast didn't include rain, and the radar even indicated clearing skies by the time we reached Missouri.

We all vowed to stick together, obeying the no-more-than-ten-miles-over-the-speed-limit rule. We agreed that we wanted to share our first impressions of Marceline as a group.

With a long drive ahead of us, we got an early start, putting Colorado quickly into our rearview mirrors.

Immediately upon entering Kansas, it seemed as if we had yet again entered a new and different dimension. No tall and slender palm trees, no barren deserts, no red rock mesas, no snowcapped mountains, no downtown skyline, just miles and miles – and miles and miles – of flat, grassy fields dotted every now and then with a farmer driving a massive tractor, or an above-ground irrigation system spitting water over freshly planted crops, or grazing livestock in endless pastures.

The monotony of the view made staying focused increasingly difficult. I opened my windows to get fresh air, just as we were passing a cow pasture, go figure, and let me say that the odor wafting through Betty would definitely not be Calvin Klein's newest scent.

I blasted music through my car's speakers, singing off-tune at the top of my lungs and playing some mean air drums on my steering wheel. I called Mollie, then talked to Mom, I dictated some ideas for the Uptown Theater in my Notes App, started my Christmas list (it's only seven months away), planned my wedding (with a faceless, yet-to-be-named groom), named my children and, just when I thought we had gotten stuck in a time warp of endless nothingness, we entered the Greater Kansas City Area and, to my abundant relief, began to see signs of civilization.

The sun rejoiced with me, breaking out from behind fluffy white clouds.

In about two hours, we should, at long last, reach our final destination.

After a quick drive through Kansas City, we left the interstate that had been our friend the last three days and merged onto U.S. Route 36. Deciding to make our last pit stop, uncertain about the distance between towns on the rest of our drive, we stumbled upon a highway marker boasting about "America's Genius Highway".

According to the marker, 'U.S. Route 36 in northern Missouri is a four-lane, east-west roadway that tourism officials have dubbed *The Way of American Genius*.'

"No wonder we're being sent here," Trevor pointed out with a chuckle.

The marker went on to say:

> *Route 36 takes you to the childhood stomping grounds of Walt Disney, the headquarters of the legendary Pony Express that delivered communications more than twice as fast as competitors and the birthplace of a life altering inventor. From St. Joseph to Hannibal, Missouri's stretch of Highway 36 covers 195 miles of rolling farmland and small towns, offering attractions from state parks, lakes and farm tours to museums, mom-and-pop eateries and shops. Some of the names are familiar, like Walt Disney, Mark Twain, J.C. Penney, General John J. Pershing and Walter Cronkite. Others are lesser known, for instance, Andrew Taylor, the founder of osteopathic medicine, Howard A. Rusk, considered the father of rehabilitative medicine and Iowan Otto Frederick Rohwedder, owner of the first commercial bakery in the world to offer machine-cut bread as a convenience that has become a way of life. Some say a trip down Route 36 is better than sliced bread.*

"I can't believe that many important people came from this area," I said, astonished after reading the sign.

Everyone agreed.

I had a new appreciation for the area and began to feel enthusiastic anticipation for what was ahead.

The highway narrowed to a two-lane road as we left U.S. Route 36 for State Route 5. After several miles, it changed once again into Missouri Avenue and the city limits of Marceline. A right on Santa Fe moved us past the Walt Disney Hometown Museum to Kansas Avenue, where we took a left and pulled into four empty spots in front of Ripley Park.

We emerged from our vehicles and surveyed the surrounding area of our temporary home.

Lush green grass spread out in front of us. A small gazebo stood in the middle of the park with a pond off to the right, a fountain springing from its center. Circling the pond's perimeter was a walking path dotted with several benches for watching ducks bob in and out of the water, and it was connected on each side by what looked to be a recently constructed, arched bridge. Budding trees punctuated the park's landscape and provided a feeling of serenity.

We walked through the park to get a better look at its main feature – two immense trains on display, a large black steam engine and a red caboose.

Hearing the roar of a moving train barreling down the tracks just on the other side of the park, we all looked up.

"I read that 70 trains pass through here a day," I told the group. "I guess that's a sound we'll be getting used to."

Leaving the park, we walked past the Walt Disney Post Office on our way to Kansas Avenue – the stoplight-free thoroughfare through town. There, we saw three blocks of downtown businesses with angled parking spaces waiting for customers.

In the center of it all stood the Uptown Theater waiting for her revival.

The street was virtually empty as it was getting late and people were settling in for the evening, although my guess was there wasn't a much bigger crowd even in the middle of the day.

Silently, we turned to head back to our cars and find our *Airbnb*s.

Lucy suddenly stopped us and pointed up.

"Look," she said.

We followed her gaze to a street sign adorned with Mickey ears that read *Main Street U.S.A.*

This is why we are here, I thought.

And if this was considered the 'Original Main Street', we had our work cut out for us.

CHAPTER 8

Following Betty's GPS directions, I pulled up in front of a cute, white-framed bungalow on North Mulberry Street. (Oh, the irony – here I am in Disney territory, moving into a house from a Dr. Seuss book – go figure!)

Flowers had been planted in window boxes creating a charming welcome.

Before I began the arduous task of unpacking, I decided to check out the inside. Retrieving the key from a Lock Box on the side of the house, I walked up three steps to a screened porch, furnished with two white rattan chairs – one a rocker and the other a stationary chair with ottoman – adorned in blue and yellow floral cushions.

If the rest of the house was anything like this porch, I'm going to love it here!

Moving to the front door, I quickly unlocked it and peeked inside. I was greeted by a large, homey living area. Dropping the keys on a round table sitting directly to my right, I started my investigation of the premises.

A faux leather sofa rested against the front wall beneath two lead-paned windows and, in the corner, was what appeared to be a working, potbelly stove with a basket of wood waiting to be burned. Directly across from the sofa was a mounted TV and off to its left the entrance to the kitchen and eating area.

A large oak table, which could easily seat ten, dominated the room along with a built-in china cupboard – a nod to the era when the house was originally built, probably sometime in the 1930's.

Beyond the table was a step down to the kitchen, which had basic appliances but also a delightful, vintage red, Formica dinette set. Off the back of the shotgun-style kitchen was a back door leading to a landing with some steps down to a medium-sized fenced-in yard. A concrete pad at the foot of the stairs hosted a fire pit and patio ensemble, beckoning our little group to gather and enjoy some fresh country air.

Back in the living area, I headed down the narrow hall. Arched entrances to each of the two bedrooms added character. The first room was filled with a wrought iron bed covered in a white duvet and multiple pillows in various shapes, sizes and colors and a small, battered dresser. The second room was a small office which would be perfect for completing paperwork in the evenings.

I had hit the jackpot! This little cottage was even better than my studio apartment back in California. It just felt … cozy.

I moved the contents stored in Betty's trunk and back seat into the house and headed straight for the bedroom and a good night's sleep. It had been a long three days, and the real challenge would begin the next day. I'll unpack later, I thought to myself as my head hit the pillow.

• • •

I woke in the morning feeling amazingly refreshed. Digging out some clothes from my unpacked belongings, I hurried up and got ready, finding most of what I needed in the overnight bag I packed for the three-day drive.

With first day jitters, Betty took me the two short blocks to Kansas Avenue and a parking space directly in front of the Uptown Theater. I was supposed to meet Taylor Lubouski, my local design assistant, at eight o'clock. For once, I was remarkably on time (Day One and I had stuck to my Marceline Mantra, which was already more than I could say for most of my New Year's resolutions). Yet ... Taylor had beat me anyway.

My first impression of Taylor was that she was pale, almost translucent, with large, round, brown eyes like saucers set in a sweetheart-shaped face. She was dressed in a quirky red, pleated skirt adorned with a large bowknot in the front and a fitted black-and-white squared neck top with three-quarter-length puffy sleeves. With fringed bangs and a long, dark braid snaking down her back, she was hard to miss.

"Taylor?" I tentatively asked, although I was sure it was her on account of the profile pic Cassandra had given me.

When I said her name, she turned and walked my direction.

"I'm Jess. Nice to finally meet you."

"Hi. I can't tell you how excited I am to be working with you. I have so many ideas and changes I can't wait to share. Not everybody agrees, but I think this is going to be really good for our town," Taylor rattled off at lightning speed. "I don't know if you can tell, but I'm kind of nervous. This is such a big break for me. I know we're going to make this into an inspiration for the other vacant shops around here. There is so much potential in these old buildings. Where do you want to begin? I can show you around, if you want to start there. Otherwise, whatever you had in mind is okay by me."

To my great relief, she finally paused. I wasn't sure how a person could talk so long in one breath, but she seemed to be fine, not blue in the face and ready to faint, at all.

"I'd love it if you show me around," I said, "but I noticed a coffee shop next door. Do you mind if I get a cappuccino first?"

"That would be great! They have the best hot chocolate. I'll get that."

Walking next door to Sunrise Coffee, I was extremely thankful that Taylor didn't appear to be interested in ordering an espresso. I couldn't imagine her on high-octane caffeine. I chose a medium Café Carmella, and she got a small Hot Cocoa. She introduced me to the owner, Shelly. We exchanged pleasantries, and I expressed how happy I was to be in Marceline. I noticed, but ignored, a couple of patrons whispering to each other and giving me wary glances.

By the time we returned to the theater, the film crew had arrived and were unpacking their tremendous amounts of equipment. Trevor was with the lead cameraman, Jonathon, going over the plans for the 'before' scene shots that Andre and I would add narration to during the editing process.

I saw the back of Andre on the other side of the lobby talking to a hulking construction worker with dark wavy hair, wearing a blue plaid flannel, jeans, and stained work boots. Based on his attire, I assumed he was one of the local construction team. Plus, the heavily laden tool belt next to his feet was another clue.

Who knows, if this assignment doesn't work out maybe I'll change careers and become a detective ... just a thought.

It appeared that they were in a deep discussion, perhaps outlining the start of demolition as soon as the initial filming was complete.

Things were really starting to roll.

Taylor started my tour in the lobby with its empty glass candy case, outdated movie posters, and paint-chipped walls.

Diane Manley

"I love the crown molding around the ceiling in here," I told her. "We definitely need to incorporate it into the new design."

"I know, beautiful, isn't it? It's original from when the theatre was built. Before we move on though, I think it's important I fill you in on some of the history of this theater."

"Wait," I said. "This might be good background information to add to the first episode. Let me find Trevor and see if he wants to get footage of you sharing some of The Uptown Theater's past glory."

Trevor liked the idea and sent a group over to set up filming.

We stood outside, under the theatre's massive neon sign, as Taylor shared with me her local knowledge of the theater's decades-long story. Her abundance of energy made her a natural in front of the camera.

"The Uptown Theater, built in 1930, seats 286 people and remained open for eighty years. The largest events held in this building were the world premieres of two Disney films shown on this theater's original screen. The first was *The Great Locomotive Chase* in 1956, in which Walt and Roy Disney, along with their wives, traveled for several days by train from California to attend. It was here that Disney announced to the world 'his best memories were the years he spent in Marceline – it's where he found the magic'."

Making brief eye-contact with Trevor, he gave me a quick thumbs-ups as Taylor continued her narrative.

"This film was special to Walt Disney due to his fascination with trains from an early age when engines roared down the tracks right on the outskirts of town. That's why it was so important to him that the debut of *The Great Locomotive Chase* be in Marceline. Even the idea for Mickey Mouse came to him while riding on a train," Taylor explained, her tone showcasing her genuine interest in the historical value of the theatre and Marceline.

"The second premiere shown in this theater was the 1998 film entitled *The Spirit of Mickey,* which was an anthology of Mickey Mouse Cartoons from the 1930's and 1940's. It was attended by 18,000 people and two special guests ... Mickey and Minnie Mouse. Although Walt Disney came back to Marceline several times over the years, one of the most important was in 1946 when he shot movies of the entire three blocks of Main Street in order to replicate our downtown for his entrance to Disneyland and its Main Street U.S.A. The Main Street Cinema in Disneyland, which shows early Mickey cartoons, is designed after this Uptown Theater."

We moved inside to the now abandoned lobby as Taylor finished her spiel and the crew wrapped filming.

"You were great," I said, and I meant it, she was. "It really helps to get to know the building. I don't know if that makes any sense, but what we want to do is modernize and repurpose her, but not completely change her. We want to keep some of her amazing history."

"That's what the town is hoping. We love our old buildings. It's just that they're a little tired and need some revitalization."

"I hope that is what we can accomplish. And it's why it's so important that we work together to keep the local personality in the renovation. I'm a television person with a creative background, you're the designer, so I'll be leaning on you a great deal for ways to mix the old with the new ... to make a fabulous, updated facility."

"Okay, I like the sound of that, so how do you want to begin?" Taylor asked.

"Well, I thought we could go over the ideas that each of us have been contemplating for the past month or so since this whole thing got the green light. For example, my producer was very clear about using the Disney theme *sporadically* throughout the building instead of all over it. She instructed us to keep in mind that this is a twenty-first century performing arts center for the people who live in Marceline *today*. The museum is a couple of blocks down the road, she said, not here in the theater."

"I agree, go on," Taylor said and then smiled.

"One idea I have," I shared, "came from a visit years ago to Disney World."

"I bet you went there a lot as kid, with it being so close."

"Yes, I went to Disneyland a couple of times a year, but I'm talking about Disney World. My family never felt the need to travel far from the coast, but one summer we were invited to a relative's wedding in Florida. We went for an entire week and made it into a vacation. While there, we decided to check out the Disney World parks. That's where I learned about Hidden Mickeys. They are three round circles grouped together to form a Mickey head placed in out-of-the-way spaces. I thought it might be fun to conceal Hidden Mickeys throughout the facility as we renovate each section."

"I love it! What a great idea! Are they located in all the parks?"

"We only went to Animal Kingdom and Epcot, but they were spread throughout each of those. I guess you could say I've seen them in my extensive travel all around the world," I said and chuckled.

Out of the corner of my eye, I saw Trevor had popped through the theater doors into the lobby.

"We were just about to call it a day," I said to him. "We've got a start on some great ideas."

"You need to be ready Monday. I've scheduled filming of the walk-through where you point out each of your planned design changes to the building's owners for their approval."

"I'll be ready," I assured him.

CHAPTER 9

After a stop at the local grocery store to pick up some much-needed food, I headed back to my new place for a quiet night of unpacking.

As I pulled up in the driveway, I saw Mona, still in her tree box, waiting for me on the porch. Leaving my bags in the car, I hurriedly unlocked the front door, dragged Mona into the living room, removed her wrapping while trying not to break off any of her precious shoots, and found a perfect spot for her next to the sofa, near the window where she would receive plenty of light. I found a plastic pitcher in the kitchen and filled it to the top.

"I bet you're thirsty, aren't you girl?" I asked her as I probably overwatered her.

About an hour later, with a full tummy of frozen pizza and salad, I started the daunting task of unpacking all my belongings.

I crammed the closet in each bedroom with my clothes, shoes, and a few fun hats then stored away the empty suitcases. Still littering the living room floor were several boxes filled with random necessities that needed to find homes.

I opened the first carton and pulled out a desk lamp and some office supplies. Rooting through the bottom of the box for my laptop cord, I saw something scuttle to the other side of the container.

Pulling my hand out as if it were on fire, I inadvertently knocked the box on its side, jumped on top of the sofa like some decathlon athlete, and screamed at the top of my lungs, just as a mouse ran across the floor into the dining room and through the kitchen.

What should I do?! Breathing so heavily I began to hyperventilate, I knew exactly what I needed to do. Call my dad! *Wait, I can't call Dad. He's in California, and I'm in Missouri.* Okay, be an adult, I coached myself. *It's only a tiny mouse. You can handle this. You are a strong, brave, rodent warrior.*

I slowly and carefully stepped off the sofa, grabbed my keys and bag from the table by the door, yelled to Mona to keep an eye (or leaf) out for the mouse, quickly locked the door and ran to my car.

I remembered seeing a hardware store on Main Street. *I'll just go buy a mouse trap. Easy.*

I made it to the hardware store a mere fifteen minutes before closing time. Having never been in the store, it took me a few tries before finding the bug spray aisle where I began looking for mouse traps.

Out of the corner of my eye, I saw Mr. Blue Plaid Flannel, Jeans and Stained Work Boots coming towards me. I looked up, and we made eye contact and smiled at each other. I continued to search for a trap, but unfortunately, they seemed to be out.

"Do you need some help?" he asked. "You look lost."

"I'm looking for mouse traps. I seem to have one in my house."

He began to chuckle, although I was fairly certain I had not said anything funny.

"You're new in town, aren't you?"

"Yes … ," I said cautiously.

"Well, you need to remember where you are. Mice are a protected species in Marceline."

He pointed to a square package sitting directly in front of me.

"This is what you need. It's a special bait box that makes mice thirsty, causing them to leave your house in search of water, without killing them. Put one under your sink and another by the washer and dryer. Place the rest around the outside perimeter, and you won't see any more mice."

"Really! That sounds easy enough."

"Really, it is pretty simple," he countered. "Hey, aren't you here with *LeisureTV*?"

"Yes. I just got in last night."

"I thought I saw you over at the Uptown earlier today. I'm Chance ... Chance Alexander."

"Hi, I'm Jess ... Jess James, Design Coordinator for the renovation."

"I got stuck working with Andre. Nothing against him, he seems like a great guy. I'm just not a fan of this project."

"Then why are you doing the demo and reconstruction work?" I questioned, out of curiosity.

"My dad is still the patriarch of the family construction business, and he was ecstatic when we got the bid. Believes this is the best thing to happen to Marceline in a long time. I happen to disagree, but business is business."

"Why don't you think this is a good idea? It's going to be great for the town."

"Just don't think we need some fancy California folks coming in here and changing everything. No offense."

"None taken. It seems to me the economy in the area is hurting, and a show like this can help give the city some exposure and the boost it needs for revitalization."

"My point exactly. You don't even know us, and you're making those kinds of assumptions. You probably think we're all a bunch of dumb hicks or rednecks or whatever name you want to use, but we're not. We're smart, innovative, tech-savvy, creative, hardworking, plus we feed you with what we grow," he said and paused a moment. "Sorry, I didn't mean to go off on you like that, it's just that this is a great community with great people, and it's hard to watch a bunch of strangers come in and try and change it. Anyway, I've got to run. Good luck with the mouse."

I took my mouse bait to the checkout counter.

A middle-aged gentleman, who had clearly been waiting to close up shop for the night, met me at the register. I could tell he had overhead our conversation and, for the second time that day, I received an apprehensive look from one of the locals.

Arriving home, I immediately placed the bait stations in the two locations Chance suggested. Even though it was now dark, I went outside to position the rest of the boxes around the house.

Just as I finished and was about to return inside, I looked up and saw a night sky alight with, what must be, a thousand sparkling stars. I had never seen anything like it. The entire sky was dotted with glowing lights.

It made me think how far away L.A. was and that, a few days ago, I was commenting to Trevor how pretty Tinsel Town's buildings looked all lit up at night. But that was nothing compared to this. I had no idea what a dark night without city lights could really look like. And it was phenomenal!

I went back inside the house and moved every belonging I owned off the floor, away from my miniature "Mickey" mouse, and headed off to bed, pondering the accusations Chance had made.

The Wonderful World of Marceline

I wonder how many people in Marceline are like his dad, happy to have us here, and how many people wish we'd just go back to where we came from?

CHAPTER 10

I started the next morning once again with a Café Carmella but added an oatmeal raisin cookie to the order. If I wasn't careful this was going to become a very fattening habit.

I headed into the Uptown Theater, with my hands full of goodies.

I was excited to see that the door was already propped open, allowing fresh air to circulate throughout the stuffy, stale-smelling old building.

After only one bite of warm cookie and a sip of decadent cappuccino, Trevor beckoned me to join him in a discussion he was having with Andre.

I set my cookie on the glass candy counter and arrived just as Trevor was explaining to Andre that he recently met with the owner of USAMade, Mr. Larry Biggs, and Mr. Biggs had requested our presence for a reception at his home on Friday night.

As this was the first, and largest, in a string of fulfillment centers he planned to open along the Santa Fe Railway, he had purchased a second home in the area to personally oversee the initial operations.

"It is a semi-formal garden party taking place on his back lawn, with drinks and hors d'oeuvres served at seven," Trevor informed us. "All of the local business owners, city council members, as well as our team have been invited for the kick-off of the Main Street Project. This is your official invitation, so let me know if you have any questions."

Leaving Trevor and Andre to continue their conversation, I took the sketches of our new design and entered the deserted theater for a better look at the current condition of the auditorium and to see if any of its contents were salvageable for repurposing.

Walking down the worn, red-carpeted aisles, I took in the character emitted by this theater of yesteryear. Its torn, hard-backed folding seats lining each angled row, a pair of speakers facing the audience, handmade steps leading up to a painted platform functioning as a stage, and behind the stage, a large sagging white screen, tacked to the back wall, were among the first items to be renovated. Anchored on the side walls were some ornamental, gold-filigreed decorations, which might be the only items worth saving.

It was easy to see how this was once the gem of the town, but that time seemed to have sadly passed it by.

As I looked at the area in front of me, I thought how different this was from the theaters I frequented at home. In fact, every experience, since leaving California – from the hot, dry desert to the multi-colored sunsets and brilliant starry nights – had been unlike anything I had ever encountered. And that realization gave me an idea, something I never thought of when working on the preliminary design in my office cubicle, a better idea than the blueprint sitting in front of me.

Taking out my phone, I looked at the clock in the upper right-hand corner of the screen. Even with the time difference, it shouldn't be too early to reach Cassandra.

She answered on the first ring and immediately wanted to know if there was a problem. She had a lot riding on the project and although she would never admit it, I think she was a little nervous about pulling it off.

"I know we have our team's weekly teleconference meeting on Monday, but I have a proposal that couldn't wait."

I described my epiphany and the new ideas I had for the theater in detail. I then posed two basic questions. "Cassandra, is the idea feasible and more importantly, can my new plan fit in the existing budget?"

"That is a significant change, Jess. We will have to cut somewhere else to pull this off, but I like it. And since the theater is the crown jewel of the entire project, I say, let's go with it. I'll contact Trevor and fill him in."

Ecstatic, I touched base with the design sketch artist in his Los Angeles office and explained what changes needed to be made to the original plans and, to his great chagrin, told him I needed the updated drawings by first thing Monday morning.

Next, I contacted Taylor and informed her about the revised design. With an infectious enthusiasm that I was quickly learning was uniquely her, she began spewing ideas to compliment the alterations I had outlined.

It seemed that everyone was on board.

● ● ●

Remaining in the theater for the rest of the afternoon, I practiced my presentation and developed what questions I would be asking Erin Langley, the current owner of the Uptown Theater, when filming started on Monday. That was when I would be meeting Erin for the first time so the camera crew could capture her true reaction to the design plans for transforming the Uptown Theater into the Uptown Performing Arts Center.

Although she and her husband owned the entire building, including the Airbnb located on the top floor, where Trevor and Andre were currently residing, we would only be renovating the lower level – the lobby, theater, and the new addition with its practice and multipurpose rooms.

Like Chance's father, Erin was hopeful that the changes happening in the area would bring new life to Marceline.

At least that makes two people in favor of us being here.

Packing up my belongings, I headed out of the theater and back into the lobby, where Trevor, Andre and Chance were conferring on the safest way to take down the large neon 'Uptown' sign gracing the outside entrance of the building. As it was original to the structure, much care needed to be given in removing it in order to renovate the theater's exterior.

Just as I was about to tell them to have a good evening, a brown spotted, medium-sized stray dog meandered in the open front door. It wasn't overly shaggy, but it was obviously hungry and looking for food.

"Hey, Chance, do you know whose dog this is?" I asked.

"Nope. I've seen him strutting around town the last week or so, but he runs away whenever I get too close."

"Here boy," I squatted, trying to entice him further into the lobby. "Where did you come from?"

He wagged his tail slightly and stared warily at the three of us.

"We need to find a leash and take him to the animal shelter," I said.

For the second time in two days, Chance started laughing and I had no idea why.

"There's no animal shelter in Marceline. If you can catch him, you can take him over to Doc Andrews on Lake Street, though."

I saw my leftover cookie sitting on the candy counter, and even though it was probably hard as a rock by now, I was pretty sure this dog would eat anything. "Want a treat? Come here big guy."

I broke the cookie in half and held out my hand, encouraging the dog to move closer. "Come on, buddy, it's yours if you want it."

The dog moved forward, sniffed and took the cookie.

"Wasn't that good? Do you want some more?" I said in a little doggie voice I didn't even know I could do.

He took the other half of my cookie, and I was able to grasp him loosely around the waist. "Hold still, cutie, and we'll get you home. Can somebody help me move him to my car?"

"I'm pretty sure I have a rope in my truck that we can make into a leash, if you can hold him a few seconds," Chance said as he jogged out the front door.

He returned quickly carrying a rope that he had already transformed into a makeshift leash.

"Any more mice?" he asked as we placed the loop over the dog's head and secured it by slightly tightening the knot.

"No, I think the bait stations worked, thankfully."

"First a mouse, now a dog. You seem to have real animal magnetism," he said with a smirk and raised eyebrow.

I rolled my eyes (a skill my mom would say I mastered at a very young age) and walked with the dog out the front door to my car.

"Let's go, boy," I said to my new friend while hoisting his twenty pounds (*an estimated weight based on my extensive knowledge of dog poundage – okay truth, I'm just guessing*) into my passenger seat. "We're going to see the nice doctor who will find your people."

Without an appointment, we had to wait about twenty minutes to see the vet. I tried to explain to the receptionist that I merely wanted to drop the dog off, but instead we were placed in an empty examination room. After another short wait, the door opened and in walked a rather young female in a white lab coat.

"Hi, I'm Doctor Andrews, but everybody around here calls me Kaitlin or Doc. I don't believe we've met."

"Nice to meet you. I'm Jess. We haven't met because I recently moved here from California to do the renovation on the Uptown Theater. About an hour ago, this sweet guy wandered in through the open front door into the lobby, and I'm here to drop him off so he can get home."

With a scowl etched across her brow, Kaitlin explained, "This little guy probably escaped from one of the illegal puppy mills in the area, which means it is not too likely a family is missing him. As the only vet in town, I'm pretty familiar with the family pets for miles around, and I've never seen this dog before. Let me give him a quick exam."

The dog sat calmly on the examination table, enjoying the attention, as Doc Andrews looked him over from top to bottom. "He is in surprisingly good shape for a puppy mill animal. It looks like he escaped at a young enough age, probably around a year old, so he doesn't have too much damage yet."

"That's good news. What breed is he?" I asked, out of curiosity.

"I'd say he's a beagle with some Jack Russell terrier mixed in. He's got great markings."

"So, what happens to him now?"

"Unfortunately, I don't have the facilities to keep dogs for more than seven days. If a dog isn't claimed, I try and find it a foster home, but after the seven days are up, the animal gets sent to the Linn County Animal Shelter. They keep it for seven more days and try to it adopt out."

"Then what?" I wondered aloud, having a strong notion I wasn't going to like the answer.

"Do you really want to know?"

She looked at me, her expression indicating that she knew I already understood how this was going to play out.

"They can't do that!" I couldn't hide my horror.

I looked at the dog, and he looked up at me and lovingly licked my hand.

"Looks like you've made a friend. It appears someone wants to go home with you," Doc Andrews said, petting him.

"I don't know anything about having a dog. I've never owned a pet, not even a gerbil."

Just as I said this, the dog rested its head on my outstretched fingers and let out a heavy sigh. And in that brief moment, I realized I had fallen in love.

"It's not hard to take care of a dog," the doc continued, "just a big responsibility. You need to feed him, let him outside, walk him, play with him and, most of all, love him. It's pretty straightforward. With you being new in town, it might be nice to have a dog. He seems like he's ready to be your loyal companion. I do need to take his picture and post it on my board for a week to make sure no one is looking for him, but if he isn't claimed by then, we can fill out the paperwork, and he will be yours."

I didn't weigh the pros and cons, and I didn't overthink it, instead, I asked for directions to the nearest pet store.

Doc Andrews laughed and said, "Get on Highway 36 and go 125 miles to Kansas City or head out of town a half hour to the Tractor Supply Store. Remember, this is rural Missouri, Jess. But I've got everything you'll need for now."

We picked out a collar, leash, bowls, crate, pillow, food, treats for training, floor cleaner (in case there were accidents), a brush and shampoo, and lastly, a few toys.

My plan had been to drop off a dog but, somehow, I was leaving the vet's office with several bags of supplies and a new friend. I did one last check and got online to verify my Airbnb was pet friendly – YES it was!

We piled everything, including the dog, into my car and made for home.

"It looks like you made the right decision when, as Granny would say, 'you flew the coop'," I said to the dog. "Hey, I like that. What do think of the name Cooper?"

Although he was shaking, I saw a slight wag of his brown and white-tipped tail.

"It really fits you."

We pulled into the driveway, I parked the car and went around to the passenger side. As soon as I opened the door, he jumped out.

"Welcome home, Cooper," I whispered.

CHAPTER 11

Our first week in Marceline quickly came to a close. And it had become quite a challenge for me to stay focused on the renovations. All I could think about was rushing home after work to play with Cooper.

He loved to chase his ball, win at tug of war, and was even responding fairly well to training. I was able to go home at lunch and let him out, which kept him from having too many accidents and earned him enormous amounts of praise. We had been working on sit-and-stay, but that was going to take a lot longer to master. My guess was he wasn't trying very hard so he could keep getting treats. *That's what I would do.*

Tonight was the reception at The Biggs' estate. I was picking up Lucy so we didn't have to walk in by ourselves (and later that evening, I was pretty sure we would also honor the unspoken girl's pact of going to the restroom at the same time).

I had not brought many outfits suitable for a semi-formal, outdoor gathering, so I decided on my vintage '50's yellow-flowered, sleeveless dress with its cinched waist, scoop neck, and V-cut back, paired with matching low-heeled, sling back, bow pumps. Keeping my hair down for a change, I loosely curled the ends, added a touch of make-up, and double checked my appearance in the mirror. *Not bad.*

I gave Cooper a kiss, put him in his kennel (with the promise of a treat if he didn't have an accident), and flew out the door.

Lucy and I drove a short distance out of the town's center to the Biggs' sprawling, hundred-year-old, Greek revival. Perched atop a knoll that was surrounded by acres of grass and open fields, the mansion stood proud, like a monument to a bygone era. The front entrance, dominated by four, ornate, white columns rising from the portico to the peaked pediment, reminded me more of the South than the Midwest. Painted white, the mansion was adorned with black shutters, towering chimney stacks on each side of its structure, and a short flight of steps leading to a glass front door. A matching car port, added to the left side of the house, gave it a sense of asymmetry.

We traveled up the circular driveway, admiring the property, and were met by a local teen hired to valet. He parked my car in a grassy area away from the house as Lucy and I made our way to the back lawn.

Standing apart from the other guests made Trevor and Andre easy to locate. With drinks in hand, they were talking amongst themselves on the lush lawn near the entrance to a formal garden.

As we walked toward them, I looked around. I did not recognize a single person in the crowd (I wasn't sure why I thought I would know anyone in a town I had lived in for a mere week, but I looked anyway.)

Some of the guests seemed to be enjoying themselves, but others appeared to be completely out of their element and looked so uncomfortable that I suspected they might bolt at any second.

Andre, Lucy, and I talked about the amazing architecture and grounds surrounding us while Trevor sauntered over to the portable bar positioned on the patio to get Lucy and me a drink.

"Thanks, Trevor," we said in unison upon his return with two glasses of white wine.

"You ladies look stunning this evening," he said to the two of us as he handed us our drinks.

His eyes lingered on me, making my heart skip a beat.

A lull crept into our conversation, so we digressed into shop talk, the one thing we had in common. We were all excited for the next week when things would really get rolling. The crew had already filmed scenes highlighting the three blocks of Kansas Avenue – or Main Street USA as it was officially renamed in 1998 – for the opening of the show. After my tour with Erin on Monday, the demolition could start in earnest from inside to outside.

"That old neon sign is going to be difficult," Andre said. "We were discussing with Chance the best way to get it down and refurbish it when you found that dog. By the way, Jess, whatever happened to him?"

"I adopted him," I said as they all stared at me in disbelief. "Well, it isn't official yet. I have to wait a few more days, but he's living with me for now."

"Jess, we're only here for six months. You can't adopt a pet. What are you going to do when we leave? I mean, does your place back home even allow pets?" Trevor asked.

"I love dogs! What does he look like?" Lucy chimed in.

"He's light brown and white with the cutest face you've ever seen. It's tan with a white muzzle and a white stripe snaking between these liquid brown eyes leading all the way from his nose to the top of his forehead," I happily answered Lucy and ignored all of Trevor's comments.

And yes, those same questions had crossed my mind … more than once. But I flatly refused to worry about them until the time came.

"How did you find him?" Lucy inquired, having not heard anything about our dog adventure of a couple of days ago.

"He wandered into the theater the other day. I think he was looking for food, so I gave him a cookie."

"And then Chance came to her rescue with a rope that he turned into a leash, like balloon art you see clowns perform at festivals," Trevor snickered.

"Saving a dog! That's so cool! I bet he will keep you busy," Lucy added.

"You need something to keep you busy around here. There's not too much going on, as far as I can tell," Andre quipped.

"I stumbled across some games in one of the closets where I'm staying. Want to have an old fashion game night at my house tomorrow night?" I threw the idea to the group.

"I'm in," Lucy said.

"I'll pop a bunch of popcorn for snacks," I proclaimed, trying to convince the other two to join us.

"Sounds alright to me. I'll bring some beer," Trevor offered.

"I'll be there, although it might be with something a little stronger than beer," Andre said.

"I'm a wine person, myself. So I'll bring a couple of bottles to share. What time, Jess?" Lucy asked.

As we were finalizing our plans for the next evening, Mr. Biggs, an imposing man with a broad face and slicked back black hair, moved to the center of his immense patio, stepped up on a small, temporary platform and commenced to coughing into a cordless microphone to get the crowd's attention.

"I would like to welcome you here today to kick off Project Main Street," he began. "Project Main Street is the start of what we hope to be a movement across this great nation of ours. I wish my daughter, Samantha, could be with us today, as much of this project was her brainchild, but she is scouting our next location in a small southwest town, also along the Santa Fe Railway. But before I expand on our mission, I would like to acknowledge a few of our special guests. First, Bob Knowell, Mayor of Marceline, along with the entire City Council."

As the mayor and council members raised their hands in a brief wave, people clapped.

"Next, I would like to recognize Herb Walker, Chairman of the Linn County Chamber of Commerce. These two organizations have worked many late nights to get this project off the ground. USAMade had several cities in mind, but we were so impressed with Marceline and the effort put forth by the City Council and Chamber of Commerce to make this project a reality, the decision wound up being an easy one. Thank you."

Another round of applause ensued.

"And to all of the business owners along the three blocks of Kansas Avenue, better known as Main Street, we're excited at the transformations you have outlined and your open-mindedness in improving the heart of Marceline."

Once again, a smattering of people raised their hands as the rest of us golf clapped.

I actually recognized two people from the small group being acknowledged – Shelly from Sunrise Coffee, who appeared to be pleased to be at the event, and the gentleman who checked me out at the hardware store who, not surprisingly, looked like he would rather be absolutely anywhere besides a fancy garden party.

"Jim, Jim Alexander, where are you?" Mr. Biggs asked.

A sturdy, attractive, gray-haired man at the back of the crowd gave a brief wave.

"There you are. We are excited to be working with Alexander Construction who will be making the downtown renovations a reality starting with the Uptown Theater. And speaking of renovations, I would lastly, like to give a shout out to Trevor Dorrington and his team who will be filming the transformation of Marceline's historic buildings for the new show *Main Street* airing on *LeisureTV*."

We raised our hands and waved to the group, whose faces displayed mixed reactions.

"Studies show people are moving from urban cities to rural areas in droves," Mr. Biggs said. "Although many reasons exist for this phenomenon, what we've experienced is that people are beginning to understand what you have always known ... small towns are special. I also know this well, having been born and proudly raised in rural America. But this small town is particularly special. From the Main Street of Marceline burst a man who exemplified an excitement for dreaming big and making the impossible, possible. Our folks from California can tell you, upon entering Disneyland and Main Street U.S.A., one evokes a sense of happiness ... not only children, but adults, and people from every walk of life, and from every nation in the world."

Looking over the crowd, from the doubters to the optimists, I could see Mr. Biggs had the group's undivided attention.

"Our goal isn't to change Marceline," he continued. "It's to give Marceline a fresh coat of paint. To reinvigorate a city with a proud history. With the addition of USAMade's new fulfillment center to the region, we see an opportunity for Marceline to add new jobs, invite new blood into the community, and expand, by using money generated from a vibrant, local economy ... all while keeping its hometown feel. Those of you with existing businesses on Main Street are sitting on prime real estate that, with a few updates and renovations, can pay great dividends. Improvements are difficult to turn into reality when business is stagnant. But as commerce increases, and it will, we say ... do what this town is known for and dream big!"

PART II

Living the Dream

CHAPTER 12

I woke the next day to a warm spring morning, the kind of morning the birds had obviously been pining for during the long, cold winter. Singing loudly, they swooped from trees to rooftop, chasing each other and grasping twigs off the ground for building their nests.

The sun was rising brilliantly over my front screened porch, turning it into a beckoning and bright oasis.

After letting an excited Cooper into the backyard, I made myself a cup of morning coffee, grabbed a breakfast bar from the small pantry and headed for the front porch. Moving to one of the rattan chairs, I watched the birds (something I had never done in my life, but suddenly found fascinating) and picked up my latest edition of *Cosmo*.

Relaxing was something I rarely did in L.A., but here, I found the peacefulness of it almost therapeutic.

Finishing my magazine, I decided to put a visit to the library I had spied near the town's entrance on my afternoon To-Do List (something else I rarely did in my life, but now found surprisingly appealing).

As the sun rose higher in the sky, I decided to try out the leash and give Cooper a walk through the neighborhood, which was laid out in a web of random, crisscrossed streets. Hooking his leash to his blue and black camo-patterned collar – one of the few choices at Doc Andrews' clinic – we practiced sitting (which earned him a Scooby Snack) before striking out on our adventure.

Once out the front door, however, Cooper was in total control. I could barely keep up with him as he tugged and pulled, dragging me to some unknown location. When he saw a squirrel run up a tree two houses away, I nearly lost hold of his leash altogether.

Stumbling down the road, I tried to keep a firm hold on his leash as I gave a friendly wave to people out cutting dewy lawns and planting spring flowers.

I wasn't sure if it was my imagination or not, but it felt as if the residents on my street were returning puzzled stares rather than warm, fuzzy, neighborly smiles.

Cooper either tugged or sniffed through our entire journey, and I was exhausted by the time we returned home. Clearly, we needed training, not only with sit-and-stay, but we could now add taking-a-walk to the ever-growing list.

As we approached the edge of our yard, I heard a small voice call out a friendly greeting. Assuming it must be for someone else, since I knew very few in Marceline, I glanced around for the source of the voice.

The street appeared to be empty except for Cooper and me. Doing a double take in every direction, I finally noticed an elderly lady, rocking on her narrow porch, waving to me.

Quickly, I opened my gate, shooed Cooper into the backyard, and traipsed next door to see what my neighbor might need.

"Hello, Dear."

I automatically loved this woman, since no one had ever called me *Dear*, except Granny.

"Hi, I'm Jess … Jess James. I moved in a couple of days ago with the group from *LeisureTV*. We're here shooting the television show about Main Street," I said as I held out my hand in a friendly greeting.

"Have a seat," she said and gave my hand a soft pat. "I have an extra rocker just waiting to be used."

Pointing to a matching chair sitting on the opposite side of her front door, I sat and automatically began to gently move back and forth.

"Oh, I know who you are," she continued. "You don't live in this town your whole life without knowing what's going on. I'm Ida Jenkins. It's nice to meet you, Jess. Sorry it's taken me so long to officially welcome you. I don't move around as well as I used to or I would have been over the day after you moved in. The day you found the mouse."

"How do you know about the mouse?" I asked, astounded.

"Like I said, you don't live your entire life in this town without knowing what is going on," she said and grinned. "Can I offer you a glass of iced tea, Dear?"

"I'd love that! Thank you."

"I tell you what, there is a pitcher on the kitchen counter and a clean glass in the cabinet directly above it. Why don't you pop in and pour yourself some? It will take much less time if you do it than if I hobble in there."

I opened the screen door and crossed a very floral-patterned living room into the kitchen with its pitcher of iced tea located right where Ida said it would be. After pouring a glass, I returned to the porch and my rocking chair.

"Looks like you've got yourself a feisty one there in that Cooper," she said and pointed toward my backyard.

Once again, I wondered how she knew Cooper's name, but this time I didn't ask. Instead, I commented how sweet he was, but that there was still a lot of training needed.

"I expect he broke free from one of the puppy mills up the highway."

"That's what the vet believes, too," I added.

"Kaitlin is sure a good person. Nice gal for you to get to know better."

"She was really helpful," I agreed.

"So, you've been here a few days now. What are your first impressions of our little town?"

I hesitated, not really sure what I thought. "I've got mixed feelings," I began. "Some people have been friendly, while others seem resentful that we are here. Some of the old buildings are inviting, while others look like they are ready to fall down. Sometimes, I think this place is a relic of the past and yet, at the same time, it seems to be screaming that it is ready for a new future. Am I making any sense?"

"Perfect sense, Dear," she nodded, a wise expression coming over her face. "Many of the good people in this town are afraid of change. Give them time. They'll come around. You'll see. Our buildings are sturdy like our residents. They have a stubborn streak in them that makes them strong like diamonds in the rough. We have a heritage that we are very proud of around here. The magic still lives in this town. It's just that some folks have forgotten how to believe in it. I've seen it all firsthand, the good and the bad, and I'm so excited to still be here and to watch Marceline's new chapter unfold."

"I'm excited too, I think," I said and then chuckled.

Finishing my tea, I thanked Ida for her hospitality and made my way home with a promise to visit her again soon. She had left me with a sense of optimism for the coming changes, tinged with a new respect for the people and places surrounding me. I needed that.

"Better water those flowers in your window boxes before they die," Ida yelled across the lawn, giving me one last bit of grandmotherly advice.

I glanced over at the wilting mini petunias, or Calibrachoa, as the internet called them when I frantically searched *popular container flowers* to learn how to care for the live splash of color hanging from my windows. Since Mona was the only plant that I had not killed, I had decided I needed some of Google's expert advice on plant care. *Maybe that's why I'm so attached to Mona. She's my one and only plant success-story, which reminds me, I probably need to water her, too.*

A few hours later, after watering Mona and her sister plants, Ruby and Violet (the mini petunias), I headed into town to grab some popcorn and other essentials for the evening's game extravaganza. Picking up everything I needed, I then visited the public library to nab some reading material for more lazy mornings on my screened-in porch.

Like so many places in Marceline, the library's façade was a tribute to its proud history. The two-story brick structure, built in 1920, was flanked with white iconic columns at its entrance and was punctuated with a sign boasting about its patronage by the Carnegie Foundation.

The first display I saw upon entering the building was a selection of books on the history of Marceline and various other regions throughout the state. I chose a past-and-present coffee table book to help me better understand the culture of the area and then made my way to the fiction section.

Not much of a reader and without a favorite author, I decided to make my selection based on each book's cover and the short synopsis on the back. I found a book that looked light and fun, but more importantly, it had a dog very similar to Cooper right on the front. With his tilted head and pleading eyes, he appeared to be begging me to read about his escapades. *Perfect!*

• • •

That evening, even though they had driven separately, Andre, Lucy and Trevor all arrived at my house at the same time. I put down my new library book and greeted them as they marched up the porch steps.

"This is really nice," Lucy commented.

Upon hearing their voices, Cooper came bounding through the doorway to greet our company.

"So, this is Cooper," I smiled, pushing his front paws off of Lucy, mentally adding one more training goal to the list – *No jumping!*

Next, he ran to Andre, giving his outstretched hand a wet welcome. Change that from one to two more training goals – *No jumping* and *No licking. Either I am going to end up with an undisciplined pup or a very fat dog.*

"Come on, Cooper, time for a nap in your kennel," I told him.

Between the walk and playing in the backyard all afternoon, he should have been exhausted. My guess was he would knock out the minute he curled up on his pillow.

Everyone followed me inside and wanted to see around my place.

"This is way better than where they stuck me," Lucy said.

"Andre and I are above the Uptown Theater, which is convenient. We each have our own, fairly spacious apartment that has some interesting original architecture, but the Mickey-themed decor is over the top for me, would you agree, Andre?"

"Pictures, sheets, dishes, even the shower curtain … yeah, I'd say it's a bit much. But it's clean, comfortable and only for six months, so I can handle it. I just have to make sure none of my friends back in L.A. ever find out, or I will never live it down. I've got a reputation to keep."

We moved towards the dining room where I had laid out the games that I found hidden in the back of the office closet.

"I can't get over how much space you have," Lucy remarked for the third time. "What did you do, pay off Cassandra?"

"Money talks," I joked, trying to change the conversation.

This was starting to make me feel uncomfortable. I guess I was wrong in assuming everyone's accommodations were relatively the same.

"These are the games they left behind."

I put *Candyland, Disney Sorry*, and *Battleship* on an empty chair, which left *Scattergories, Bananagrams*, and *Catch Phrase* on the table as possible choices.

Agreeing on *Catch Phrase*, Trevor read the directions, so we were all following the same rules. (For the record, I've seen accusations of cheating turn into raucous brawls between some very competitive friends of mine.)

I brought the popcorn in from the kitchen and coasters for everyone's beverage of choice, which I found in the back of a drawer.

"Let the games begin!" I announced.

It was guys against girls in a battle of the sexes.

Trevor and Andre didn't buy it when I told them that they didn't stand a chance against our superior intellect, so game on!

As predicted, Lucy and I destroyed them.

Truth: We won the best two out of three, but the second game was a landslide. It did make for an easier path to victory with words appearing on our screen like *candle* and *turkey* while our opponents were required to describe *smidgen* and *scoundrel*. But being such clever girls, I'm sure that we would have been able to guess those, too. At least that's what we told them. They didn't agree!

We decided to change partners for the next round. Trevor and Lucy switched seats, which made Trevor my new clue giver/receiver.

As we played, all four of us got sillier, laughed louder, and debated more answers. It was our final game, and we were tied. It was neck and neck. One more point for either team would win it all.

Andre was holding the game console, so he got to start the round.

"Um, let me think," he said calmly, feeling no pressure as only the person who starts the round can get away with.

"I know ... what Jess gave Cassandra to get this place," Andre described for Lucy.

Tick.

Tick.

Tick.

"Cash! Money! Favors!" Lucy screamed out possible answers.

"Right ... money!" Andre yelled out, tossing the game device to Trevor.

I gave them both playful, dirty looks.

Trevor looked at the new word and uttered his clue with urgency as the timer began to tick more rapidly.

"What the wind does ... "

Tick.

Tick.

Tick.

"Blow," I quickly respond.

"Another form of the word."

Tick. Tick.

Tick. Tick.

Tick. Tick.

"Gale. Breeze," I continued to guess.

"No, make it bigger."

Tick. Tick. Tick.

Tick. Tick. Tick.

Tick. Tick. Tick.

"Hurricane! Tornado," I said, trying again.

"No, make the first word bigger."

Tick. Tick. Tick. Tick.

Tick. Tick. Tick. Tick.

"I don't remember the first word," I said, beginning to panic.

"What the wind does."

Tick. Tick. Tick. Tick. Tick. Tick.

"Oh, never mind," he said, bringing his hand to his mouth.

He smacked it with his lips, pointed his hand toward me and, with a wink, blew a kiss my direction.

"Blowing a kiss," the three of us screamed in unison, just as the buzzer went off, allowing Andre and Lucy to win the final, championship game.

Shaking his head in mock disgust, Trevor turned off the game device, and I slipped it into its packaging. Lucy then placed it on the chair with the rest of the games.

"Wow, *Disney Sorry*. I had that as a kid," she said enthusiastically. "Let's play!"

She brought it to the table, removed the pieces and set up the game board.

It took less convincing than it would have earlier in the evening to get us to join her.

Lucy taught us the rules, which she found hard to believe we didn't know from our childhoods.

As we made our way around the board, my Bambi literally knocked Trevor's Buzz Lightyear back to 'Start'. *And the crowd went wild!*

Andre's Hades was the first through the 'Safety Zone'. *Booooo!* And eventually, Lucy slid her last cardboard figurine of

Ariel home to victory. Jeers and allegations of unfair advantage filled the room since she had grown up playing the game.

After finishing our games, we sat talking easily for a while, but soon, my guests packed up their belongings and prepared to leave for their short drives home. As I walked with them outside to their cars, they thanked me for hosting what we decided was our 'first game night' with more to come.

"I left some beer in your frig. Do you mind if I go in and get it?"

I heard Trevor ask as I was heading inside.

"I'll find it," I said as I rushed back in the house

When I returned, Trevor was waiting for me on the porch.

"Thanks again for having us, Jess. Hey, I was wondering if maybe you'd want to do dinner tomorrow night?" he asked and then paused before continuing, "I don't really know places to eat in town, but I make a mean vegetarian and avocado pizza with Greek salad."

"Sure, that sound delicious," I said as calmly as I could manage, as if the man of my dreams had not just suggested dinner ... for two!

"My apartment over the Uptown is pretty small, so would you mind if we cooked in your kitchen ... if that's not too much of an imposition?"

"It's not an imposition at all," I said. *It's fantastic!*

He gave me a quick kiss and immediately strolled off to his car.

For the second time since our adventure began, he had left me with a jolt of electricity moving through my entire body.

CHAPTER 13

I decided to take Cooper to Ripley Park for his morning walk. The path around the man-made lake wasn't very long, but that was great because there was only so much tugging and pulling I could stand. It would also give me a chance to see how he behaved around people and other dogs. Hopefully, the fresh air (and a couple of aspirin) would help me get rid of my nagging hangover headache, I thought as I packed Cooper into Betty's passenger seat.

I pulled into a spot near where Trevor, Lucy, Andre and I parked the night we arrived in Marceline, a short week ago. If you told me then, that in a week's time, I would be returning to the park with my dog, I would have never believed you. And yet, here I was.

Cooper jumped excitedly out of the car, bouncing around anxiously to begin our trek. I had brought a few treats so we could practice 'sit' when we were near other pedestrians on the path.

The park was virtually empty, except for a small cluster of people gathered near the gazebo, taking directions from someone who appeared to be the group's leader. As she pointed to sections of the park, people carrying large bags, gradually dispersed to those areas.

Immediately, Cooper and I began our battle between running and walking. I worried that, at some point, he might pull my arm out of its socket, but overall, I was winning. We basically trotted (a compromise) the entirety of the lake.

Deep in my own thoughts, contemplating a second go-round, we passed a stand of trees when I heard someone yell my name. Startled out of my reverie, I saw Chance exiting from behind a large evergreen.

Pulling out a treat, I enticed Cooper to sit-and-stay. He got it on the first try. *We are definitely improving.*

"I see you kept the dog," Chance said as he reached down to pet the top of Cooper's head.

"Cooper, this is Chance. Chance this is Cooper," I introduced them. "What are you doing here?"

"It's the annual Spring Clean." He pointed to the half-full bag of trash in his left hand. "A group of us, 'The Neighborhood Beautification Committee', ready the park for the upcoming summer festivals."

His use of air quotes made me think he was trying to indicate he had no part in naming the organization, which made me chuckle to myself.

"Several festivals are scheduled here every year … Summer Kickoff, Music on the Green, Arts and Crafts Extravaganza, the annual Train Show, Independence Day festivities. Toonfest is our big one, and in the fall, a Chili Cook-off, just to name a few. You have to give one a try while you're here … if you don't have anything better to do," he said.

Was he daring me to break out of my insulated cocoon and immerse myself in the local community?

"Who knows, it could be fun," I said, balancing my skepticism with my curiosity. "That's a lot of festivals."

"I guess it averages about one a month. Most of them are fundraisers for one organization or another, but really, it's just an excuse for people in the community to socialize. I mean, who doesn't love smoked meat, a cold beverage and live music on a Saturday night? It's pretty hard to beat!"

"We'll see," I said as Cooper began to grow restless. "I'd better be going."

I pointed to Cooper. "He can't sit for too long, but we're working on it. Good luck with your clean up."

I waved as Cooper and I walked back to Betty for the short drive home.

Even with a walk, the minute the car door opened, Cooper sprinted to the backyard for more play time. Opening the gate to let him in, I saw Ida hunched over a flower bed pulling a few errant weeds.

"Good morning, Ida," I called out to her from my side of the fence.

"Good morning, Dear," she said as she looked up from her task. "Did you have a good walk?"

She shuffled over to lean against her fence post.

"How do you do that? How do you know everything that is going on? It's like you have a crystal ball."

"Well, Dear, you are holding a leash in your hand, and most people do not carry one of those around unless they have walked their dog, but if you want to think I see into a crystal ball, go right ahead. I must admit, I have never in my life had anyone suggest I possess supernatural powers. This is a first and, at my age, that is saying something! Did you kids have a good time last night?"

There she went again. But it didn't feel like she was a nosy neighbor, more like she had some sort of all-knowing aura.

"Thanks for asking. Yes, we had a great time ... a lot of laughs. Trevor's coming back over tonight for dinner." *Why did*

I just tell her that? I was sharing my social calendar with my next-door neighbor! What was happening to me?

"Is he the blond one? He is quite a looker, that one," she carried on, without my confirmation.

As I told her about Trevor, I began to understand how she knew so much about the goings on of the town. Ida could draw information out of you that you never intended to reveal, and somehow, you were glad you did.

"So even though he gives signals that he might be interested in me, he hasn't officially asked me out on a date, so I'm sure there is nothing. He's just a co-worker, after all, who is coming to dinner tonight ... so maybe it is something...," I said, realizing I had been rattling on and on.

Ida listened without interruption until my monologue trailed off. She smiled at me, patted my hand and took a deep breath.

"Jess Dear, don't think so much. You will worry yourself to death. Just enjoy the moment!"

How was that for some parting words of wisdom?

●　●　●

Heading off to bed after a long day, I picked up my phone, opened my messages, selected the first name on the list, and started typing:

Me: Guess what happened tonight?

(I didn't have to wait long before my phone dinged with a response.)

Mollie: You won the lottery and are coming home with Cooper to a new mansion you can now afford that will allow you to keep ur dog – amirite

Me: No better!

(Well ... until I get to the end of the evening, I thought to myself.)

Mollie: Tell me everything but I want the real version not the Jess – I have to read between the lines to figure out what really happened – version

Me: Ok I'll keep it boring for ur sake

Mollie: No matter what happened I'm sure it won't be boring

Me: So u know I hosted game night last night

Mollie: How was it

Me: Actually super fun but here's the good part. Trevor stayed a few minutes after everyone left and suggested we have dinner 2nite so of course I said yes

Mollie: It's only taken u a week to work ur magic on him – that's a record

Me: What are you talking about in CA I tried for months to get him to notice me

Mollie: It's late and ur dinner with him must be over so what happened? Please tell me he isn't still there and you are texting me!

Me: No he's gone ☹

Mollie: Stop keeping me in suspense – what happened

Me: Don't rush me – ur the one who wants details

Mollie: smh

Me: Trevor showed up at my house with peppers, red onions, fresh basil, avocados, mozzarella and a bunch of other ingredients to make dinner. It was like a scene out of a romantic movie where we laugh and talk easily while cutting vegetables together in my kitchen

Mollie: You can buy all of that stuff in Marceline

Me: I'm not in some third world country and ur missing the point

Mollie: Sorry I didn't mean to insult ur new home

Me: So he baked this amazing gourmet pizza and used the rest of the ingredients to make the best Greek salad I have ever tasted. We decided to eat at my expansive dining room table where I parked myself at one end sitting in the same spot I sat in for game night, like it was my assigned seat. Trevor chose the chair next to mine moving it so close that our legs were touching under the table which I thought was a good sign. I was really glad he didn't pick the chair at the other end of the table or I would have felt like we were the Lord and Lady of some ancient castle although that would be fun too. Anyway there is this weird dimmer knob on my dining room light switch so I lowered the lights and we had like this fake candlelight pizza dinner. It was actually quite romantic

Mollie: What did you and Lord Trevor speak of during your royal feast and please don't say the peasants at work

Me: lol You name it we talked about it and you'll be happy to know that the only time we talked about work was when we were discussing where we would like to be in five years. He's hoping this show will boost his resume enough to get him a higher position with a bigger network. He's really ambitious!

Mollie: So you had dinner, played footsie under the table and he left? I hate to break it to you but so far this is not better than winning the lottery

Me: I'm not finished! Patience!! We cleaned up our dishes and shifted into the living room to find a movie on *Netflix*. He was pretty astounded by the size of Mona and made jokes about her eating him like Audrey II from Little Shop of Horrors. I tried to explain what a good companion Mona has been and how she would never do anything to hurt someone unless provoked of course but he made me sit next to her anyway

Mollie: I have to admit I've always been a little afraid of Mona and Justin won't go anywhere near her. There's a reason you couldn't get anybody to keep her while you were away

Me: Ur just jealous bc the plant you bought that day died within a week. Anyway we both like James Bond movies so we picked Casino Royale. I know it's old but it was the only one showing on Netflix. We flipped off the light, sat snuggly next to each other, turned on the movie, and while it's still in the first scene Trevor leans over and starts nibbling on my ear

Mollie: I need all the details, Jess, leave nothing out!

Me: My entire body was tingling as he moved from my ear to my neck. Next thing I know we were kissing like we couldn't get enough of each other. His hands are rubbing my shoulders but slowly moved to the front of my shirt. I was conveniently wearing that cute chambray striped, button down so he easily unfastened the top button. His kisses got even deeper which I didn't know was possible. He got the second button undone and was working on the third when disaster hit

Mollie: No! I want more of the juicy stuff

Me: It seemed I'd been only paying attention to Trevor and not Cooper. He'd been laying in his kennel with the door open and decided at the most inopportune moment to remind me he hadn't been out all evening. So Cooper walked up to the couch, lifted his leg, and peed all over the rug. I screamed, jumped up, ushered him out the back door and grabbed my cleaning wipes to remove the large spot before a stain formed on the carpet. Since it wasn't my house, I needed to clean up every bit of urine, which took quite a bit of deep scrubbing. In the end, Trevor sat on the sofa by himself as I was on the floor acting like some handmaiden. Even though I apologized over and over again, the mood had been completely broken. I'm not sure if it was my pee cleaning hands (even though I washed them thoroughly) or the residual smell of urine, but Trevor decided since we had to work in the morning that it was time for him to head back to his place for the night

Mollie: Get rid of Cooper! jk

Me: I'll ignore that comment. Anyway, Trevor didn't seem mad, we had a really good time and he did say we should get together again. I just hope it's sooner rather than later!

Mollie: My bet's SOONER!

Me: ✌

Mollie: Keep me posted

Me: I will. CIAO

CHAPTER 14

Although Erin Langley, the current owner of the Uptown Theater, and I were the only ones being filmed, everyone associated with the show was present for its official kick off. Energy and excitement filled the lobby where we were all gathered Monday morning for our final instructions.

Jonathon, our lead cameraman, and the entire film crew were setting up outside where shooting would begin. Andre, Chance and another member of the construction team were there to determine the feasibility of my changes to the plans, in case Erin or Mr. Biggs had any major objections to the proposed design. Taylor, dressed in floral-printed, washed denim overalls with pink tennis shoes, would be taking notes as Erin and I went through each room of the property.

Since Lucy had not seen all the recent updates, she was there, too, hoping to garner some fresh ideas for promoting the new Uptown Performing Arts Center. She had also been hinting about a big announcement in the works and was standing off in a corner with Mr. Biggs sharing some of the news. As a major investor in *Main Street,* he would be keeping a watchful eye on our progress (and budget), beginning with today's design reveal.

And Trevor, well Trevor, kept glancing my way with a sly grin, which was making it inordinately difficult for me to concentrate on my agenda. He was talking with a person who I presumed to be Erin. She appeared to be in her mid-forties and had a mass of bouncing, shoulder-length brown curls which framed her perfectly smooth, round face. A smile, accentuated by two deep dimples, moved all the way to her sparkling brown eyes giving her a look of continual cheerfulness. I had a feeling that working with her was going to be a pleasure.

We moved outside and filming began.

Erin was directed to walk down Main Street toward the Uptown Theater where I was waiting to meet her.

"Hi, I'm Jess. Great to finally meet you," I said as she approached.

"I'm Erin," she said as she shook my hand and smiled broadly in a way that lit up her entire face. "I'm so excited, but have to admit a little nervous, about our meeting today."

"I'm also excited about the renovation of this amazing, soon-to-be century-old building," I added. "Are you ready to see what we have in mind?"

"So ready!"

"We're going to start with the exterior," I began. "Our goal is to modernize the building, to make it an inviting structure that people want to visit, while keeping its original integrity. The first step will be to convert the iconic Uptown sign to LED. We will do this by removing the sign's face and existing neon tubing. After extensive cleaning, LED strings will be installed, and the sign's face will be reattached. Not only will the sign now have a brighter glow, but this will also save money by decreasing power usage. As an added bonus, since LEDs are more durable, less maintenance will be required in the future."

"That sounds great, and decreasing our electric bill is a definite plus!"

"I thought you might like that part," I nodded. "Next, our plan is to freshen the exterior and make this building look as it did in Walt Disney's eyes. We know how he saw Kansas Avenue by looking at Main Street U.S.A. in Disneyland. It is a place to which people are drawn, so our design goal is to replicate that feeling in your building, on the original Main Street. The golden brick exterior on the top two floors, accentuated by the rest of the building's red brick, gives the theater an inviting appearance for visitors. As it is the central focal point of Main Street, there are no changes planned to the building's façade. We also plan on keeping the two finials standing tall at the top of the building as well as the decorative rosettes framing each window, so as to retain the classical architectural feel we are looking to achieve."

"The main changes will occur to the entrance area," I continued, explaining to Erin and our television audience, "where we will be removing the awnings, one on each side of the entrance, and replacing the marquee over the doorway with a canopy in the shape of a half hexagon with three defined sides. The words Performing Arts Center, in large bold lettering, will dominate the front rectangular section. We'll create an eye-catching outline to the sign by dotting its perimeter in small light bulbs. The other two sides, facing up and down Main Street, will display the current or upcoming production schedules. What do you think?"

"So far, so good," Erin replied.

"Next," I said, relieved that so far she seemed pleased with the proposal, "we will be moving the beloved ticket box. We should be able to keep this piece of history intact, but instead of front and center, two ticket boxes will be inset on either side of the entrance doors, facing each other, rather than looking toward the street. Employees will be able to enter the boxes from the lobby and, once inside, you will see the flexibility this offers by allowing tickets to be purchased at the window outside or, on a cold, rainy night, from an area indoors."

"But where will the original ticket box go?" Erin asked with a look of genuine concern.

"You're one step ahead of me," I said and laughed. "Once inside, I'll show you our plan to give this piece of history its place of honor."

As I paused to let Erin digest this change (the one modification I feared she might find objectionable), a train whistle blew, and the rumble of the engine passed on the nearby tracks.

"I'm worried some of the town's people aren't going to be happy about the modifications to the front of the building, but I, personally, love them."

Luckily, the passing train substantially muffled her remark. Not that I wasn't worried about the same thing, but I was pretty sure that comment would end up on the cutting room floor. Our type of show didn't go over as well with viewers and advertisers if the reactions to our ideas weren't full of awe-filled praise and enthusiastic approval.

I let the noise of the train, which was turning into a very familiar sound, lessen before continuing, "The last adjustment to the exterior of the building affects the doors leading into the theater. Three sets of wood and brass double doors, adorned with semicircular, ornamental fanlights, will enrich the entrance and allow easy access to the lobby for visitors."

I pulled out the sketch sent from our California team and showed Erin a visual of the design I had just described. The look of joy and the radiance of her infectious smile as she viewed my drawing of the new exterior relieved me.

The film crew followed us as we moved indoors, and I began my description of the lobby's updated appearance. The rest of the team stayed near, but away from the camera's lens.

Looking in Trevor's direction, I could see he was pleased with how things were going so far. *Yeah!*

"Due to the acquisition of the land and the structure next door, our plan is to more than triple the size of the lobby."

"Wow, that will be huge," Erin said, looking surprised.

"Let me explain our vision," I said, excited about this part of the renovation. "Just as you see in front of us now, we will continue to have a concession stand in this area. We will modernize the front by mixing glass blocks with the traditional candy case. On nights of live performances, this area will turn from a concession stand into a small wine and beverage bar, giving the theater a more sophisticated feel."

"To the right of the entrance will be an indoor ticket window available for use during off-peak times when the Performing Arts Center has a skeletal staff or on busy nights as a will-call window."

Unable to hide my enthusiasm, I kept on going with my plan.

"We will keep the doors on either side of the concession stand leading into the theater, and by adding new paint, floors and lighting, we can easily, and fairly inexpensively, update the look of the lobby. We would like to keep the crown molding, if possible, since it gives the interior that classic architectural feel we are trying to incorporate throughout the building."

"It all sounds very chic," Erin said and beamed.

"That's our goal," I replied. "So, I bet you are wondering why we want to increase the size of the lobby by such a large amount."

"It did cross my mind."

"If you'll notice, to the left of the main entrance and concession stand, you will find most of the lobby's square footage. This space will be utilized for three main purposes. Next to the theater's left entrance, we plan to wall-in office space and add a reception window. Since The Uptown is now a theater and educational center, the building will need to house some permanent staff. This space will serve the dual purposes of providing employees a work area in the front of the building and also function as a Help Desk for anyone who has a question regarding show schedules, availability of classes in the educational wing, or possibly a visitor wanting information regarding the theater's history."

"Perpendicular to the office will be a set of double doors," I continued. "Bold letters above the doors will invite students to enter into the educational wing where rooms will be waiting to teach music, dance, film, photography, painting or any other visual or performing art. We won't be going into that section today since it is currently vacant, but I'm sure you can visualize basic classrooms as well as a multipurpose area for larger meetings."

"I can see that," Erin replied.

Happy she seemed to be grasping and appreciating my vision, I proceeded.

"The third section of the lobby will be directly across from the office and about twice its size. Our idea is to create a small museum dedicated strictly to The Uptown Theater and its rich history. I've seen a great deal of memorabilia scattered throughout the theater. We would like to house all of the pictures and collectables, along with some new items, in one location and make them accessible for public viewing. It's here, at the entrance to the museum, that we plan to move the Uptown's iconic ticket booth. And don't worry, this area is not meant to be competition for the museum down the street, but instead be a complement to it ... a way to give visitors a different look into Main Street's past."

Once again, I showed Erin the initial sketches, but this time of the proposed lobby. And once again, she seemed delighted.

With her approval of the design, we all moved for our last stop into the theater itself.

"Here is where the bulk of the renovations will occur," I explained. "With the size of this auditorium, we will be aiming to offer an intimate theatrical experience for the audience. By replacing the seats, carpet, curtain, stage floor, and lighting, we can provide an optimal setting for live performances. To enhance the film experience, we will include some new soundproofing, acoustical ceiling tiles and the addition of a state-of-the-art sound system. These are pretty standard changes, but we've added a few exciting developments to make a visit to The Uptown Theater a completely different experience.

"First, in place of a projector and screen, we will mount a 34-foot-wide LED television on hydraulics so it can fold into the ceiling when not in use. Samsung, in collaboration with all the major film studios, has recently developed a new, digital, 8-k resolution television, specifically designed for theater new releases. Because it is similar to your standard television, it can also play movie classics, television shows or documentaries. This technology is cost-effective, and its high resolution provides an amazing picture and is ideal for a smaller venue like The Uptown."

"Second," I paused and took a breath.

None of the team had heard this portion of the proposal. *Fingers crossed they like it!*

"To enhance the experience of live performances, we also want to offer something different and turn this into a classic Atmospheric Theatre. Once the curtain is ready to open and the lights are dimmed, the ceiling will subtly sparkle with thousands of twinkling, inset lights. The auditorium will still be dark enough so as to not detract from the stage, but it will give the feel of sitting under the stars. A gentle breeze coming from the air vents and subliminal sounds of trees rustling in the wind will make the audience feel as if they are enjoying an outdoor performance in an open-air theater. So, what do you think?!"

"It all sounds amazing. The people around here are going to love it! I can't wait to see it when it's finally completed, although I know that's still many weeks away. I'm so excited for The Uptown Theater and Performing Arts Center to come back to life and be a vital part of the town once again!"

As the cameras stopped rolling, I released a breath I didn't even know I was holding and sneaked a peek in Trevor's direction.

The broad smile on his face told me I had nailed it!

He held that smile and then gave me a small wink that felt much more sensual than a basic acknowledgment for a job well done.

I could feel the color rise in my cheeks.

How can this man continue to make my heart stop, with even the smallest of gestures?

● ● ●

A few days after the renovation walk-through, Taylor and I began our quest for items needed to modernize the Performing Arts Center's interior. After selecting as many pieces as possible from the USAMade product line, we still needed to purchase some large upgrades not carried on their website. Taylor highly recommended a local decorating and design center about a half hour down Highway 5, so we decided to take the drive south and see what they had to offer. With hundreds of flooring and lighting styles, we should be able to find what we needed.

I was beginning to look forward to each meeting with Taylor. She was competent, compatible, and highly imaginative, and I also loved seeing what she had pulled together for her outfit de jour. Bordering between fashion risk and fashion disaster, somehow, she could turn crazy combinations into stunning works of art. Today, she showed up in purple, gray, black and white camo pants, a plum knotted t-shirt, white high-top tennis shoes with florescent orange laces and her long hair in two bouncy pigtails.

I, on the other hand, was wearing jeans, a basic black V-neck top and black ballerina slippers. A person would guess that Taylor was the one from Los Angeles, not me.

Bursting with ideas, Taylor chattered away during our short trip while I listened intently to each of her creative suggestions. She credited many of her ideas to the training she received at the Kansas City Art Institute, where she graduated with honors. And although she thoroughly enjoyed living in Downtown Kansas City, she was thrilled when offered The Uptown Theater design position, even though it meant moving back home and away from her beloved KC. She was hoping this opportunity would help launch her carer. And I planned to help her advance, any way I could.

Reaching our destination, I was pleasantly surprised to discover a fully stocked and finely decorated showroom available for us to peruse.

Starting in the lighting section, we focused on finding a fixture for the lobby and decorative lights for the theater walls. We immediately agreed on black and white, triangular, art deco wall sconces to illuminate the aisles, but were unable to obtain what either of us had visualized as the perfect fixture for the theater's entrance.

Moving into the flooring area, we flipped through hundreds of samples and were nearly ready to give up when we both spotted a sample square in the perfect design. Red, orange, and gray swirls, like incomplete Mickey ears, appeared to be swimming on a black background punctuated with flecks of harvest colors. It coordinated perfectly with the black, faux marble tile we chose to surround the concession stand and the red plush audience chairs being installed in the theater.

Our drive back to Marceline, after a successful buying trip, generated more of a conversation rather than a one-sided, nonstop spew of Taylor's thoughts. She asked a lot of questions about what it was like growing up on the West Coast, and I enjoyed talking about my family and friends, the area where I lived, and the vibe of the beach and Downtown L.A.

Between staying so busy with work and training Cooper, and meeting new friends, I suddenly realized that I had not found the time to get as homesick as I thought I might.

CHAPTER 15

Who knew that a day of searching through carpet and lighting samples could make a person so hungry? I was ravished!

A friend once explained to me that you can only use the term 'make' with dinner if you mix ingredients to create an edible dish, whereas if you open a box and put it in the microwave, that is called 'preparing' your meal. Based on the contents in my pantry and refrigerator, I was trying to decide what filling meal to 'prepare' when I heard a faint knock on the screen door.

Happy for the distraction, I pushed my tasty choices aside and ran to the front of the house, excited by the idea of an unexpected visitor, while keeping my fingers crossed that it turned out to be Trevor.

Upon seeing Dr. Andrews on the porch steps, my initial surprise rapidly changed into fear and worry that she was here to inform me that Cooper's long-lost owners had been found. I invited her in, with trepidation, as Cooper, never far from my side, jumped up to greet her.

"Down," I said as I gently pushed Cooper off the good doctor. "Sorry, we're working on that."

"Hi, Buddy," she said, bending down to pet him.

He immediately rolled onto his back with his legs in the air, begging for belly rubs.

She obviously was a natural with animals. Probably why she became a veterinarian. But, all the same, Cooper melted in her hands.

"Hope you don't mind me stopping by unannounced. I was reading through our records and saw your address listed not far from the clinic. I also noticed you've called several times inquiring if anyone has made claim to the dog that, as I understand, you've named Cooper."

"I admit, Dr. Andrews, I have been curious and more than a little anxious to know if his family has turned up. I've grown pretty attached to this guy."

"Well then, let me be the first to offer you congratulations, as you are now an official dog owner. As I suspected, no one has claimed him, so he is yours, if that's what you still want," she grinned and handed me a small present.

"Yes, that's what I want!" I gushed, giving Cooper a big hug.

"What's this?" I asked, pointing to the box in my hand.

"A little something from the clinic. Go ahead, open it."

I opened the small black and white bag decorated in paw prints and inside found a bone-shaped tag with *COOPER* etched on its face and our address engraved on the back. I squealed in delight, immediately adding it to Cooper's collar.

"Thank you, Dr. Andrews, for the thoughtful gift."

"Now, he should never get lost again," she explained.

She handed me some paperwork. "So here are a few items that need to be completed, just a formality, along with a vaccination schedule. You need to make an appointment to get Cooper his required shots and also get him microchipped."

"I know you're new in town," she continued. "I've been there myself, and it can feel pretty lonely. I was wondering if you would be interested in grabbing something to eat, since it is around dinnertime."

"I'd really like that," I replied.

"We can go … on one condition," she stated.

I looked at her quizzically.

"You are required to call me Kaitlin and never Dr. Andrews."

"Deal," I said. "Let me put Cooper in his kennel and grab my bag."

As I ran into the kitchen to turn out the light, I saw the boxes of dinner choices on the counter (none of which seemed even remotely appetizing) and realized how delighted I was to be going out to eat. It appeared to be the case that I was going to get a 'made' meal tonight after all!

"Have you been to the Corner Café yet?" Kaitlin asked.

I shook my head.

"It's the first place you need to dine in Marceline. It's a local legend."

I followed her back to Kansas Avenue, where we parked a few spaces down from The Uptown Theater.

Walking inside The Corner Café was like turning back time and entering an old fashion diner.

Taking a seat in one of the red vinyl booths, we were immediately greeted by a waitress.

"Hi, Kaitlin. Haven't seen you in all week."

"Linda, I'd like you to meet Jess. She's here with the group filming down the road."

"Nice to meet you. Is this your first time in?" she smiled.

"Yes, it is," I replied. "The number of people I see coming in and out of here all day has made me anxious to give you a try. Kaitlin was nice enough to invite me to dinner tonight, so here we are."

"Well, what can I get you ladies?"

"What do you recommend?" I asked.

"Everything," she said and laughed, "but whatever you choose, you have to leave room for a piece of our famous homemade pie."

We each decided on the chicken sandwich – mine with fries and Kaitlin's with tater tots – and an iced tea.

"How's the renovation going?" Kaitlin asked, once Linda departed with our order.

"Great! Erin Langley, the owner of the building, loves all the design ideas as well as Larry Biggs, the main backer of the project, which is even more important. Erin's husband Chris wasn't able to join us for the unveiling of the initial proposal, but he came by with Erin a couple of days ago, and he was also thrilled with the plans."

"I know the Langleys. They're great people. They own a black Lab named Magic. Hazzard of the trade," she said and chuckled. "I identify most of the folks around here by their animals."

She took a sip of her tea. "So how long will it take to complete the remodel? I can't wait to see it!"

"We're in the demolition phase right now. It's pretty messy over there, but the building will shape up quicker than you'd think. Since we're on the fast track, I bet we're done within twelve weeks."

"Hey, Doc."

I heard a voice boom from behind my left ear.

A family with two school-age children stopped at our table on their way out of the restaurant.

"Hi, Jimmy. How's Maisy doing?"

"Just fine, thanks."

"Have you picked a name for the calf yet?" Kaitlin directed her question toward the boy and girl standing with their father.

"I want Matilda," said the girl.

"Zelda's a way better name," immediately countered the boy.

"Charlie plays a few too many video games," his dad said, ruffling the boy's hair. "I think either *we're* going to have to choose a name," he said and pointed to his wife, "or flip a coin, because there is no compromise happening between these two."

"I vote for Zatilda or Melda," Kaitlin said, "but I guess I'll have to wait until next week when I come out for her check-up to learn her official name."

"Alright, you heard the doctor, we have to make a decision by next week," he told his children as he waved goodbye and ushered his group out the front door.

"Everyone is so friendly with you. Unfortunately, I haven't experienced that same warm reception from the people I've met so far. Some, like my next-door neighbor, and you, have been great, but others are almost hostile ... not a lot of people, but a few. For example, yesterday, I tried to mail a package at the post office, but no one would wait on me, so eventually, I left."

"Give them time. You really can't meet better people than those who live around here. They're uncomfortable with change and, to them, that's what you represent – uncertainty and change."

"You are the second person to tell me that. I guess I'll just have to wait and see."

"Being a newcomer myself not that long ago, I understand your doubts, but it will happen. I promise."

"How did you end up here anyway?" I asked.

"Well, I was born in St. Louis but left when Mizzou accepted me into their veterinary program. Once I graduated, I did some research, saw a need for a vet in this area and opened a practice. I always wanted to live away from the city and work with more than dogs, cats and an occasional bird, ferret, or other exotic pet. When I'm in need of my city fix, I go home for a long weekend. It works for me. I've come to really love it here ... the people, the countryside, the small-town atmosphere. I'm part of a community and not just a doctor on call at some large veterinary chain."

We remained in our booth well after our meal was finished, easily conversing about various topics. It almost felt like I was talking to Mollie.

"You remind me of my best friend, Mollie, from back home," I told her. "She's smart, fun, loyal, brutally honest and also getting married. I love her fiancé, but things have changed since she started sharing more of her life with him than me. We still text every day, and she's talking about flying in for a girls' weekend, but we haven't settled on a date. It would be a lot of fun, so I hope we can make it work."

"The same thing happened with my best friend. Unfortunately, I don't talk to her as much as I'd like since she's crazy busy with three kids under the age of five. For me, right now, I'm married to my practice, and I like it that way. How about you? I bet you broke someone's heart when you moved here."

"Not a chance," I said and laughed. "There's a guy who came to Marceline with our group that is…actually, I'm not sure what he is. We're kind of talking, but who knows if it will go anywhere," I said, starting to gather my belongings and ready myself to leave.

Since we had stayed at Linda's table well after our pie plates were cleared away, I put down a large tip.

"I've really enjoyed this evening. Thanks for inviting me to join you for dinner," I said as we left our booth.

Everyone in the restaurant nodded or waved to us, correction – everyone nodded or waved to Kaitlin – as we walked out the door of the Corner Café and headed for home.

CHAPTER 16

Curled up in a chair on the porch, reading my newest novel from the library and drinking a cappuccino, I was enjoying another lazy Saturday morning. Cooper joined me, laying in a patch of sun, for what was becoming our weekend routine.

It was predicted to be another beautiful day. And I had not decided on my plans yet, but whatever I chose, it would definitely be something outdoors. Ida told me that summers in Marceline were stifling, but so far, the weather had been ideal – cool mornings and evenings with warm afternoons.

Engrossed in a particularly steamy section of my book, I was startled back to reality by the ding of a text. With the time difference, I knew it wasn't Mom or Mollie, my usual texting partners, so I wondered who would be contacting me this early on a weekend. Maybe it was Kaitlin. We had been texting frequently since our dinner the other night.

I looked at my phone and, to my surprise, I saw Trevor's name appear on the screen.

Trevor: Hey, what are you up to today?

Me: I haven't decided yet, why?

Trevor: What do you think of getting out of this godforsaken town for the day? One of the local crew told me about a winery not too far from here. Want to go?

Me: Sounds great. What time?

Trevor: I'll pick you up at 1:00. Does that work?

Me: Perfect

Trevor: sys

After finishing my chapter and coffee, I jumped off the chair and moved toward the shower. It felt as if Trevor had read my mind about wanting to spend the day outdoors. And I took that as a positive sign.

With a towel wrapped liked a turban on my head, I rummaged through the bedroom closet trying to decide on the perfect outfit for a day trip to a winery. I thought about wearing my navy striped T-shirt dress and sandals but was afraid that, even though the outfit was pretty casual, it might look like I was trying hard to impress him (which to be honest, was exactly what I was trying to do). Instead, I chose my light rose skinny capris matched with a bold, flowered top and a pair of pale pink chucks. Very springlike, I thought, as I looked in the mirror.

After adding some understated jewelry, I was back in the bathroom to blow dry my hair. Since I wore a ponytail to work every day, I decided to actually curl and style it for a change.

After twenty minutes and a couple of burns, I remembered why I never did this and usually just wrapped the brown mass in a scrunchie or piled it on top of my head.

Adding a quick touch of make-up, I was ready and had forty-five minutes to spare. *Has someone stolen Jess and replaced her with an on-time double?* Maybe Trevor would be good for my personal punctuality challenge (positive sign #2). I had pretty much kept my promise to be on time for work and appointments, but early?! Now that had never happened until that very moment!

Trevor pulled in my driveway at exactly 1:00. Sauntering up the front porch steps, he was carrying two helmets, one in each hand. Since I had only seen him drive his car lately, I'd forgotten he had his motorcycle shipped with Mona on the equipment truck.

"Hope you don't mind if we take the beast," he said.

"Not at all. It seems like a perfect day for a ride," I replied, relieved that I had changed my mind at the last minute about wearing a dress, although I was totally bummed about the amount of time I had spent fixing my hair. I was going to look stunning with helmet head!

After locking the front door (probably the only person in Marceline to do that in broad daylight), he handed me the hair-smashing helmet, and I climbed on the cushioned seat behind him.

He started the bike, which was very loud.

"Hold on tight!" he yelled.

I grabbed his waist just as he bolted out of the driveway and onto the empty road in front of my house.

We flew down the street, whipping around the corner, bobbing and weaving as we went. It would actually have been quite thrilling if I wasn't scared out of mind.

Screeching to a halt at a stop sign, he looked back at me and asked, "What do think?"

The lack of color in my face must have answered his question because he slowed to a much safer speed as we drove through the center of town.

On the other side of Kansas Avenue, we passed what looked to be a fairly new salon and spa, just as Lucy exited the building. She recognized Trevor's motorcycle and waved as we continued zooming down the highway to our destination.

The drive along the winding, two-lane country road was exhilarating. Trees were bent over the pavement creating a canopy of new foliage, wildflowers were springing up on either side of the highway, and large birds soared overhead. We passed a few cars going the other direction, but for the most part, it was a peaceful journey.

The entrance to Vista Vineyards was up a steep hill, which allowed the chateau-style tasting room to sit high above the vineyard.

Trevor parked the motorcycle in an empty space under a shade tree, and we gracefully dismounted the bike.

Truth: Okay, he gracefully dismounted the bike, and I practically knocked myself to the ground trying to pull my leg over the seat. I managed to salvage what dignity I had left by cleverly acting as if I meant to look like an interpretive dancer. Or at least I hope I did.

After regaining my balance, we made our way to the building and walked into an impressive tasting room.

Tables, scattered throughout, allowed for plenty of indoor seating. A large bar dominated one end of the area and a massive, brick, wood-burning fireplace sat at the other. The room had a cozy, rustic atmosphere. Its shiplap vaulted ceiling, oak beams running each direction, large wooden fans, and strings of fairy lights gave the entire space a relaxed, open-air feeling. I immediately loved the place!

Walking up to the bar, we studied the wine list and, to our surprise, saw that they had quite a variety of choices. Not only did they carry local wines, but they also offered an assortment from various parts of the country and even some European selections. I chose a local Vignoles, a Riesling from Washington State, and a French Bordeaux to sample. Trevor selected one California wine and two from Europe, including the same Bordeaux I was tasting.

"What do you think of the Bordeaux?" he asked.

"It's good, not too dry," I replied.

"Why don't we find a place to sit on the patio and order a bottle?" he suggested, moving through the tasting room to a pair of double doors leading to the back of the property.

We picked a table overlooking the sprawling vineyard below. It reminded me of our night in Utah, but with a different, yet just as beautiful, landscape.

Rows of tethered grapes wound from just beyond our perch, down a rolling hill, to the base of a small pristine lake surrounded by flowering trees of pink and white. The tranquil view stretched as far as my eyes could see. I sat back in my chair and watched two swans serenely glide across the lake's glasslike surface. This was exactly what I had in mind when I was trying to plan my day outdoors.

A waitress arrived and Trevor ordered a bottle of Chateau de Boyer while we scanned the menu.

"I thought the local wine was pretty flavorful, nice and crisp." I remark.

"I didn't try any of them," he commented, looking up from his study of the house selections. "I always opt for the most expensive wine since it inevitably turns out to be the best choice. Anyway, I had the impression you also liked expensive wines."

I gave him a quizzical look, wondering where he got that idea.

"I just think it's nice to support local businesses," I said, evidently not of the same opinion, at all.

"We are supporting area businesses. We're patronizing this local establishment, aren't we?"

"I guess you have a point," I said, still wishing we would have ordered a local variety.

The waitress arrived with our bottle of wine and poured us each a glass of the deep red Bordeaux. We ordered the Meritage Spread, which included a selection of specialty cheeses, cured meats, dried fruits, nuts, and a brown sugar mustard, as an appetizer.

Relaxing in the mid-afternoon sun, we quietly sipped our wine while looking out over the countryside.

"I bet this is even more beautiful in the fall," I said, breaking the silence.

Trevor counted out the months. "That would be right before we return home. We'll have to come back and check it out."

That was positive sign #3. And wasn't '3' supposed to be a lucky number?! (That is if I didn't subtract one for his wine snob comments, but then I'd have to do math which was not an option on weekends.)

A two-person band, setting up on a small stage in the corner of the patio, began to play its first set. Their Southern rock harmonies were a perfect choice as background music and added to the patio's laidback atmosphere.

Although I found myself gently moving to the beat of each song, the duo's minimal decibel level was low enough for Trevor and me to continue talking without shouting over each other.

We spent a lazy afternoon eating, drinking, listening to live music, laughing and solving all the world's problems. As time passed, Trevor's chair magically scooted closer to mine, our heads almost touching as if we needed to lean in to hear one another over the music.

At one point, Trevor asked me if I had been grilled by any of the locals about the number of famous people I knew. Relieved, I told him that so far, I had luckily avoided those kinds of conversations.

We discovered that neither of us were remotely starstruck, probably since we had grown up so close to Hollywood and Beverly Hills, and couldn't understand the rest of the world's fascination with movie stars. It was both our opinions that celebrities were nothing more than regular people who selected acting as their career choices, not the demigods the rest of the world made them out to be.

"I was out one evening with Mollie, right before we moved here, going to a club not far from her apartment," I told him. "... and a group of female tourists in front of us spotted James Franco walking not more than ten feet away from them. You would have thought they found a long-lost relative the way they were carrying on. It was just James Franco, for goodness sakes. Anyway, they were pointing and getting all excited."

I demonstrated their actions by wildly swinging my arms in the air.

Laughing, Trevor grabbed my wrist, just as my hand nearly sent his glass of wine flying off the table.

"Watch it there, you crazy tourist lady," he jokingly scolded me.

"My Dad always says if you tied my hands behind my back, I wouldn't be able to talk," I said and giggled as he loosened his grip from my wrist and slowly moved his fingers down to my hand.

As we resumed our conversation, he gently stroked the top of each of my fingers in a sensual way that made it not only difficult to concentrate on what he was saying, but to also feign any sort of coherent reply.

He must have felt the same electricity I was because suddenly, a lull crept into our conversation.

"Are you ready for me to drive you back to your place?" he asked with a wicked smile before tracing a finger up and down my goose-bumped arm.

The sun had begun to set over the lake in front of us, the music had ended an hour ago, and the crowd was changing from afternoon groups to evening parties.

"I'm ready," I replied, my voice shaky.

The ride back to Marceline, as so often happens, seemed shorter than the ride out to the winery. I sat a little closer and held onto him a little tighter.

With his assistance, I dismounted the bike with much more grace than the first time.

Running ahead to unlock the front door, I quickly let a waiting Cooper into the backyard.

I hurried back to meet Trevor just as he was entering the house. He immediately pulled me to him, giving me a long, deep kiss.

The heat between us had been growing all day, and I suspect that we both felt a sense of urgency.

We continued kissing with more passion than I have ever experienced. Our hands both tugged and caressed, trying to touch every part of each other's body as our clothes began to peel away.

Trevor paused, stepped back and stared at me.

"You are really beautiful, Jess," he said.

I blushed as he gently took my hand and led me down the hall.

CHAPTER 17

With demolition of The Uptown Performance Center complete, the actual renovation phase had shifted into full swing. Andre and I were meeting in the lobby of the theater, along with the film crew, to discuss remedies for two problems that had arisen. As always, Trevor was in the background to approve any changes to the original plan, pending Cassandra's final authorization.

I dashed into the coffee shop next door to order a shot of caffeine before facing the cameras.

"The usual?" Shelly asked as I approached the counter.

"Yes, thanks. I should probably get a double. We're filming today, and I could use the extra energy."

"I could talk to customers for hours, but I could never speak in front of a camera the way you do. Don't you get nervous?"

"To be honest, I don't pay much attention to the film crew. With so much constant activity happening inside the building, it feels more like they're part of the construction team rather than the production staff assigned to shoot Andre and me. It's not like having to memorize a script. I don't think I could do that. Instead, I just talk to Andre, like I do all the time. The only difference is we've discussed the topics in advance. And you know the best part? If I say anything really goofy, we just do another take."

She nodded and had that look of "Okay, I hadn't thought of it that way, but that makes sense" as she finished making my latte.

"I can't tell you how many times I've wished for a retake in real life," I added with a chuckle.

Handing me a double Café Carmella, I thanked her again and turned to leave.

"Good luck," she cried, as I headed out the door, drinking my liquid energy.

● ● ●

"Hey, Jess, I've got a couple of issues we need to discuss," Andre said as the cameras began to roll.

"What did you find?" I asked cautiously. "I hope nothing too big."

"First, we've worked as carefully as possible in dismantling the lobby's existing crown molding," he said, pointing to a place high on the wall with half the molding down and the other half still intact.

He directed my attention to some pieces leaning against the wall.

"Unfortunately, the molding is so old that it continues to break off into small pieces, no matter how meticulous we are about its removal. I'm afraid it's going to be impossible to reattach once the new construction is complete and the walls are repainted."

"That's too bad," I said, truly disappointed. "I was really hoping to keep something original from the lobby. I'll have to look around and see if I can come up with a different idea to retain some of the theater's nostalgia."

"With enlarging the size of the lobby, I was curious about your design strategy for integrating the molding into the new section, so in a way, this solves that problem," he replied, his voice tentative.

"You have a point," I agreed.

Suddenly, I had a creative solution! *I love it when that happens!*

"Andre, don't trash those pieces of molding yet, I have a thought on how I might use some of the larger sections. I'm also still looking for an authentic light to beautify the lobby entrance," I continued, "so I'll keep an eye out for some antique-style crown molding while I'm on the prowl for the perfect ceiling fixture … one that captures the guests' attention when they first walk through the doors."

"That brings us to our second and much bigger issue," Andre resumed. "We've found dry rot throughout both buildings. Due to the lack of ventilation and use of radiant heat, it has been able to grow for years behind the plaster and under some floorboards."

"How bad is the damage?" I asked, not sure I wanted to hear the answer again, even though we'd already discussed it before the filming began.

"By installing a new HVAC, thankfully already included in the plans, we will be eliminating the source of the moisture, which is the first step. Then we need to remove and treat the sections of wood that have been destroyed. That, I'm afraid, can get pretty pricey, but it has to be done in order to pass inspection," he informed me.

"We have some emergency funds in the budget. Get me an estimate, and I'll see if we can cover it. If the repair is too expensive, I will, unfortunately, have to make some uncomfortable phone calls. Keep your fingers crossed."

Having made our decisions on how to deal with the renovation issues, we did our closing remarks, and the cameras stopped rolling. Andre left to share the updates with the team of construction workers who had been watching from the sidelines.

As everyone was returning to their construction posts in the lobby and new wing, a hand grabbed mine and pulled me into the entrance of the dark theater.

"Hi, beautiful," a voice whispered in my ear.

Then I felt small kisses moving down the side of my neck.

"Stop that! We're at work," I said, not really meaning it.

"You were great out there," he murmured.

His breath softly caressed my neck and sent a chill down my spine.

"Thanks, boss," I somehow managed to say.

Next thing I knew, not only was he kissing me, but his hands began moving to places that, with anyone else, would have constituted sexual harassment.

"You're incorrigible," I giggled, swatting his hands away.

"I'm not that kind of girl," I said with my best fake haughtiness. "Besides, someone could walk in here any minute."

"Come on, Jess, nobody is around," he protested.

I pulled away from him, moving toward the exit and into the lobby with a dejected Trevor trailing behind me.

"Hey, Jess, just the person I was looking for," Lucy called out as she rounded the corner and entered the main lobby.

"See, I knew we'd get caught," I muttered to Trevor under my breath as Lucy eyed us suspiciously.

"Not if we would have stayed in the theater," he countered, almost pouting.

Shooting Lucy a brief wave, he headed down the newly-constructed hallway and into the educational wing to speak with Andre.

"I wanted your opinion on some changes to the museum," Lucy said.

We moved to a quiet spot, where her questions began. But that was okay because she usually had good ones.

"Was that you I saw on the back of Trevor's bike Saturday?" I did say usually.

"Yeah, we went to a winery not far out of town. You should go there. It's really nice," I answered, trying to deflect the topic to the 'winery' rather than the 'you and Trevor on his bike' part of the question.

"So … what's going on, girlfriend?" she probed.

She proceeded to nudge me with her elbow, clearly looking for some good gossip.

"I thought I felt some chemistry between you two even on the drive out here, but definitely during game night. How long has it been going on? Tell me everything!"

I like Lucy, but I was not close enough to her to 'tell her everything'.

"We both just wanted to enjoy a beautiful day outside, and a ride to the winery was a perfect little get away. Like I said, you should really visit there. The setting is as nice as some of the Napa locations."

"Okay, I can tell I'm not going to get any details, but I want you to know I'm really happy for you. I think you two make a super cute couple."

"Thanks," I said, still not about to give her an ounce more. "So, what changes do you want to make to the museum?"

"I was thinking about altering the focus of the museum from The Uptown Theater to the era of the Movie Palace. The history of the Picture Palace, as it was also sometimes called, is an interesting story in itself. Hundreds, like this one, were built every year between 1925 and 1930. We can design an exhibition hall to chronical the effects these theaters had on society and on towns like Marceline. For example, during the hard days of the Depression, weekly visits to the movie theatre were considered an inexpensive release for the struggling people of the community. Obviously, we will still highlight The Uptown Theater, its roll in Marceline and Walt Disney's appearances and film debuts, but focusing on the bigger theme of the Movie Palace will give more depth to the museum and feel very different from the Disney Hometown Museum up the street. What do you think?"

"I absolutely love it! What did Cassandra say?"

"I'm going to call her next. I wanted a second opinion before I pitched it to her."

"She was totally open to my changes, so I'm sure she will want to go with it, particularly if it doesn't add to the budget," I said as the front door opened.

Taylor came in wearing her newest accessory – a pair of oversized, crimson glasses. Riding straight across her brow then curving well below her eyes, they covered half of her pale face, reminding me of the tree frog featured in the Nat Geo documentary I had watched last week, 'Amazing Rainforest'. (Evidently, I was still eating way too many dinners alone in front of the television). Matching streaks of red ran through her long, dark tresses and as usual, she had pulled off the frog look beautifully.

"Hi, Jess. Hi, Lucy." Taylor bounced into the lobby with her characteristic exuberance. "I talked to Mrs. Davison at Yesterland Treasurers, and she's expecting us there in a half hour."

"I guess I'd better get going," I said to Lucy, grateful for the out. "Good luck with your call to Cassandra!"

CHAPTER 18

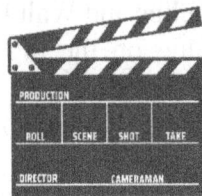

Taylor and I had arranged to spend the afternoon, a block from Uptown Theater, antique shopping for interesting items that would help to generate an aura of past and present intermingled throughout the renovation. Mrs. Davison, the owner of the shop we were going to, had been kind enough to close her doors to the public for two hours while we filmed our visit and hunted for unique pieces of memorabilia.

It is always easier to secure a favor when people know they are going to be featured on television.

My first impression was that the three-story brick building, built in the early 1900's, was an antique itself. Like many of the structures along Main Street, it had great bones, retaining its original architectural features. But unlike other edifices up and down Kansas Avenue, this one had been recently modernized with the addition of striped awnings, benches situated on either side of the entry for weary shoppers, and etched glass windows announcing to the world that inside could be found countless *Antiques*.

Our entourage entered as a cheerful Mrs. Davison appeared from a back room to greet us. I wasn't sure if she had heard our arrival from the jingling of the ancient bells dangling down the front door or from the banging noises of several people and heavy film equipment being hauled into her store.

"Hi, I'm Jess James. I believe we talked on the phone," I greeted her. "Thanks so much for having us today."

"It's so nice to meet you," she gushed. "Taylor has told me all about you and how much she is enjoying her experience."

Mrs. Davison gave Taylor a sweet smile, obviously proud of the local girl. "And please, call me Carol."

Carol took us on a narrated tour of the building, describing the origins of various pieces, pointing out new arrivals and highlighting her favorites for the camera. She led us through rooms full of dishes, glassware, jewelry, figurines, clothing, toys and an assortment of old furnishings, all from a bygone era.

"I'll leave you two alone to dig through the inventory. To me, that's always the best part, discovering a hidden gem," Carol said, ending her television debut.

As she walked back to the front counter, Taylor and I began our search, poking around the shop, rifling under stacked items, looking in out of the way corners and high up on dusty shelves while the cameras followed behind, filming our every move.

"Hey, look at this," Taylor said, calling me over. "This old chest would be perfect for the drama classroom. We could fill it with costume props."

She grabbed a black-laced pillbox hat off the top of a turn-of-the-century, mirrored dresser, placed it on her head, added some imaginary opera gloves and brought a pretend cigarette holder to her mouth, mimicking Audrey Hepburn in *Breakfast at Tiffany's*.

"Darling, what are your thoughts on the idea?" she asked, employing her best socialite voice.

"I love it," I said and laughed at her while she strutted around looking for other items to fill the chest.

Draped over a wooden rocker, Taylor took a crocheted shawl and wrapped it around her shoulders. Removing the elegant hat, she dropped it in the chest and continued her search while hunched over, old lady-style. With each item she found, she changed her character to fit the prop. *She really is a natural in front of the camera.*

Filling the chest with more hats, a cane, a boa, then a long strand of pearls, a gavel, and finally a magnifying glass, we decided to leave the trunk half empty so future classes could add more items to fit their needs. We also settled on a red and gold damask parlor settee that would fit perfectly inside the theater's lobby.

But my favorite find was a red crystal chandelier, tiering downward like an inverted birthday cake. It was the exact kind of dramatic fixture I was imagining for greeting patrons as they entered The Performing Arts Center.

Before leaving, I spoke with Carol about my desire to replace the crown molding around the lobby area. She informed me that a few of her networking connections, made over years in the business, might be able to help us out and that she would be more than happy to make a couple of calls. I left her my contact information with a request to be notified if she was able to secure any decorative cornices.

We purchased the rest of our items and thanked her profusely for inviting us into her treasure trove.

After a successful hunt, Taylor, the film crew, and I split up.

Since we had been in Yesterland Treasurers longer than I expected, I needed to hurry home and pick up Cooper for his scheduled veterinary appointment. Although I was sure Cooper wouldn't have complained about postponing his shots, it appeared we would just make it.

• • •

We had to wait about fifteen minutes before being ushered into our exam room. Apparently, someone unexpectedly dropped off a litter of kittens that needed immediate attention. Eventually, Kaitlin arrived and gave Cooper a good once-over.

"Everything looks great," she said to me then shifted her attention directly to Cooper. "Buddy, you need rabies, distemper, parvovirus and adenovirus shots today to keep you nice and healthy. You will only feel a little stick, so if I can get you to hold still for me, we'll get started."

She soothingly ran her left hand down Cooper's back while using her right hand to expertly inject him in his side with his first shot.

Cooper didn't even flinch.

I felt myself releasing a breath I didn't even know I was holding.

"This cocktail combination might make you a bit lethargic tonight," she continued talking to him, "but by tomorrow, you should be full of energy again and wearing out your mom, as usual."

Cooper took all four shots like a trooper. *If a doctor gave me four shots, I would be crying and requiring sympathy from anyone who would listen. He or she would be telling me to put on my big girl pants and insist that I stop whining.* (As you can guess, I have heard those phrases spewed in my direction more than once in my lifetime, probably one reason I haven't seen a doctor in over five years.)

Kaitlin told me to watch for certain signs that would indicate an adverse reaction to any of the shots, but she didn't expect any issues. She still recommended a quiet evening inside.

We thanked her and were about to leave when I thought, from the expression on her face, that an idea was crossing her mind.

"Jess, I'm going to try and adopt out the kittens who were dropped on our doorstep today at this Saturday's Summer Kickoff Festival and could use a second hand. Would you be willing to help me out in my booth?"

I thought about it for about a half second.

"I'd be happy to! It sounds better than sitting around the house, plus I'd love to return the kindness you've shown me since arriving in Marceline."

"Thank you," she said with a big smile on her face.

After all, Chance had practically dared me participate in a community event the day I ran into him in the park, so I figured I should check one out.

CHAPTER 19

I was only a few blocks away from Ripley Park, so I decided to walk to Kaitlin's booth located on the south end of the lake. I figured it would take less time to walk than to drive and fight for one of the limited parking spaces, which would mean I would also wind up walking the same number of blocks anyway.

Having worked from home the previous day, I was shocked by the transformation of Main Street and Ripley Park. The first, and impossible to miss, change was the giant water slide rolled down the middle of Kansas Avenue.

I had been so busy with the Uptown renovations that I hadn't paid attention to the flyers and signs posted all over town advertising the Summer Kickoff Festival. Deciding I had better remedy that, I stopped in front of Sprinkles, Main Street's frozen yogurt and sweet shop, and read about the day's events; food, games, bounce houses, live music, vendors and the 1000-foot inner tube slip and slide – *fun for all ages*!

I had never seen anything like it. Giant firehoses were attached to lime green tubes spraying water through the length of the two-lane slide. The festival didn't officially start for another fifteen minutes, but a long line was already snaking down Main Street's three blocks, as far as the eye could see. I didn't even know there were that many people in Marceline.

To avoid the crowd, I walked down the opposite side of the street toward the lake, searching for Kaitlin's booth.

Hearing a bunch of meowing, I realized I was in the right spot before I ever saw Kaitlin.

In two, three-tiered cat cages were a total of six gold and white striped, pink-eared kittens with bright blue eyes actively playing, pawing and jumping from level to level. It was a good thing I had found Cooper first, otherwise, I'm pretty sure I would be a cat owner rather than a dog mom.

They were so adorable!

Kaitlin wasn't going to need my assistance for very long.

"Hi! How can I help?" I asked as I approached Kaitlin's booth which was no more than a white, folding banquet table covered in brochures.

"I'm pretty much set up. If you could man the table while I talk to people about the kittens that would really help."

"What is all this?" I asked, picking up one of the leaflets.

"I try to encourage people in the area to be conscientious of their animal's health and safety. Not everyone treats their animals like beloved pets, so I want to get the message out that regular veterinary checkups and preventive care are as essential as food and love to an animal's well-being. If you look on the back, I offer a free first visit so I can talk to the owners about their specific animal's needs. Sometimes, that's in the office and, other times, I travel to their farms and homes, depending on the animal. I've seen a real improvement since I first moved here. I'm working to spread the message to everyone and having a booth at the festivals helps me get the word out. It also helps people to know me better and allows me to answer some simple veterinary questions. It's been a real win-win."

Just as she was finished explaining about the pamphlets, a family stopped to ogle the kittens. They held, pet and played with one whose tan stripe ran from the top of its head to the tip of its nose, but eventually they moved on to other activities.

People continuously stopped throughout the morning and by lunch, four of the six kittens had been claimed. Contracts were signed, veterinary visits were scheduled for the next week to ensure the little guys would be well taken care of, and excited pet owners walked away with new family members.

I knew that amazing feeling well!

By noon, the park was filled with people mingling, laughing, and enjoying the festival. I recognized some of the film crew in the crowd, along with a few locals whose names, unlike a few weeks ago, I even knew. Most of them were working booths like Carol from Yesterland Treasures, but others like Erin Langley, owner of The Uptown, and Bob Knowell, the Mayor, were with their families enjoying the festivities – most of the kids were soaking wet from the waterslide, which seemed to be a big hit.

"Is Trevor going to be here today?" Kaitlin asked when we got a small break from curious kitten lovers.

"This isn't his thing. He's not a big festival person," I said, adding air quotes to *festival*. "How about I grab us a couple of burgers from that stand over there?"

I wanted to change the subject from Trevor. I had tried the day before to talk him into stopping by our booth, but he wasn't remotely interested.

"If I give you some money, would you mind grabbing me a sandwich, too?"

The request came from the other side of Kaitlin.

Next to our booth was Mandy Kirk, a local real estate agent, who Kaitlin had introduced me to early that morning. Due to the steady flow of traffic in front of our table all morning, we had not been able to socialize. (That's what happens when you have six kittens that become the center of attention.)

"I hate to leave my table empty," Mandy continued.

"Not at all," I said as I got her and Kaitlin's orders.

A large grill had been filling the air with the aroma of mouthwatering barbecue, causing long lines to stretch from the food tent.

Standing as part of the herd, I surveyed the park and the people milling about. This really was a happy place, I thought to myself. These people were not wealthy, and they were not trying to climb the corporate ladder. They weren't dressed in designer fashions, nor was I waiting in line with them for fancy food and bottled spring water. The residents of Marceline were just nice, down-to-earth people, who cared about their families, neighbors and community.

"I see you came, after all."

A deep voice broke me away from my thoughts.

Chance, carrying a paper food boat with a partially eaten bratwurst covered in mustard, onions, and relish plus a side of fried chips, approached me as I moved one step closer to the source of smoke wafting my direction.

He had changed with the season from his standard flannel to a charcoal tee stretching over biceps that had, unfortunately, previously been covered by his long sleeves. His wavy hair looked fake-ruffled like a sexy fashion model posing on a sailboat in the middle of the ocean. Only I was confident he had put zero effort into the look and placed no product in his hair to make it fall that way. Too bad he still had that annoying smirk on his face when he talked to me, as if I were a constant amusement to him.

"I'm helping Kaitlin with adopting out a litter of kittens," I stuttered, pointing toward her booth just in time to see another kitten leave in one of the pop-up nylon carriers she provided for the new families.

"I can't believe how many people are here," I said, looking over the crowd.

"This is somewhat larger than our typical festivals," he conceded. "We've been advertising the Summer Kickoff and giant slip and slide in Brookfield and surrounding communities for the past month. What's the movie line, 'If you build it, they will come'? Apparently, that's true. The city council wanted to go all out today as a way to welcome some of the new residents starting at the Fulfillment Center. It's my opinion they also wanted to impress a certain group of people filming a television show based here. Although no one has voiced that out loud, I've lived here long enough to know how things work."

"I would say they succeeded," I exclaimed as I reached the point in the line where I was about to be asked for my order.

"I think you're next," Chance said, pointing to the gap between myself and the person in front of me.

"Hope you enjoy the rest of your day," he said before taking a large, messy bite of bratwurst and strolling into the crowd.

Juggling our sandwiches, chips and drinks, I patted myself on the back for making it back to the vendor section of the park without having dropped one morsel of food. My journey might have ended successfully but being as five different people asked if I needed help in the short walk from the food tent to our booths, I seemingly didn't make the trek too gracefully.

"Thanks," chimed Kaitlin and Mandy simultaneously as they helped me untangle our drinks and meals.

"I see you've already made friends with our resident hunk," teased Mandy as she savored her first bite of pulled pork.

"Who's that?" I asked, not willing to take the bait.

"Chance Alexander, the most sought-after guy in Linn County," she retorted. "How have you two already gotten to know each other?"

Mandy had an inquisitive trait that I was quickly learning was common in Marceline. That curious-minds-want-to-know thing.

"He's working as lead construction for our renovations, but I'm not so sure I agree with your assessment of him. I actually find him rather condescending," I said, thinking of the way he continually mocked me.

"Well, I can assure you, you are the only female around here to feel that way," she replied.

"Mandy was just filling me in on the exciting development announced at last night's city council meeting," Kaitlin said and turned to me.

I was so grateful to her for bailing me out of a conversation that I was more than happy to terminate.

"I've been working with the mayor behind the scenes," Mandy explained, "but it was revealed to the public last night that an established real estate developer, Westhoff Group, from Kansas City, wants to rent out second and third floor properties above businesses on Main Street and turn them into lofts. They like the changes that are occurring in town and believe the area has real potential."

Hmmm ... I wonder if that will make us more popular around here?

"Originally, jobs at the new facility were being filled by people from the area," she continued, "but recently, USAMade has begun interviewing an influx of candidates from other regions outside the county. Many of these new employees are moving to Brookfield ... it's a bigger town with a Walmart, hospital, more retail and dining, plus it's only about twenty minutes from the fulfillment center. But Mayor Knowell, the city council, and now this Kansas City development company want to attract people to Marceline also. They want to create a completely different vibe from Brookfield. Their vision is to keep Marceline quaint ... small specialty shops, local independent dining options, and entertainment, all contained in a vibrant, three to five-block area."

"That fits right in with what we're doing on Main Street," I said, unable to suppress my excitement.

"I'm pretty sure the changes being filmed by *LeisureTV* are part of the appeal for the development firm, but whatever the reason, it's good news for Marceline," Mandy added.

"I can't believe it," I exclaimed.

"I can," Mandy countered, rather defensively. "Marceline may be small and off the beaten path, but this is a nice place to live and has tons of potential."

"No," I said and laughed, although I didn't think it was funny and felt bad that she thought I was knocking Marceline, "I CAN believe that a property management firm is interested in Main Street development, what I CAN'T believe is that Trevor came to the festival!"

I pointed toward the two men walking our direction.

"What are you doing here?" I greeted Trevor, who with Andre, was walking with beers in hand toward our booth.

"That's a nice hello," Trevor said and chuckled.

"I'm just surprised to see you," I said, introducing them to Kaitlin and Mandy. "I thought you were busy all day."

"Andre dragged me to the Country Club for a round of golf this morning. I thought with the festival going on, there wouldn't be many people on the course to see how bad I am at the world's most frustrating sport."

"He isn't kidding," Andre agreed. "What did you shoot, a 150? We quit keeping score after the second hole so he wouldn't be embarrassed at the end of the round when he had to admit he couldn't add that high."

"Very funny, Andre," Trevor said sarcastically. "He even gave me a 36 handicap, and I still owe him money for every hole but one. So, I thought I'd drown my sorrows and make this guy buy me a beer for torturing me. We saw your table and thought we would say a quick hello. Besides, we can't go back to our apartments for a shower ... we have no water pressure. It seems all of our water is running down Kansas Avenue on that giant slide outside our building."

"You could grab an inner tube and take a three-block bath, if you're really desperate," I proposed.

"I think we'll wait it out, but thanks for the brilliant suggestion, Jess. Maybe we should be going," he said to Andre, "before she comes up with any more bright ideas. Besides, I see an empty cornhole game over there, and I need to earn some of my money back."

"See you later?" Trevor asked me, his twinkling blue eyes boring straight into my core, full of innuendos that were impossible to miss.

I nodded as Trevor and Andre left us and walked toward the game area, breaking out into a sudden sweat, even though I was sitting under a leafy shade tree.

"So, I finally get to meet the famous Trevor Dorrington," Kaitlin teased me. "He's clearly as smitten as you are. I think it's cute ... I mean, I think he's cute."

"Stop it," I said, blushing. "We're just getting to know each other better, that's all."

"I bet they're getting to know each other better," Kaitlin mocked me, along with a giggling Mandy.

"I'm going to leave and not help get this last kitten adopted if you don't stop," I said, unable to keep from joining their giggles.

And with that, a family approached the cat cage asking if it would be possible for their daughter to hold the kitten. *Saved by the cat!*

The family and the last kitten were a perfect match. The day had been a huge success, not just for the veterinary clinic, but for the town as well. It was obvious the festival had been a big hit and, even though Kaitlin didn't need my help at the booth any longer, I stayed a while chatting with her and Mandy.

I, too, had enjoyed the day immensely and was slow to leave for home.

"I better get going," I finally said, rising from my chair behind the table. "I've got a long walk, you know. With this crowd, my time to reach home might increase from five to six minutes."

"The band is going to start in about an hour, why don't you stick around?" Kaitlin suggested.

"Trevor's coming over tonight for dinner and a movie. We're both James Bond junkies, so we plan to finally watch *Casino Royale*. It's leaving *Netflix* after this weekend. I love the car chases, mystery and intrigue. I think Trevor just likes to watch the sensual women, with and without all their bling. Anyway, I still need to shower and get ready, but thanks for the offer. I'll remember to keep my evening open for the next festival so I can hear the band. I love live music. Anyway, thanks for including me today. It was fun."

"Thank you for your help today," Kaitlin countered. "I could not have handled those kittens and the booth by myself."

Moving around the table, I told Mandy how nice it was to meet her and began my trek through the park toward home, thinking about what a pleasant afternoon it had been. I finally allowed myself to look forward to the evening ahead. I had tried not to fixate on our 'date' since Trevor had asked me on Thursday. *In my world, nothing can slow down time quite like counting down the days, hours, and minutes.* But now, I permitted my mind to jump from dinner and the movie to envisioning where our night might end – a deep, passionate kiss turning into…

"What the?!"

Unable to finish my thought, I suddenly felt my arms flailing, as I tried to regain my balance, but it was of no use. Next thing I knew, I was lying on the ground with a sharp pain shooting through my ankle.

Mortified, I looked around, only to see a crowd quickly surrounding me.

Two men, I had never met, helped me to my feet, asking if I was alright, while a mom, obviously experienced in boo-boo's, yelled that she was going to get Joanie. *Who's Joanie?*, I wondered.

"I'm fine," I said to the men, who were still holding my arms to steady me.

I put my right foot down as another pain seared through my ankle, making me wince and nearly stumble a second time.

"What happened, Jess?" screeched a concerned Kaitlin as she, Mandy, and Joanie (whoever she is) broke through the crowd and rushed towards me. "One minute you were practically skipping home and the next thing we see, you're crumbling to the ground."

"I don't know," I said and looked around again.

"I know. Look at this rut," Mandy said, pointing to a large, fresh divot, dug deep in the grass.

"Sit over here and let me take a look," said the lady I presumed to be Joanie, as she directed my human crutches to help me hobble over to a picnic table a few feet away.

I plopped down on the bench as Joanie gently took my ankle in her hands, feeling around for broken bones.

"Hi, I'm Joanie Newstead. You must be Jess?"

"Ouch, yes," I answered as she twisted my ankle slightly to the left.

"I'm a nurse at Brookfield Community Hospital. Looks like you've got a nasty sprain, but luckily nothing seems broken.

You're going to need to ice your ankle, stay off it and keep your foot elevated for at least the rest of the weekend ... maybe longer, depending on how it feels. Can you put any weight on it?"

I stood, gingerly, lowering my foot to the ground. It hurt like crazy, but I was able to put some pressure on it without the intense pain I originally felt.

"I'm fine," I said and grimaced.

The crowd, realizing that I had only sprained my ankle and not busted my head open and didn't have any gaping, bloody wounds, began to disburse for more exciting activities, leaving me a path to walk/limp a few steps on my own.

"I can make it home," I told the small group who stayed behind, sweetly still concerned about my well-being. "It's only a few blocks away."

"I'll tell you what," Joanie said, "I live a couple houses down from you. I've seen you walking that dog of yours, or should I say, I've seen that dog of yours walking you." She chuckled. "How about I accompany you home? I just need to let my kids know I'll be gone for fifteen minutes or so. They're over at the slip and slide where they've been all day."

"That's a great idea," Kaitlin interjected. "Thanks, Joanie. We'll stay here with Jess until you return."

I thanked the two gentlemen (Kurt and Henry) who helped me to my feet and had asked me a hundred times if I was sure I didn't need their assistance getting home.

"Really, I'm fine, but thanks again. I cannot tell you how much I appreciate all your help, and I honestly mean that!"

They reluctantly left me with Kaitlin and Mandy to wait for Joanie's return.

"So, I give her a 9.5," Kaitlin said.

"No, definitely a 9.8," countered Mandy. "Did you see that landing?"

"Thanks for the high marks, but I really should have a 10 by now, with as much practice as I've had falling lately," I said, shaking my head in frustration.

We saw Joanie approaching, and I hobbled her direction, assuring Kaitlin and Mandy that I would be fine. *It's just a sprain.*

As we pushed through the crowd, Joanie walked close by my side in a way that would normally feel like she was in my space, but this afternoon, it gave me comfort, knowing I had someone to grab onto in case I started to fall again.

"So, you live on Mulberry Street too?" I asked, breaking the ice.

"Yes, I'm two houses down from Ida Jenkins. If I know Ida, she made it a point to meet you within your first week here. Am I right?"

"That's about how long it took," I said and laughed. "She's a great neighbor, but sometimes I feel like she is clairvoyant. She seems to know everything."

"Oh, she's a character, all right, but you couldn't meet a better person. My kids love her. She's always giving them cookies or some kind of homemade treat."

"How many children do you have?" I asked, truly interested.

"Two, twin girls. They're in middle school. I totally embarrassed them, and I'm pretty sure ruined their lives, by telling them in front of their friends that I was leaving for a few minutes to walk you home. Being seen talking to your mother is a mortal sin at thirteen. One day they love all over me and the next day, I can't do anything right."

"I'm sorry."

"It's okay, Oliva and Emily are just figuring out their independence. My husband and I have tried to teach them to be strong, confident young ladies, but I have to admit, we do cherish those moments when they're still our little girls."

As we reached our street, Joanie pointed out which house was hers and I realized that I had seen her working in her yard when walking Cooper. Only I didn't recognize her in the park without the floppy sunhat covering half her face.

"You know, I have some Extra Strength Tylenol inside. Why don't I get you a couple of pills for tonight? They'll help alleviate the pain and allow you to relax. Resting that ankle is vitally important if you want to be back on your feet soon."

I leaned on her white picket fence (really, she has a white picket fence surrounding her yard!) and waited for her to bring some drugs before hobbling the last three houses to my front porch steps, which I was sure were going to be a major challenge.

After Joanie got me settled in my house, I thanked her profusely for all the help home.

"It's no problem," she assured me as she headed back to the festival and to her humiliated daughters.

● ● ●

Deciding I had better text Trevor and see if he even wanted to keep our date now that I was injured, I reached for my phone.

> **Me**: You're never going to guess what happened to me after you left the festival

> **Trevor**: You decided to go down that slip and slide, you didn't slow at the finish and crashed headfirst into the barrier at the end of the slide

> **Me**: You're on the right track, only your version sounds like more fun

Trevor: I was joking. Now you have me worried

Me: With all the people running through the park today someone accidently created a hole the size of Rhode Island in the ground which I conveniently found and tripped in and once again humiliated myself by swan diving in front of a large crowd

Trevor: Are you okay

Me: No I sprained my ankle and it really hurts. My neighbor Joanie walked me home and gave me some Extra Strength Tylenol so now I'm sitting alone on my couch with my leg elevated as instructed by Nurse Joanie (she really is a nurse) bummed about spoiling our date tonight

Trevor: How about I run to the grocery store, pick up a bottle of wine, some ingredients for seafood linguini, play Dr. Trevor and keep you off that foot

Me: Now that sounds like a plan!

CHAPTER 20

"Come in, the door is unlocked," I yelled from my perch on the couch.

Trevor entered, groceries in hand, and Cooper danced at his heals, both of them making a beeline for the kitchen.

Sitting helplessly on my throne, I heard the bang of the back door (as Trevor let Cooper out), the clinking of pots, the running of tap water and cabinets opening and closing, all the while feeling guilty, thinking I should be the one making him dinner.

Poking his head around the corner, Trevor smiled, holding two glasses of chilled wine.

"Which one?" he asked.

"I would love the full one, but should probably have the smaller glass since I had an appetizer of Extra Strength Tylenol earlier."

Trevor laughed, sitting next to me on the couch, stealing a long, slow kiss, before handing me my splash of wine.

"Does that make it any better?" he asked.

"More of that, and I won't need any drugs," I said and sighed, looking forward to our long evening together.

"So, how is the ankle?"

"Throbbing, but better than it was when I first got home. I'm really sorry about ruining tonight's plans," I added, so disappointed.

"You probably need to start watching where you are walking, Jess. It seems like you fall a lot."

"I know. My mind begins to wander, and I quit paying attention to my surroundings. It's always been an issue for me. Did I ever tell you about my first day of college when I walked into Intro to Psych, dreaming of how I was going to become an expert at analyzing all of my friends' problems, and then tripped over a chair jutting into the aisle, falling on top of a guy seated in the next row? Not exactly the way a girl wants to start her college career, but it made quite a first impression. Ethan and I later became good friends, and he never tired of telling people how the first time we met I gave him a 'lap dance'. I'm sure it's one reason I decided against Psychology for my major … turns out I made a better subject for the class than student of the field."

Silently, staring at me as if I had three heads, Trevor nodded politely and abruptly announced he needed to check to see if the water was boiling on the stove, leaving me to wish I'd kept that story to myself. (Oversharing – another of my issues which has led to countless embarrassing moments.) If I kept going, I could have Trevor running for his life before the night was over.

"How can I assist you?" I asked a startled Trevor as he quickly grabbed a chair from under the kitchen table and directed me to take a seat, sensing I had depleted all my energy moving from the living room to the kitchen hopping on one foot.

"I want to help," I said, hobbling over to the counter. "It's boring in there by myself. Besides, I need to move around or I'm going to fall asleep. So, what can I do?"

"You can sit your cute little behind on that red chair and tell me where you've hidden the olive oil," Trevor instructed.

"I hate sitting here while you do all the work," I argued, but I wound up doing as I was told, giving directions from my post while Trevor created a culinary masterpiece.

Since I was already seated, we decided to eat in the brightly lit kitchen rather than the dining room with the flickering candles, soft music, and the romantic atmosphere I had been envisioning all week.

Talking ceaselessly (without me sharing any more embarrassing stories), we moved seamlessly from one topic to the next until we were both comfortably full from the exquisite meal and totally relaxed from the bottle of wine. I figured with food in my stomach, what was one (ok maybe two) more small glasses of wine.

"Should we move into the living room? I probably need to elevate this ankle. I can feel it starting to swell again," I suggested, picking up my plate and staggering toward the sink, my balance off.

"Let me clean up these dishes, and I'll meet you in there, unless you need any help getting to the couch?"

"No, I've got this. If you haven't noticed, I'm pretty bullheaded. I've never been a fan of people waiting on me. I'd rather do things for myself."

"Oh, I've noticed. Actually, I'd call you a bulldozer more than bullheaded," he smiled.

I don't know if it was having spent the entire day in the sun, the wine, the full belly, the medicine, or the stress of the fall, but walking from the kitchen to the living room utterly exhausted me. I found our movie on *Netflix* while Trevor cleared the dirty dishes and put the leftovers in the refrigerator before joining me on the couch.

Sitting at the far end of the sofa (away from Mona), I nuzzled in the crook of Trevor's outstretched arm with my legs stretching the length of the couch. Turning on *Casino Royale*, I watched the initial scene ... and remember nothing else.

• • •

Opening my eyes, I discovered I was in bed, fully-clothed, lying next to, an also fully-clothed Trevor, the sun peeking through my bedroom curtains and an only slightly throbbing ankle.

Thinking back to the night before, I couldn't recall anything past the black-and-white opening to the movie. Beyond that, everything was a complete blank. This had never happened to me! Even the times when I had too much to drink, I never passed out.

I rolled over and saw Trevor's eyes beginning to open.

"Good morning," I whispered.

"Good morning," he said and smiled back.

I wasn't sure how someone's teeth could be so white and hair so perfectly tousled that early, but somehow Trevor looked as good waking up in the morning as he did coming through my front door last night. I, on the other hand, had hair sticking out in all directions, make-up smudges under my eyes, and the breath of a dragon – assuming my appearance was the same as the reflection I saw every other morning in the mirror after stumbling out of bed.

"What happened last night?" I asked, not sure I wanted to hear his answer.

"The minute you relaxed on the couch, you knocked out cold. You were so out of it, I was afraid to leave you alone. I hope you don't mind that I spent the night?"

"Not at all! That was really thoughtful! Taking medicine always makes me sleepy. I guess that's what happened, but the good thing is, I'm wide awake now, and my ankle feels much better."

"Then maybe we should pick up where we left off last night," he rolled over and kissed me.

We may have slept all night in our clothes, but as Trevor's hands began to explore every inch of my wanting body, I got the feeling that's not how we would be spending our morning.

● ● ●

Still full from the previous night's feast and our morning indulgence, Trevor and I made coffee, toasted a couple of "everything" bagels, and sat across the kitchen table from each other, eating our breakfast and talking about our plans for the rest of the day.

Unfortunately, my plans were nothing more exciting than sitting in a chair with my foot elevated. Although significantly better than yesterday, I found myself limping my way around the house on a still-tender ankle. I had a major filming session scheduled for Wednesday, so it was imperative I got my foot healed quickly.

Trevor was presenting the plan for our third and final project – a farm-to-table grocer with a small outdoor bistro, located at the other end of Main Street – to Mr. Biggs, the mayor, and select members of the city council the next day, so he needed to work on the final touches of his presentation.

After a passionate goodbye, Trevor left me to shower and settle in for a long, lazy day.

I got the feeling Cooper was glad Trevor was gone so he could once again become the center of my world. Unfortunately, no walk today for him or for the next week. *How do I explain that to a dog staring at me, then staring out the door, staring at me again, and then staring out the door again?*

"I'm sorry, Cooper, but we're just going to have to enjoy the porch today."

He must have understood because his tail curled between his legs, and he slowly walked toward his favorite sunny patch of warm, wood flooring. He probably figured if he couldn't walk, he might as well nap.

Grabbing my newest novel, I settled into what had become my favorite reading chair and followed Nurse Joanie's orders, propping my foot atop several pillows stacked on the ottoman.

I was deep into the third chapter when I heard a faint rustling of footsteps coming from the sidewalk outside my front window leading directly to my porch.

Cooper, raising his sleepy head, leapt to the door and began excitedly barking while I, having sat too long in one position, stretched and limped to the screen door to check out the source of the commotion.

Hobbling, worse than I was with my silly ankle, was Ida, slowly approaching the porch steps. In her hand was a red-speckled, oversized mug covered with a plastic lid.

I pushed Cooper back, opened the door and ushered Ida onto the porch.

"Let me take that from you," I said and helped her to the rocker.

"I thought some of my famous, homemade chicken noodle soup would be just the ticket for a speedy recovery. There's nothing a hot bowl of soup can't fix, including a sprained ankle," she said as she lowered herself into the chair.

"How thoughtful! Thank you so much! Let me put this in the refrigerator so I can heat it up later this afternoon. It sounds delicious," I said, heading to the kitchen. "Can I get you anything to drink?"

"No, I'm fine dear. I can't stay long. My daughter will be here to pick me up soon. She is taking me to her house for the afternoon. I spend most Sundays with her and her family."

"That's nice," I said, recalling her telling me of her small, but close family.

If I remembered correctly, it was herself, a daughter, her daughter's husband, and a grandson.

Limping back to the porch, I sat in the rattan chair and propped my leg back up on the pillow-stacked ottoman.

"So, I am not even going to ask how you heard I sprained my ankle," I chuckled. "Once again, I'm visited by the all-knowing Ida. Luckily, when Joanie Newstead brought me home from the festival, she gave me strict instructions to relax and elevate my foot all weekend, and I think it's actually working. Wait until I eat that soup, there will be no stopping me!" I giggled.

"Joanie is a wonderful nurse and neighbor. You're lucky she was there."

"That is so true," I said. "I was sitting here earlier marveling at how nice everyone was to me yesterday and now you have even brought me a bowl of soup! I can't get over how helpful people are here. I fell on the sidewalk back in L.A. right before we came to Marceline and, no one was rude – kicking me while I was down, jeering at me, etc. – yet no one helped me either, as I picked my humiliated self up off the ground. They just walked around me, in a hurry to get to their own destinations. I didn't think much about it at the time, but after seeing how many people rushed to my aid yesterday, I can't believe the difference," I said with a catch in my throat.

"Of course, people were there for you. That's what neighbors do! We help each other."

"MOM," we hear a voice calling out from next door.

"It looks like Kathy is here," Ida said and smiled as she slowly rose from her chair. "Just remember how it felt when a stranger was there for you. Someday, you'll be given an opportunity to … what's the expression you young people use today … pay it forward? And I know you will."

"Over here," Ida yelled from my porch door.

Walking toward the steps was an attractive brunette in her mid-fifties, dressed casually in white capris with a variegated purple and white, boat-neck tee and white canvas loafers. I was having trouble seeing Ida in her until she entered the porch, and I noticed the same strong jawline and chocolate brown eyes with wrinkles etched in the corners, just not as deep as her mother's.

"Hi, I'm Jess," I stretched out my hand to greet her.

"I'm Kathy," she said, shaking my hand, offering a warm smile, identical to Ida's. "And no introductions needed," she said and laughed. "I know all about you."

Apparently like mother, like daughter.

CHAPTER 21

"We're taking time to step away from The Uptown Performing Arts Center renovations," I spoke into the camera, "to visit the local Walt Disney Hometown Museum ... the crown jewel of Marceline."

It was Wednesday, and my ankle was nearly mended. Luckily, I was able to do the day's shoot without a noticeable limp. Unfortunately, though, I couldn't wear any of my cute sandals yet. Choosing my denim shirt dress, I was able to spice it up with some accessories and still look presentable for television. A bold, collar necklace, pink and blue plaid slip-on boat shoes and a fedora with pink ribbon from the back of my closet completed the ensemble.

"I'd like to introduce Nancy Carmichael, curator and local historian."

The idea was for Nancy to take me on a tour through the modest museum, highlighting its most interesting pieces and sharing some unknown facts about Disney and his time in Marceline.

"This stately, red-bricked building standing before us," Nancy began, "was a bustling train depot between 1913 and

1989, but now houses our museum dedicated to the four years Walt Disney lived in this town. Although four years doesn't seem like a long time, to Walt, they were the best four years of his childhood and would influence him during his entire life. He would tell you they were actually the only four years of his childhood, since he immediately went to work delivering newspapers for his father after moving with the family to Kansas City at the age of nine. Walt's father, a perfectionist, woke Walt and his brother, Roy, daily at 3:30 a.m. and required them to place a newspaper behind each customer's storm door, not toss the paper on the lawn the way other newsboys did, even in the frigid Kansas City winters. It was a big change from his lazy summers spent on the Marceline farm entertaining his younger sister, Ruth."

I could tell Nancy was going to be a wealth of information. And she had a relaxed style in front of the camera and was enthusiastic about showing off her pride and joy to the rest of the world. The only issue I foresaw with the interview was too much content. Since we had only slotted nine minutes for this section in our one-hour (actually forty minutes – due to commercial breaks) episode, I would have to keep her moving through the exhibits.

Traveling with the film crew inside the train station, we began our official tour of the museum.

"The ground floor is dedicated to the history of railroading. This room," Nancy continued, "describes the importance of coal mining in the area and highlights the significance of the Marceline stop on the Santa Fe line. Not only did Marceline house the Missouri Railway Division offices, but it also served as an important crew change point, where the employees received their coveted pay."

Our main focus, for the shoot, was to be the second floor which was primarily dedicated to Walt Disney's formative years.

Lugging the camera equipment up a twisting stairwell, we found ourselves immediately immersed in Disney memorabilia.

"Our goal of the museum is to highlight where the magic began and the influence Marceline had on Walt Disney throughout his life and career," Nancy said, continuing to provide narrative as she walked us into the main room. "We're very appreciative to Walt's younger sister, Ruth, who left most of these letters, personal belongings, and artifacts to the town. She understood how important Marceline was to Walt and how proud we are to have helped mold Walt's dream. What we've tried to do is focus more on Walt the man, who he was, and where he came from, and less on the parks and Disney films."

This woman is a natural. She moved through the displays without missing a beat. It was difficult for me to ask any questions as she simply flowed from one exhibit to the next. *Fine with me!*

"Here are miniature replicas of the original Disneyland, built to scale using actual blueprints of the park," Nancy said, pointing to several glass cases in the middle of the room as we walked around to get a closer look. "A careful examination shows how the buildings in Marceline correspond directly to those on Main Street USA at the entrance to the California theme park."

"The detail in these buildings is amazing," I said, instructing the cameramen to zoom-in on the display of Disneyland's Main Street.

"They were created by noted miniaturist Dale Varner. He began with Sleeping Beauty's castle and continued for forty years to recreate sites throughout the park until his death in 2009. He corresponded directly with Walt Disney and hoped to replicate a small version which embodied what Walt originally wanted the park to be, a place where fantasy came to life and families could have fun."

Continuing through the museum, Nancy pointed to personal family letters, photographs, original illustrations, early Mickey Mouse dolls, recreated portions of Walt's school, studio, and front porch, a light table from one of his first illustration jobs, and even a track panel from the play railroad he built for his daughters in their California home's backyard.

For a small museum, I was shocked by the amount of personal artifacts packed within its walls.

"Walt Disney not only designed a personal, small-scale train ride, but he also created a child-sized race track, Autopia, within the park." Nancy now pointed us to a miniature, jade-colored, two-passenger car with a large, red steering wheel in front of each seat.

I smiled to myself, remembering how, as a kid, I felt like such a grown up when I sat behind the wheel of an updated Autopia car in Disneyland.

"When the speedway was dismantled and replaced with *It's A Small World*, Walt had the ride moved and reinstalled at the Marceline municipal park. It's the only attraction ever removed from Disneyland and operated elsewhere. The ride only ran in Marceline for a couple of years, but here we have on display, one of its historic cars. Donating Autopia is another outward example of Walt Disney's love for this town."

"Your exhibits make that abundantly apparent," I replied. "Why don't you show us a couple more highlights before we go? We could spend hours looking through all the memorabilia, but unfortunately, we need to get back to The Uptown Theater. There's a renovation project waiting to be completed," I said and laughed.

"Two of our guests' favorites are this way," Nancy said as she walked us to the other side of the room. "First, is a piece of the Dreaming Tree. This is a branch from the original cottonwood that sat on the Disney farm. Walt, tasked with minding his little sister, would sit under this tree and create stories or draw his surroundings into flip books used to entertain Ruth on long, hot summer afternoons. Many of these sketches included barnyard and field animals … a familiar theme in so many of his movies. The Tree of Life in Animal Kingdom is modeled after Walt Disney's original Dreaming Tree."

"And across the way," Nancy led us to our last stop, "is Walt Disney's primary school desk from the early 1900's. Walt had a habit of drawing on most anything, and if you look closely, you can see his initial carved into the top of this wooden desk."

She paused while the camera once again zoomed-in for more detail.

"These are just a few of the hundreds of artifacts within these walls that commemorate an extraordinary man. It was an honor to show you some of the museum's memorabilia today. I hope you'll return and browse all the exhibits at a more leisurely pace."

Nancy was not only extending an invitation for us to return but was shrewdly inviting everyone watching our episode of *Main Street* to make a visit to the museum.

I gave her a silent "You go girl!"

I walked with her downstairs, back into the reception area and gift shop, thanking her again for the wonderful tour and willingness to be filmed today.

Noticing the placement of Mickey's arms on the clock hanging behind the information desk, I realized that if I returned to The Uptown, I would barely get started before it would be time to wrap-up for the afternoon. I decided instead to go home and elevate my foot since it was beginning to throb from standing on it for far too long.

Slowly limping my way out to my car, I unlocked Betty, throwing my belongings into the passenger seat, and was about to climb in when I heard a deep voice call out my name.

I looked up to see Chance leaning out his truck window, stopped on the street directly behind my car.

"I thought that was you. Nice hat."

"Thanks," I replied, surprised by his compliment.

"So, what's your impression of our museum?" he asked, moving his head in the direction of the train depot.

"It was nice. I can see how a Disney junkie would eat this place up. You could spend hours in there reading all the information on his family, early life and inspirations, plus I love the way they tied it in with his fascination of trains by housing it in such a beautiful historic building," I said as one of the many, daily trains came thundering our way.

"So, what was your favorite?" Chance shouted over the roar of the approaching engine.

"I would have to say the Dreaming Tree touched me the most," I yelled, walking closer to his truck so we didn't have to keep screaming over the train. "There is something inspirational in the notion that a boy, sitting under a tree, with nothing more than paper, pencil, and a head full of ideas, can pass on to generations his belief in imagination as the magic to making dreams come true."

"Do you have a few minutes? I want to show you something."

"Sure," I replied, hoping my ankle agreed.

"Hop in," he said, leaning over to pop open the passenger door. "Surferboy won't mind if I take you somewhere, will he?"

"No," I said, wondering how and what he knew about Trevor and me while feeling heat creep into my cheeks.

I clicked my key fob, threw my keys in my bag, and climbed into the cab of his truck.

"What did you just do?" he asked as I buckled in.

"I locked Betty, I mean, I locked my car – I affectionately call her Betty," I explain, sheepishly.

"You do realize, yours is probably the only locked car in over a hundred miles, right?" he chuckled.

"It's a habit, and not a bad one," I added, on the defensive. "What are you doing over here, anyway?" I asked as we ambled down the road in his bouncy truck headed for an unknown destination.

I was pretty sure that this was the exact scenario my mother warned me against – getting into a stranger's car with no idea where we were headed. *Maybe this isn't such a good idea, after all.*

"We're ready to paint the rooms in The Performing Arts Center tomorrow, and I needed to pick up the supplies so we can get an early start. Looks like we're going to make the deadline, so you should be able to film your 'Big Reveal' in a couple of weeks, as scheduled."

"Wow, that's great! I'm glad you didn't run into too many unexpected snags. Keep your fingers crossed that our luck continues on the next two projects."

We were only a couple of miles out of town when Chance pulled over next to a charming, barn red, two-story home. Two dormers protruded from its gray roof while white trim accentuated the windows and door, all surrounded by a lush green lawn.

"Here we are," Chance announced as he parked the truck and opened his door to exit.

"Where, exactly, is here?" I questioned, climbing out of the truck.

"This," he pointed toward the house, "is the Disney farm. It's a private residence, but the owners are gracious enough to let visitors walk about the property and see what the town likes to call 'the birthplace of dreams'."

"What a beautiful farmhouse," I said in awe. "Was it always this big?"

"No, an addition was built a few years back as well as a complete renovation to update the over one-hundred-year-old property. They built the current home around the original structure, but left bits of the earlier farmhouse intact, like crooked doors and frames, some flooring, doorknobs, and other antique features that preserve the home's history, but allow it to be a functioning residence. Our company was lucky enough to have been contracted for the job, which is how I'm familiar with the changes made by the family."

"But this isn't why I brought you out here. Follow me," Chance continued as he walked towards a stretch of land hidden behind the house.

Walking down a matted grass path, we stopped next to a signpost describing the large cottonwood in front of us as the *Son of the Dreaming Tree.*

"As Nancy probably told you during your tour, the original tree was diseased and eventually destroyed by a lightning strike. In 2004, Walt Disney's grandson ceremoniously planted a sapling grown from a seed dropped by the original Dreaming Tree, and this is that tree ... planted just feet away from where the initial cottonwood stood for so many years. Even though this tree is considered full grown, it's unfortunately not nearly as majestic as the one Walt Disney sat under as a boy. People visit from all over, believing that being in the presence of or touching the tree that triggered so much imagination, will encourage them to follow their own dreams."

"That is so inspiring," I said, pressing my hand to the bark, expecting to feel a current run up my arm releasing sparks of ideas into my brain.

Instead, I felt a sense of calm and serenity, perhaps from the peacefulness of the open field and the gentle breeze blowing through the leaves of the tree. It was easy to see how a young boy could sit here, lost in his daydreams, and sketch for hours.

"You just touched the tree, so what dreams are you hoping to realize, Jess?" Chance asked, looking deep into my eyes.

"I'm trying to figure that out," I answered honestly, surprising even myself. "I've always planned on being part of the fast-paced city life, moving my way up in the film industry, and being someone 'important'. But in my short time here, I've adopted a dog, slowed down my hectic lifestyle, and enjoyed afternoons lazily chatting with my next-door neighbor, Ida. I'm sure you know Ida. Everyone seems to."

"Oh, I know Ida."

Chance barely got four words out before I cut him off to continue my rambling. Now that I had started to express my hidden thoughts out loud, I couldn't seem to stop myself.

"My life in Marceline is the exact opposite of my life in Los Angeles, but not in a bad way. When I moved here, I was counting the days until I could return home, but I don't feel that way anymore. I guess I'd like to take the best of both worlds and make them into something positive and satisfying. Does that make any sense?"

"Perfect sense, and now you know where to find the Dreaming Tree if you need help figuring out how to combine the visions from your two opposing worlds into something ideal for you. I'm going to guess you don't have anything like that to help you in Los Angeles."

"Well, I don't actually have a Dreaming Tree. I have more of a Therapist Plant, named Mona. She is a giant Monstera houseplant I brought with me, and she is currently residing next to my couch on Mulberry Street. When I need a little advice, Mona and I have a heart-to-heart and before I know it, all my problems are solved."

Chance actually belly laughed loud enough to echo through the canopy of trees, breaking the peaceful silence surrounding us.

"Leave it to someone from La La Land to have a Therapist Plant. Sorry, I'm really not laughing at you. I think it's great. Probably saves on doctor bills plus, if it works, why not? I don't know how you do it, Jess, but every time we talk, you find a way to make me smile."

"More like smirk," I said and glared at him.

"You're reading me all wrong, Jess. Believe me, I'm smiling. Come on, let's continue the tour, shall we?"

He led me further down the path to a replica of the Disney farm's old barn.

"Did you know the California studio, where Walt Disney did all his work, was modeled after this barn? Well, not this exact barn, since the one in front of us was built in 2001," Chance said and paused. "Now that was quite a weekend. The entire town came out for a three-day, old-fashioned barn raising. It was as big of an event as any of our festivals." Chance chuckled. "OSHA would have had a field day with all the regulations that were broken."

"Anyway," he continued, "the barn was the setting of Walt Disney's first show. He dressed some of his pets and farm animals in costumes and called it the Disney Circus. He charged the neighborhood kids ten cents for admission. But like so many other successful people, his initial try was a miserable failure, and his mother made him refund all the money. He said that experience made him understand that giving an audience more than they expected would always lead to a better response."

"Wow, you really know your Disney history," I said, impressed.

"Not really. I'm just good at paraphrasing the visitor signs," he confessed, pointing to the marker in front of the barn door. "So, now you've seen all of our Disney landmarks. What do you think?"

"It actually confuses me," I answered. "It seems to me the people of Marceline are more proud of Walt Disney than they are of the actual town ... the very place Disney bragged about inspiring him, the 'happy place' that gave him his vision."

"Once again, you read us wrong, Jess. The people of Marceline are fiercely proud. You said yourself that the town's people weren't overly friendly when you first arrived. That's because we are proud of our rural Missouri town and, in turn, somewhat skeptical of change coming from outsiders. We know we have something special here."

"If this place is so special, why do only locals get to enjoy it? Why not update and improve areas like Main Street and share all of this with the rest of the world? I can't imagine Walt Disney would have found inspiration in a downtown lacking in activity. I bet during his time here, Main Street was bustling with commerce. Would it be so bad to capture some of that excitement again? Why should Marceline only be about the past? Why shouldn't it also be about the present?"

"We tend to be stubborn, proud, and a little stuck in our ways. Random change is hard for many of us."

"But Mr. Biggs and the City Council have an actual plan which is significantly better than random developments here and there. They are focused on keeping Marceline a quaint community. After the renovation of the old Allen Hotel, Lucy's idea is to court Kansas City residents into choosing Marceline for their weekend get-a-ways. A little history, a winery, some shopping and, of course, the theater."

"I must admit, the improvements to The Uptown Theater have turned out really nice. You've done a great job, Jess."

"You're the one who has done all the work. I just had to come up with ideas, shop for antiques, and redecorate. I have the easy job," I said and laughed, thinking of the many nights I had stayed awake reconfiguring designs for the buildings on Main Street.

"I probably need to be getting back," I said, realizing that we had been gone much longer than I expected. "If The Performing Arts Center is going to be ready on schedule, I have a lot of work to do before we reveal the renovations to the Langleys. Thanks for showing me around today. I really enjoyed the tour. You make an excellent guide. Once Marceline hits it big again, maybe you can quit your construction job for a post as a Walt Disney Hometown Tour Guide. I see a whole new career in your future." I giggled.

"I'll stick with my day job, thank you."

We walked (well, he walked, and I limped) back to his truck.

As we moved down the uneven path, he took hold of my elbow.

Who does he think I am? Some 90-year-old woman? Or maybe he has me figured out – an uncoordinated klutz who might fall over a small twig hiding in the grass. I'd sure hate to trip and give him another reason to 'smile'.

CHAPTER 22

I'm actually nervous. Today is it ... the day we have been waiting for, the big dance, the main event, the grand debut ... the much-anticipated reveal!

Erin and Chris Langley would be there within the hour to see, for the first time, the completed renovations of the Uptown Performing Arts Center.

Living on the other side of town had made it possible for the Langleys to circumvent Kansas Avenue for the past several weeks, although it was my understanding that staying away had been a real challenge for them. With Trevor and Andre as long-term residents of the rooms above the theater, they had not needed to clean or restock the lodgings for new guests. So, today's unveiling should be quite a surprise for the couple.

For me, sleeping or concentrating on anything other than the day's filming was completely out of the question, so I arrived early, with a Grande Café Carmella in hand (*I needed the big one today*). Dashing from room to room, I added a few last-minute touches and picked up random items left behind by the construction crew.

Andre and his team had already moved all their equipment and supplies to our next project – The Allen Hotel.

Our second episode of *Main Street* would focus on the abandoned set of rooms sitting above the three businesses located at the corner of Kansas and Ritchie Avenues. I had already seen a large 'Open During Construction' sign in front of the Corner Café, readying patrons for the loud, overhead noises they were going to be subjected to for the next several weeks. The sign also let customers know that Bangers & Mash (sausages served with mashed potatoes and onion gravy) was this month's special. *You've got to love their sense of humor!*

Unlike Uptown Theater, this historic building was owned by Charles and Jazelle Victor, who rented space to the restaurants and shops on the ground floor. A few businesses had moved in and out of the upstairs spaces, but nothing had stayed long, so The Victors were looking forward to converting the place into a small period hotel, but with state-of-the-art, twenty-first century amenities.

Once again, I wouldn't be meeting with the clients until we were ready to film the walk-through, but I had heard they already had plans to outsource the day-to-day operations of the hotel to a reputable management company. I hope they were as easy to work with as the Langleys.

Leaning over the new, glass-block concession stand to hide an errant hammer found in the corner of the lobby, I suddenly felt a hand on my thigh, slightly above the hem of my houndstooth, flared skirt. Startled, I whipped around, coming face-to-face with a smiling Trevor.

"I love your skirt," he said with a mischievous grin as he gave my lips a quick, but tantalizing kiss.

I wasn't very comfortable with his bold display of public affection, but he was so cute. And when he offered me that irresistible smile of his, somehow, all was forgiven.

"Good luck today. I know you will do a fabulous job," he added.

I wished my insides felt as confident as Trevor seemed to be.

Andre, Taylor and Mr. Biggs all arrived at the same time to watch and critique the final filming of Episode 1. As they walked in the front door, I could see a group of locals beginning to gather across Main Street, waiting for the shoot to finish so they could take a peek inside their new performing arts center.

Lucy had just text saying that she would be there, with the blindfolded Langleys, in five minutes.

The camera crew was outside, set up and ready to begin shooting.

Here we go!

I met Lucy, with Erin and Chris Langley, in front of the theater, where I took over and the filming began.

"Are you ready to see the new Uptown Performing Arts Center?" I asked.

"We can't wait," Erin replied as she nervously bounced up and down.

"Alright then, remove your blindfolds!"

Erin and Chris slowly lifted the bandanas from their eyes, each squinting and scrunching their faces into grim scowls.

What?! Scowls?! Thinking they were exceedingly disappointed in our renovation, my heart skipped a beat.

"I'm speechless," Erin softly uttered, reaching into her bag and pulling out a pair of tortoise shell sunglasses. "It's absolutely beautiful!"

Realizing their scowls must have been from adjusting to the sunlight after removing their blindfolds and not because they didn't like our work, my shoulders immediately relaxed, and I exhaled a breath I didn't know I had been holding.

"The marquee is stunning," added Chris, who was staring at the three-sided canopy over the doorway.

The words *Performing Arts Center*, in bold lettering, dominated the rectangular section directly in front of us.

"Normally, the runner lights wouldn't be on in the daytime, but we wanted you to get a feel for how eye-catching the sign will appear on performance nights. And if you notice, on the two sides facing up and down Kansas Avenue, we have listed the date for the pilot of *Main Street* to be shown live from the theater."

"Chris, look at that gorgeous entryway!" Erin pointed to the three sets of wood and brass double doors and the semicircular, decorative fanlights. "You can see them so well without the ticket booth blocking the way. Keeping the box office out front would have definitely taken away from the new exterior. Thank you so much for that suggestion, Jessica. It's been here so long I wouldn't have had the nerve to place it inside, but it was totally the right move."

"Would you like to walk through those doors and see the inside?" I questioned, elated by her compliment.

"Absolutely," they replied.

"First, we would like to take a picture of the two of you in front of the new Uptown Performing Arts Center," I said as the film crew began to move their equipment indoors.

After positioning Erin and Chris in a way that showed them as well as the new LED sign, marquee, and entry, Brandon, one of our cameramen, snapped several pictures for posterity.

Gathering the Langleys, we walked together into the newly refurbished lobby, and seeing the delight on both of their faces, I was filled with a sense of pride for what our team had accomplished.

"It's so spacious and open," Erin said, stopping in her tracks and staring at the reconfigured room. "Oh, and I love the whimsical design in this carpet, the swirls almost look like mouse ears!"

She laughed and then gazing from the patterned floor to the antique settee, to the punched tin ceiling, she slowly took it all in.

"And Chris, look at that chandelier," she said, pointing to the ornate, red fixture illuminating the lobby.

"Carol Davison, from Yesterland Treasures, had that piece in her shop. Isn't it stunning?" I asked.

"It's perfect. I can't wait for Carol to see it hanging in here."

Chris was running his hands over the expanded concession stand, checking out its solid construction and updated design.

"Very nice, very nice indeed," he said under his breath.

What a relief that, so far, he seemed as satisfied with the renovations as Erin, I thought, unable to keep from smiling.

"Remember your concession stand is set up to transform into a wine bar on live performance nights. We designed it to be more than a candy counter, making it adaptable for various types of scheduled events. Now if you look through the door off to the right of the concession stand, that's where you will find your office space," I explained, directing their attention to the new addition.

"Oh, Chris, it's perfect! We won't have to work from home and carry our paperwork back and forth in folders. There's an actual desk and file cabinets, and I love this window cut out! We can greet visitors to the center and easily answer any questions without ever leaving the office. You have thought of everything! Thank you so much," she gushed.

"There is still a lot to see. Don't thank us yet," I said and giggled, moving their attention from the office to the next section of the renovation.

"I'm surprised you haven't asked where we placed the original ticket window," I mentioned as we crossed the lobby. "Like I told you when we first met, our goal was to modernize and repurpose the Uptown Theater, but not completely change her. We wanted to mix the old with the new, keeping some of her amazing history, while adding amenities that make her a valuable asset to today's Marceline community. If you will follow me, I would like to show you one way we tried to accomplish that goal."

As we walked through an arched doorway, trimmed in red velvet curtains held open by golden tassel tie backs, the first item to greet us was the Uptown's iconic ticket booth.

"We've dedicated this area, containing two large rooms, to The Movie Palaces of the 1920's and 30's, including Uptown Theater. The first room, where we are currently standing, outlines the colorful history of Marceline's Uptown Theater, including displays highlighting the two Disney movie premieres shown in this very theater. The pictures along this wall depict Walt Disney's visits, like this one of him on the Uptown Theater stage singing the Mickey Mouse Club theme song to an audience of mesmerized children. Other photos," I said, pointing to a second grouping of pictures, "highlight occurrences at this theater through the years."

Erin and Chris walked slowing through the rooms, gazing at the wall of photographs and cases of collectables, many of which had been haphazardly placed throughout the theater, but were now in chronological order with placards detailing the events pictured and items displayed.

"Each picture in this room is framed in the original crown molding from the theater's lobby. Unfortunately, we were unable to save the decorative trim when we repainted, but we had enough pieces to turn the ornamental molding into beautiful frames for these special pictures," I explained.

"I love that!" Erin commented.

"If you look at the last frame in that grouping," I said, pointing to a set of prints delineating the history of Uptown Theater, "you will notice that particular frame is empty. It's waiting to be filled with the picture we took outside this morning of the two of you ushering in a new era in the theater's history as The Uptown Performing Arts Center."

The Langleys appeared to be in awe as they read their names already engraved on the plaque below the empty frame.

"I can't wait to add new pictures to this wall. I have a feeling that we will be hosting many more notable events in the future," exclaimed Erin with a note of pride in her voice.

"If you will follow the red runner into the next room, we have a display highlighting the era of the Movie Palace. Hundreds of theaters, like The Uptown, were built every year between 1925 and 1930. We wanted to memorialize these grand buildings as well as outline the effects these theaters had on society and towns like Marceline."

Lucy really had outdone herself, I thought, as I looked around. This small, but amazing area, dedicated to the period of the Movie Palace, was a perfect addition for those visiting Main Street and the Disney Hometown Museum.

While Erin and Chris moved from exhibit to exhibit, I glanced at some of the room's tasteful displays. A series of red velvet ropes, connected by antique stanchion with art deco fluted caps, stretched in front of a collection of equipment used during the height of the Movie Palace era, including a motion picture camera, projector and authentic film reels. In the corner was a 1930's popcorn machine, which surprisingly hasn't changed much in style, with the exception of it being made from wood and accented in green instead of red.

A small row of the seats, moved from inside The Uptown's gutted theater, were placed in front of a screen mashing clips of classic movies. The short detailed the progression in film from black and white 'talkies' (what played in most of the theaters when they were built) to the use of Technicolor, and of course, the introduction of animation.

In the last corner was a display of marquee styles and the history of these lavish signs dating as far back as 1690. And to keep the little ones busy, next to the exhibit, was a huge Lite-Brite with large, colored pegs for kids to create their own colorful marquee.

"When you indicated that a small museum dedicated strictly to the history of Uptown Theater was going to be added to the center, I had no idea this was what you had in mind. I'm speechless. This is remarkable!" Erin gushed, again, shaking her head in astonishment.

"What a well-done display exemplifying the iconic movie era. Simple, yet captivating," Chris added in his unassuming manner.

I had to chuckle at their yin and yang reactions – Erin full of exuberance, and Chris so reserved. It always amazes me how often opposites attract.

"Well, we aren't done yet," I said, moving them along.

We had twelve minutes allotted for the walk-through, and we still had two more areas to inspect.

Returning to the lobby, I ushered Erin and Chris through a set of double doors where we stepped into the educational wing of the building.

We peeked into several classrooms devoted to various forms of visual and performing arts, including a dedicated dance studio with wooden floors, mirrored wall, and ballet barre; an art room with drafting tables and supply cabinets ready for classes in painting, drawing, and of course, animation; and a room containing a moveable stage and the trunk of costumes Taylor found at Yesterland Treasures, both waiting for acting, improv, and film classes. At the end of the hall was a community, multipurpose room designed for larger meetings, which we also took a brief look at.

"One of my favorite items in this part of the building is the artist copy of the Dreaming Tree stenciled across the entire back wall," I said as we entered the multipurpose room.

Modular chairs were arranged haphazardly to allow kids a place to read, reflect, or imagine under the painted tree.

"Another nuance throughout the building" I continued, "are multiple hidden Mickeys strategically placed in various locations around the center. As I'm sure you know, Disney arranged the three iconic circles all over his theme parks and in movie clips. So, as part of the renovation, we continued that concept and hid them throughout the center. If you look closely at the dreaming tree, you'll see the leaves just above the trunk are shaped into Mickey ears."

We all walked closer to examine the drawing.

"I see them! Do you see them, Chris?" Erin excitedly exclaimed, pointing to a group of leaves formed into the shape of the distinctive Mickey symbol. "I can't wait to search the rest of the building. Maybe we could even set up a scavenger hunt for the kids during our summer camps," she suggested with her contagious enthusiasm.

I noticed Trevor off to the side motioning for me to pick up the pace. We were running out of time, and it was my job to keep the Langleys moving.

"So, are you ready to finally see the new theater?" I asked.

Erin and Chris eagerly turned back toward the lobby and entrance into the theater, which answered my question.

"This way," I said, turning them around and ushering them toward a door near the back corner of the multipurpose room. "We've designed an entrance onto the rear of the stage through here. So, while performers wait to go on stage, they now have a place to gather, apply make-up, practice lines, rehearse dance moves, or run through musical numbers. A Green Room of sorts."

As we walked through the door and across the stage, a full view of the redesigned theater opened before us.

The new stage curtain, polished wood floor, plush red audience chairs and designer sconces lighting the freshly carpeted aisles all gave the theater the facelift it needed, along with an intimate, playhouse feel.

"If you look up, you can see the motorized lift holding the massive television screen which makes this a versatile venue for both live and recorded performances. And wait until you hear the new sound system! It will immerse the audience in sounds from every direction to help them feel as if they are part of the production."

"Every bit of this renovation has been better than we ever dreamed," Erin said, grabbing Chris's hand.

I motioned to Brandon (whose role had morphed from still photographer to light crew chief) to lower the theater's lighting.

As the house lights dimmed, stars on the ceiling began to subtly glow, creating a warm ambiance in what was now a very cozy theater.

"Absolutely amazing," Chris said, the awe in his voice unmistakable.

After a few minutes of simply soaking in all the changes, we walked down the aisle, exited through the audience doors, and returned to the lobby.

"It's been a real pleasure working with you," I said to the Langleys. "And I can't wait to be one of the first people to see a show in the new theater."

"You are always welcome. Maybe you can even sign up for a class this summer over in the educational wing," Erin suggested.

"I might have to do that. I've always wanted to learn to paint," I said as the camera crew began to put away their equipment.

The filming was done. Let the editing begin.

Erin and Chris decided to walk through each room again, only this time slowly, so they could inspect every detail (and probably look for some hidden Mickeys along the way).

I joined my crew – Trevor, Andre, Lucy, and Taylor – to hear their take on the day's shoot. And they were as pleased as I was. *Yay!*

"I can tell I've made a wise investment," Mr. Biggs announced, as he approached our group. "Nice work, all of you."

"Thank you," we said, talking excitedly over one another, relieved that we pulled off the first project without any major hitches.

We were so involved in our conversation that it took a minute to realize the front doors had finally been opened to the public. The lobby started to fill with people anxious to get a look at the new theater, our group all at once enveloped by the noisy crowd.

"You were perfect," Trevor whispered in my ear, grabbing my hand and pulling me toward the front doors. "Let's go celebrate!"

PART III
Worlds Collide

CHAPTER 23

Cassandra was due to arrive, in Marceline, in fifteen minutes!

I liked Cassandra, but to say that she intimidated me was an understatement.

Arriving on a morning flight from California, she was on her way from Kansas City to join us for the live showing of *Main Street (Episode 1)* at The Uptown Performing Arts Center that evening. While in town, she also planned to meet with our team and tour the two renovation sites currently under development, giving us her honest assessment of each building's makeover.

Always fair, I was sure her critique would contain both praise and constructive criticism. Yet, somehow, I would still be reduced to feeling like a child with a demanding mother I was anxious to please, which is ironic, since my own mother was neither demanding nor hard to please.

Trevor, Lucy, Andre and I had been on edge for the past few days, wanting perfection during Cassandra's visit. Thankfully, it was a short stay, with her returning to Kansas City after the premier, so she could hop on a plane back to L.A. the next morning.

It was much easier to deal with her through emails, over the phone, or as part of a teleconference, rather than in person.

She is staying for less than twenty-four hours. I can handle this!

While chatting casually with Erin Langley, who had graciously offered her new office space for our meeting, Cassandra walked through the front doors. I immediately felt my spine prickle.

In her signature stilettos, she was rocking a classic black suit with a white silk, V-neck tank peeking from beneath her single button, impeccably tailored jacket.

Looking around the room, envisioning the people who would be in attendance at the premiere this evening, it reminded me of the old *Sesame Street* song – *One of These Things is Not Like the Others*. In this laidback town, Cassandra was going to be extremely easy to pick out of the crowd.

Before our meeting, I took Cassandra on the same tour I had given the Langleys the day of the reveal, a couple of weeks ago.

She wrote some notes on her tablet, posed a few questions, muttered a 'nice' or 'excellent' under her breath, but mainly just listened and observed. Ending the tour back at the office, we joined the other three team members patiently waiting for our meeting to begin.

"First, I want to congratulate you on a job well done," she began. "The Uptown Performing Arts Center is beautiful, but more importantly, it was completed on time and within budget. That was your main task, Trevor, and I'm impressed with the way you were able to meet our goal. Let's make certain that we achieve the same results in our next two projects.

"Lucy has done an excellent job of advertising our *Main Street* pilot. Not only has *LeisureTV* been promoting the show, but Lucy has worked with the Disney Corporation to purchase airtime on its networks (*ABC, A&E, The History Channel,* and

Lifetime) to advertise tonight's pilot. After such outstanding promotional efforts, I'll be anxious to see the final viewership totals. I have a good feeling about the numbers.

"Jess, as requested, you have successfully combined the charm of the past with the cutting-edge technology of the present. I'm impressed with your eye for decorating and design. What we have here is a model for other abandoned theaters, a classic movie house merged with a high-tech theater and well-designed educational center. The museum is an added bonus, fitting for this historic town.

"Not to minimize any of your efforts, but in your case, Andre, no news is good news. I like the way you were able to handle the dry rot issue locally with minimal disruption to the work schedule. Continue to stay on top of any unforeseen developments that might occur in the other older buildings. You never know what you might find."

Cassandra paused as the four of us sat silently nodding our heads.

"Are there any questions for me? If not, I'd like to head down to The Allen Hotel and see how that property is progressing."

We gathered our items and left the theatre for the half-block walk to The Allen Hotel.

Since the hotel comprised space solely on the second floor, its main entrance was off Ritchie Avenue rather than Main Street. Main Street entrances were reserved for the restaurant and retail shops located on the first level, who relied heavily on foot traffic for business.

I had been elected by the team to give Cassandra the same basic tour I gave Charles and Jazelle Victor, the proprietors of The Allen Hotel, when filming their walk-through of the premises a couple of weeks ago.

"A burgundy domed awning," I began, "will be placed over the entrance, with the distinctive cursive 'A' logo above the hotel's name, all printed in a classic, white script lettering. Since the hotel's entrance is off Main Street, we wanted to draw attention to the building's entrance, not only for guests, but for visitors who want to get a peek inside."

"Two other important updates are scheduled for the building's exterior," I continued. "Cleaning the faded, brick façade is a high priority. Brightening the outer surface will make the hotel appear new and more welcoming to guests. As with Uptown Theater, we will also be replacing the old entry doors with a classic wood and glass design, beckoning guests to see what grandeur lays upstairs."

As we walked through the doors and up the steps to the future hotel's lobby, I gave Cassandra some background on the original Allen Hotel. I cheated, however, the same way Chance did when describing the Disney barn to me, by summarizing the plaque posted near the hotel's entrance.

"The original Allen Hotel was constructed in 1906. At the time, it was both a hotel and upscale restaurant. Walt Disney recalled an instance when the entire family, dressed in their Sunday best, ate in the hotel's dining room for a special occasion. His younger sister Ruth spilled her entire plate of food, causing quite a scene in the quiet, highly fashionable establishment. After the humiliating incident, Disney doesn't remember the family ever being allowed to eat at the hotel again."

Cassandra briefly smiled at the story, which caused me to enjoy an inner sigh of cautious relief. *That's what I was aiming for today ... a happy Cassandra! So far, so good!*

"The incident with Ruth didn't diminish Disney's love for this grand hotel," I continued. "The Hotel Marceline, found on Main Street USA in Disneyland, is a replica of this exact building, once again showing Disney's devotion to his roots in Marceline."

We each grabbed a required hard hat to continue our inspection of the property.

The construction crew was currently configuring each suite on the second floor to include a bedroom, a luxury bathroom and a small sitting area. If I was going to be heard over all their hammering, drilling and general banging, I was going to have to raise my voice for the rest of the tour.

"As we accomplished with Uptown Performing Arts Center," I yelled over the noise, "our goal is to create a period hotel, but with all the amenities today's guests require. Taylor and I have been scouring for antiques to strategically place throughout the property. We have also designed an ornate check-in desk which will immediately greet visitors as they exit the elevators and step into the spacious lobby. But upon entering their rooms … completely furnished with products distributed by USAMade, of course … guests will quickly realize they are still in the twenty-first century."

"Why don't we head back to the lobby area, away from the noise so we can talk a little easier?" suggested Trevor, his voice booming over the sound of a nearby saw splitting a piece of lumber.

"How is the timeline coming along?"

Cassandra shifted her attention toward Trevor as we turned to leave the main construction zone and walk back in the direction from which we came, leaving me in their dust (literally!).

"Nice hat, Jess," a voice grabbed my attention.

Even without seeing the face attached to it, I immediately knew who it was.

Turning, I watched Chance emerge from a group of workers just beyond where our team had been gathered.

"It suits you even better than the one you were wearing the other day," he said with his signature, smirky smile.

"Unfortunately, I notice several other people have chosen the exact same style as mine. I prefer to be unique, so maybe I should attach a pink ribbon around the brim. Don't you think that would add some panache to this stunning yellow, hard plastic accessory?" I asked playfully, adjusting my hat and angling it jauntily to one side. "You don't happen to have any ribbon laying around, do you?"

"Let me look, but I'm pretty sure all we have is yellow caution tape. Although, now that I think about it, I believe caution tape might be a perfect addition for you," he said and laughed. "It could warn people to watch out in case you decide to repeat your park performance. I'm sure you could find plenty of places to trip or slip in this mess."

"Very funny!" I said, nodding my head in Cassandra's direction. "She's my big boss, so I better not stumble and fall today. We get along really well, but I still feel this perverse need to impress her. Somehow, I don't believe performing one of my acrobatic tricks would be the best way to demonstrate my professionalism."

"Don't the infamous 'they' always say there is no such thing as bad publicity? I'm sure that same sentiment holds true for impressing the boss. There is no bad way to get remembered by your superior," he jokingly advised. "Slipping on sawdust is one of the most common ways to fall on a construction site, maybe you could use that tactic as a new way to promote yourself."

"I'll pass, but thanks for the tip. Speaking of impressing the boss," I replied, "I'd better rejoin my group before they think I got lost in this maze of construction or 'fell on some sawdust'."

"Just trying to help!"

Once again, I got a flash of that irritating grin of his.

"I'll remember that," I said. "Also, thanks for your approval regarding today's hat selection. I'll keep it in mind as an option when choosing my outfit for tonight's showing of *Main Street*."

"Maybe I'll see you there," he said, sounding almost hopeful. "The guys from work are going to the show as a group and then getting a few cold brews afterwards. We believe in a balanced life! And by the way, good luck with your boss."

"Thanks," I said, tipping my helmet at him before returning to my party.

Reappearing as part of the group, Trevor gave me a quizzical look as he explained to Cassandra the last portion of our plan for the hotel.

"This elevator," he pointed out, "will take guests to the top of the building where we are adding The Allen Hotel Rooftop Garden."

He glimpsed my way.

We shared a brief, intimate glance.

That was our idea! After spending two enjoyable evenings at The Roofstop in Los Angeles, Trevor and I proposed creating the same type of romantic spot in the hotel's initial plan.

"The original hotel included a dining room, as I explained earlier," I said, taking over for him, since visually painting the design of our project was my specialty. "With Corner Café as a very popular tenant right below us, it didn't make sense to add a restaurant inside the hotel. Instead, we wanted to develop something different; something that wouldn't compete with the Café. The bar atop the hotel will be a place to sip a mixed drink in the evening while relaxing with friends, sit with a group around a glass fire pit in the fall, or enjoy an afternoon appetizer and the local scenery."

"I saw this in the plans and thought it was an outstanding addition," Cassandra commented.

"The setting is ideal, with one side facing Ripley Park, another with a view of Main Street and a third section partitioned off to watch the multitude of trains passing through town."

"We are highlighting the bar in our promotion of Marceline as a relaxing get-away from the stress of urban life in Kansas City," Lucy added.

"Excellent," Cassandra said, nodding approvingly.

"Even though I found them hard to read as I conducted their walk-through," I continued, "the Victors also seemed extremely excited about the addition of the rooftop bar to the premises."

"So, what do you think, Cassandra?" I asked, ending our second building tour of the day.

"I think I picked the right team," Cassandra said, paying us the ultimate compliment.

We all left The Allen Hotel and departed our separate ways to prepare for the evening's premiere of *Main Street* at The Uptown Theater.

Trevor and I walked together on the way back to our own places where we each wanted to change and relax a little before commencing with *Act II* of our day of impressing Cassandra.

"So, how do you know that construction worker?" he asked with a slight edge to his voice.

"I've gotten to know a lot of people in this town, and Chance happens to be one of them," I answered, surprised by his abrupt, almost abrasive, comment.

"I've watched you become friends with the residents here, and I don't get it, Jess. We're leaving in three months, so why are you all chummy with these people?"

"Because they are nice and interesting, and I like them," I said defensively.

"You mean, they are boring and lack culture," he countered. "Unlike you, I can't wait to get out of here and back to civilization."

"Don't be rude, this is civilization just as much as L.A., only different."

"Well at least we agree on that, this place is definitely different!" Trevor retorted as we reached The Uptown Center and his place.

"I'll see you in a couple of hours," I said and continued walking, uncomfortable that he and I had our first small argument.

• • •

Choosing my indigo mini dress with its cold shoulders, double spaghetti-strap detail and three-quarter length bell sleeves, I added a double-strand, silver teardrop necklace and silver sandals (one of the few matching pairs Cooper had yet to destroy), hoping to appear formal enough when standing next to Cassandra representing *LeisureTV*, but not too formal when talking with the rest of the crowd, as a member of the Marceline community.

Walking through the front doors, the lobby looked just as I had envisioned when designing the renovation – people with drinks in hand, cheerfully mingling before the start of a show.

I joined Cassandra and Lucy who were chatting near the wine and snack bar. They were going over some last-minute details regarding the short speech Lucy would be delivering to the crowd before announcing the start of *Main Street's* live debut.

From my vantage point, I happily recognized several faces in the crowd.

The Langleys were talking with Sunrise Coffee's Shelly, Charles and Jazelle Victor, and other individuals I presumed also owned businesses along Main Street. Ida was coming through the doors, assisted by her daughter Kathy. Carol Davison was pointing out the chandelier which came from her shop to a group of friends who were oohing and aahing over its beauty. Mayor

Bob Knowell was exiting The Movie Palace Museum with members of the City Council. And Trevor was speaking to a stunning, raven-haired model, who I had never seen before.

"Do you know who that is over there, talking with Trevor?" I asked Lucy and Cassandra.

"That's Samantha Biggs," Lucy informed me just as Larry Biggs, with an adoring smile plastered across his wide face, joined his daughter and Trevor in their conversation.

"Jess!" I heard my name being called from across the room.

Turning, I see Taylor in a cinched waist, mini dress covered in what appeared to be paint swatches from the entire color wheel.

"I wasn't sure that was you," she prattled on. "I've never seen you with your hair down and curled. And your dress ... it's a great color for you. You look fabulous!"

"Thanks, I love your dress too," I said and actually meant it, although I wouldn't have personally owned it for a million dollars. *Okay, maybe for a million dollars, but it's not something I would ever choose to buy or for that matter even double click on to get a closer view.* But as usual, it suited Taylor perfectly.

"I want you to meet my parents, Rhonda and Steve," Taylor said as she ushered forward two bubbly clones of herself, only twenty-five years or so her senior.

"It's so nice to finally meet you," Rhonda said.

She grabbed my hand and vigorously shook it. "Taylor talks about you nonstop. 'Jess said this, Jess found the perfect piece for the lobby, Jess decided ...'"

"Stop, Mom, you're embarrassing me," Taylor said and giggled as the three of them laughed, seeming to share a family inside joke.

I got the feeling that embarrassing Taylor had been a lifelong occurrence for the Lubouskis and that, secretly, Taylor loved it.

This had to be the happiest trio I had ever met!

Seeing the Lubouskis together made me think of home. I touched the diamond infinity bracelet adorning my wrist, as I did so often when I wanted to feel the closeness of my parents.

Talking to Mom earlier in the week, she had informed me that Dad had already bought and installed the new, bigger screen television and that they were up to twenty confirmations from their closest friends and family for tonight's *Main Street* watch party, hosted in their living room. Taylor wasn't the only one with proud parents!

Lucy headed down to the stage as I introduced Taylor and her parents to Cassandra.

"It is very nice to meet you, Taylor," Cassandra addressed her cordially. "I was telling Jess earlier today, how happy I am with the selection of this team and the work you have accomplished. Jess has spoken highly of your contributions, which makes me anxious to see the completed designs in our next two properties."

"Thank you for your confidence," Taylor replied respectfully. "It is nice to finally meet you. I hope you enjoy your time in Marceline."

The overhead lights flickered, indicating it was time for us to move toward the auditorium and our front row seats, reserved for us as 'Guests of Honor'.

"Hi, Jess," I heard as we passed a group of women finishing their wine before entering the theater.

"Hi, Maggie, nice to see you this evening. Enjoy the show," I replied as we continued walking.

"Was that someone connected with tonight's production?" Cassandra asked curiously.

"No, Maggie is in charge of the Carnegie Public Library down the street. My friend, Kaitlin, talked me into working at the annual book fair a couple of weekends ago and that's when I met Maggie. She's a super nice lady."

"You wouldn't believe the number of books they had for sale," I continued. "Tables were piled high, plus boxes of books were placed underneath each table to refill the stock when space allowed. It's the largest book fair in the county, so people from all over donate books, magazines, music, movies, even puzzles and games, throughout the entire year. On their website, they boasted that it made over $40,000 this year. They are using the money to fund future library programs, mainly for kids."

"I'm impressed, Jess. I asked all of you, before you left, to blend in here. You have gone above and beyond my expectations, taking a real interest in the area and people. I'm sure it will show in tonight's pilot."

I was beyond thrilled by Cassandra's comment as we found our seats and got ready for Lucy's opening.

Turning around, I saw that the theater was almost filled to capacity.

I waved to Kaitlin a few rows behind me, placing my nails to my mouth in mock nervousness.

She sent me a thumbs up, her way of reassuring me that it would all be fine.

Trevor silently slid into the reserved seat next to mine as Lucy entered the stage and began to speak into the microphone.

"You look beautiful," he whispered into my ear and then lightly kissed my cheek.

All remnants of our earlier argument melted away.

"I'd like to welcome everyone here for tonight's premiere of *Main Street*. I not only speak for myself, but the entire team at *LeisureTV*, when I say it has been an honor and a pleasure to film the restoration of The Uptown Theater and the construction of the Education Center. But none of this would have been possible without the sponsorship of USAMade and owner, Mr. Larry Biggs. Mr. Biggs, if you would please stand."

The crowd applauded as Larry Biggs rose from his seat, also in the front row, and acknowledged the crowd.

"Thank you, Mr. Biggs, and thank you for sponsoring tonight's pilot which, in a few minutes, will be broadcast live from this stage. Before we dim the lights and begin the show, I have an exciting announcement to make. As you all know, in 1906 a production of *Peter Pan* played in Marceline and was the first live theater performance ever seen by a young Walt Disney. The story formed such a lasting impression on him that after seeing the show, he even reprised the role at his own elementary school. Legend has it, *Peter Pan* was one of Disney's lifelong favorite plays because Walt Disney saw himself as Peter Pan, the boy who refused to grow up."

Not a sound could be heard from the enraptured audience.

"With that in mind, the Disney Corporation has agreed that Marceline's newly renovated Uptown Theater will be an ideal location to launch the premiere of *Peter and Wendy*, it's new live-action remake of the Disney classic, scheduled for release in late September; making this the third movie debut to show in this iconic theater."

A rumbling of excitement rolled through the audience as Lucy continued.

"The premiere also comes with some star power who will be in attendance for the occasion … most notably Jude Law, who plays Captain Hook in the movie."

With this added announcement, the audience's decibel level advanced from an excited rumble to a thundering round of applause that lasted several minutes.

As the crowd began to settle, Lucy brought the microphone back up to her lips and announced, "Without further delay, we'd like to present *Main Street*."

She moved into the wings as the 34-foot-wide, LED Samsung television screen slowly unfolded from the rafters above the stage. The lights dimmed, and magically, the ceiling began to twinkle with a thousand stars.

You could hear a collective sigh as the audience began to relax in their plush theater seats, getting ready for the opening of the show.

The projector lit the screen, the pilot of *Main Street* began, and Trevor grabbed my hand, holding it affectionately.

Life doesn't get any better than this!

• • •

The lobby rapidly filled with chatter as everyone began to spill out of the auditorium.

Separated from Trevor by the enveloping crowd, I was caught in a swirl of townspeople raving about the pilot and its portrayal of Marceline.

I recognized one of the group members as the gentleman who waited on me at the hardware store when I first arrived and who was more than a little wary of our presence on Main Street, but who was now adulating the finished project. Maybe Ida was right about needing to give people time to embrace change.

"Hello, movie star."

I heard his now familiar voice behind me.

"Hello, refurbisher of old buildings," I said, turning around and coming face-to-face with Chance. "So, honest opinion, what did you think of the show?"

"Overall, a typical rehab show, but with an exceptionally hot, female hostess. I'm pretty sure she used to be a Laker Girl or actress or *Sports Illustrated* Swimsuit Model. I'm not sure which, but I know I've seen her somewhere."

"Very funny," I said, punching him in the arm as if we were still in third grade. "Seriously, I'd love your take on the final cut."

"Seriously, the show was good. It really exposed the potential in these century old buildings and what they can become, even on a limited budget. Not every change you made was over the top like the theater screen, although, I must admit, the retractable screen is pretty amazing."

"That's a good idea, actually," I said. "Maybe in the next episode, I'll focus on some inexpensive, yet tasteful, pieces used throughout the updated building. And to be honest, the theater screen wasn't as expensive as you would guess."

"Hey, Chance, we're leaving."

I recognized one of our construction team members yelling from near the exit.

"I better run. You did a great job, Jess, and I just wanted to let you know."

"Thanks," I said, blushing as he left to join his colleagues.

Compliments have always made me uncomfortable (unless they are from Cassandra!).

I focused my attention on finding Trevor.

He, Lucy and Andre were coming over for a small celebration, and I wanted to change into something more comfortable before they arrived.

Scanning the crowd, I saw him by the antique settee, schmoozing with Cassandra, Mr. Biggs, and his daughter Samantha. Realizing I also needed to say good-bye to Cassandra before she left for Kansas City, I decided to briefly join their group.

"I hope in the next episode, we can highlight some pieces being used in the hotel that are available from USAMade," Mr. Biggs said as I approached.

"That shouldn't be a problem. I'll talk to Jess and get her to focus some camera time on promoting the USAMade products scattered throughout the hotel," Trevor stated as I moved closer, merging into their tight circle.

"Did I hear my name?" I said, sneaking into their conversation. "I overheard your last comment, Mr. Biggs, and I would actually like to take it a step further," I said and continued. "What if I point out items that would be great finds for the viewers? Let them not only see how easy it is to redecorate with USAMade products, but also how easy it is to redecorate without incurring enormous expenses, be it in a historic building or a typical home?"

"I love it," Cassandra exclaimed before he could even answer. "Great idea, Jess. I think the viewers will love it, too. Ideas they can incorporate into their own homes … yes … it will make the show more personal for our audience."

"I'm always a fan of an idea that promotes our products," Larry Biggs said, followed by a very boisterous chuckle.

"Thank you, Chance," I whispered under my breath.

"Cassandra, I was really just stopping by to wish you a safe trip back to L.A. I'm glad you were able to tour the buildings and see the renovations in person."

"It will be much easier to discuss updates to the plans, now that I have seen the properties and the improvements taking place," she said. "I'm glad I made the trip. But don't forget, even though I was just here, we still have our teleconference meeting on Monday."

"I'll be there and on time," I promised, and then realized I actually didn't need to add the 'on time'. Surprisingly, it had not been an issue lately.

• • •

"Cooper, we did it! Tonight's show was a huge success," I told him as I changed from my dress into comfortable shorts and a soft T-shirt.

Walking with him into the backyard, I lit some tiki torches to fend off the hordes of summer mosquitos and waited for the crew to arrive.

Plopping down in one of the cushioned patio chairs, it was the first chance I had had to check my phone.

Several text messages awaited me, but the one I was most happy to see was from my mom.

Mom: You were wonderful tonight.

Me: ty – are you still by your phone

Mom: Yes. Granny wants me to tell you that you knocked it out of the park.

Me: lol – leave it to Granny to use a sports metaphor

Mom: And your dad is about to bust all the buttons off his shirt bragging to everyone about how talented and independent you are.

Me: Who was at your house watching the show

Mom: Just a few neighbors, some friends, Mollie and Justin, the MacInerneys, Aunt Patsy, Uncle Gary, your cousins and of course Granny.

Me: Sounds like you crammed a lot of people into the house. I guess they were able to watch ok with the new TV?

Mom: The picture is amazing. I could even spot that little red mark on your cheek when you were interviewing the lady from the museum. It must have been from your fall.

Me: Good to know all my blemishes were on display for the world to see

Mom: I'm kidding, you looked lovely.

Me: I missed you guys tonight!

Mom: If you were still here, you wouldn't have been on television. There are always tradeoffs, sweetheart.

Me: I still miss u

Mom: I hear Mollie is coming for a visit in a couple of weeks.

Me: It's official she got her tickets today. I can't wait

Mom: You girls will have so much fun.

Me: I know. Hey, gotta run. Trevor and the others are coming over for a celebration and I just heard someone pull in the driveway

Mom: We'll have to meet this Trevor when you move back home.

Me: It's a deal. Love you!

Mom: Love you too, sweetheart!

CHAPTER 24

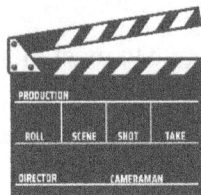

It was only nine in the morning, and it was already too hot to sit on the porch and read. With no breeze, the air was so heavy and sticky that just turning the pages of my newest novel made me break into a sweat. Even switching the ceiling fan to high provided little relief.

My weather app was warning everyone to stay inside during the afternoon to avoid the dangerous heat, and it appeared that it was going to be spot on.

Deciding if I didn't take Cooper for a walk now, it would be too late, I put my book aside.

Seeing me grab his leash, he bounded excitedly toward the screen door, unaware of the sweltering temperatures.

"Sorry, buddy, but it's going to have to be a short one today," I told him as we scampered down Mulberry Street.

I waved to Joanie as we passed by, who was also out early trying to beat the heatwave that was clearly already here. Donning her usual floppy straw hat, she was busy pruning the immaculate flower beds surrounding her home, which reminded me I needed to water my wilting window boxes. (Yes, they were still alive – barely.)

Diane Manley

We took a quick jog around the block and ended where we so often do – on Ida's front porch. She was already sitting in her rocker with a cool drink, as if she knew we would be arriving at that precise moment. Following what had become our customary routine, I hooked Cooper's leash to the newel post at the top of the banister and headed inside her house to get a glass of lemonade for myself and a bowl of water for Cooper.

He had mastered sit and stay and was now able to calmly join us on Ida's porch. (Our training appeared to be working!) He had also mastered napping, which is what he did most of the time we were there.

"Dear me, it's a hot one today," Ida said, cooling herself with a cardboard hand fan and gently rocking back and forth in her chair – the only way to feel any breeze.

"We don't have this kind of heat in Los Angeles," I said, taking a long sip of my lemonade. "It is so humid here, it's almost hard to breathe."

"It may feel that way today, but most days, nothing beats fresh country air," she boasted.

"Unless you're near a cow pasture," I said and chuckled.

"Well, it should cool off in time for tonight's festivities," she continued.

She was referring to the Independence Day fair starting that evening with live music in the park and ending with fireworks the next night.

"I remember looking forward to the Fourth of July all year. Almost as much as Christmas. We had so much fun as kids, running around the park and staying up past our bedtime," she reminisced. "Tell me you are going to the fair."

"Yes, I'm going to the fair. And then Trevor and I are meeting Kaitlin and some friends from work for the concert. I'm looking forward to it. Trevor and I heard the band out at the winery a couple of months ago, and we really enjoyed their music."

"So, you like this boy?" Ida probed.

"I do," I replied, honestly a little taken aback, as I so often was, by her direct questioning. "He's different than other guys I've dated."

"In what way is he so different, dear?"

"I don't know. He prefers to live life more on the edge. He's driven to move up in his career, and he seems more sophisticated."

"You mean he likes money."

"Well, that too," I said and laughed, "but who doesn't."

"I'd say your Betty and his fancy motorcycle speak to the differences you two place on the importance of material objects," she stated pointedly.

Had I ever told her my car's name is Betty? I don't believe so. How does she do that, I asked myself, marveling once again at the all-knowing Ida.

Still bewildered by her awareness of all things, I thanked her once again for the lemonade and informed her that it was time for Cooper and me to head home. There were chores I needed to accomplish, and the first one was watering the plants in my window boxes, before my pretty multicolored flowers shriveled into ugly brown sticks.

• • •

Ida was correct (shocking, right?), the temperatures had cooled and a slight breeze had turned it into a pleasant evening for sitting outside and listening to live music in Ripley Park.

We spread a couple of large blankets across the lawn and plopped down with our coolers securing the perimeter.

Everyone around us was in a festive mood, happy for the long weekend and ecstatic that the oppressive heat had finally broken. The band played its first set and was as good as when we heard them at Vista Vineyards.

"That was a fun day at the winery, wasn't it?" I asked Trevor, snuggling into the crook of his arm.

"Yes, it was fun, and I don't mean to be rude, but Jess, could you not sit so close? It's really hot out here," he said, sounding slightly annoyed.

"Oh sure," I said, moving myself and my slightly hurt feelings to my own space.

I spent the rest of the evening talking with Kaitlin about our upcoming trip to Kansas City. After picking up Mollie from her morning flight, we were going to be off for a girls' day of shopping and lunch in Country Club Plaza, before returning to Marceline that evening. I couldn't wait for Mollie and Kaitlin to meet. They were going to love each other!

I had thought that after the concert I would invite everyone over to continue our party on my back patio, but I changed my mind. I had been ignoring Trevor all evening as a childish punishment and decided, as any mature adult would, I'd rather go home alone and sulk. Besides, I didn't need Trevor when I had Cooper and Mona to keep me company.

Instead of a party on the patio, I ended up grabbing a bag of chips and settling comfortably on my sofa, prepared for a night of falling asleep on the couch while watching reruns of old sitcoms.

I woke to brilliant sunshine, a stiff body, and the ping of a text.

Trevor: Sorry about last night. I was feeling irritable and took it out on you. Forgive me?

Me: You were irritable and I was childish. We're even.

Trevor: I'd like to make it up to you. I know how much you like these celebrations, so how about I take you to the parade, we hit the festival, and tonight watch the fireworks together. What do you think?

Me: I would love it. ty

Trevor: The parade starts in an hour. Can you make it?

Me: If you don't mind me in a baseball cap

Trevor: Has no one ever told you that girls in baseball caps are sexy as hell

Me: Maybe I'll start wearing a baseball cap every day. lol See you in an hour

The procession slowly traveled down Main Street, led by Grand Marshall, Mayor Bob Knowell, perched high on the folded convertible top of a refurbished, red, classic Mustang. Followed by your typical, hometown Independence Day parade groups, we watched and cheered as kids and adults alike scrambled for pieces of candy, colorful bags filled with snap pops, and red, white and blue beads, thrown into the crowd.

(Thankfully, this was not a New Orleans Mardi Gras-style parade, but a G-rated family event.)

ATVs whizzed in and out of parade walkers; homemade floats were pulled by trucks and tractors; the local high school band marched by, playing a patriotic medley; and finally, bringing up the rear like Santa in the *Macy's Thanksgiving Day Parade*, was the Uptown Performing Arts Center's float. The local Hawthorne Players, housed in the Uptown Educational Center, had decorated a flatbed trailer being pulled by Chris Langley's massive pickup truck. Promoting the upcoming Disney movie debut, the trailer had been transformed into the island of Neverland, with Peter Pan, Wendy, and the Lost Boys waving to the people lining Main Street.

As they passed, the crowd applauded wildly, caught up in the excitement and anticipation of another movie premiere in Marceline.

We enjoyed the rest of the day, overeating delicious, yet completely unhealthy, fair food. We walked around the festival grounds, talking with people we had met over the past few months, and then relaxed back at my place.

I tried to give Cooper some time to run outside, but upon hearing the crack of fireworks, he immediately rushed back into the house and straight for his kennel. Since he had seemed content to sleep throughout the afternoon in the safety of his comfortable den, I didn't feel too bad leaving him again for the fireworks show.

Laying our blanket in nearly the same spot we had chosen the previous night, we sat and waited for the show to begin. This time though, it was just the two of us.

Not having learned from last night's fiasco, I once again leaned cozily into the crook of Trevor's arm, but he didn't push me away. Instead, he wrapped his other arm around me and tenderly kissed my cheek, causing a shiver to run the entire length of my body. It's amazing how sometimes the simplest gesture has the biggest effect, I thought.

"Lucy says they are going all out for this premiere, setting it up to be a formal, invitation-only affair, with a red carpet rolled out for entering the theater, photojournalists from some of the bigger magazines in attendance and a grand reception at the Biggs' mansion afterwards," I said, breaking the comfortable silence. "Then the day after the premiere, in the spirit of Walt Disney, Disney Corporation is going to run the movie *Peter and Wendy* continuously in The Uptown Theater, free of charge."

"That's what Cassandra said, too," Trevor stated. "I talked to her yesterday. She was ecstatic. Said the viewership totals came in, and the numbers were even higher than anticipated."

"What great news! Let's hope *Episode 2* does as well. The Victors are nice, but they lack the same camera presence the Langleys projected. I'm afraid filming the reveal is going to be quite a challenge," I said, expressing my concerns. "I'm considering bringing Taylor along, since she's a natural in front of the camera. I plan to run the idea of using her, as a sort of sidekick, by Cassandra at our next teleconference meeting."

"By the way," I asked Trevor, "have you heard if Cassandra will be traveling to Marceline for the premiere?"

"No, it turns out she has a major conflict that weekend. Her only sister is getting married and according to her, blood relatives are not allowed to live when they miss an Italian family wedding," he said and rolled his eyes. "I told her we'd send updates throughout the night."

Trevor paused.

"I assume 'we', but since it is a formal event, maybe it would be polite if I asked you formally. So, Jess, would you allow me to escort you to the movie premiere and after party of *Peter and Wendy*?" he requested, ceremoniously taking my hand.

"It would be an honor, Trevor," I replied as the first bursts of color lit the sky.

CHAPTER 25

Kaitlin and I gassed up Betty and hit the road for Kansas City.

Mollie, who never took off work, was flying in for a long girls' weekend, and personally, I couldn't wait! It had only been three months since I had seen her, but it felt more like three years.

The drive passed quickly with Kaitlin and me talking nonstop the entire way. I filled her in on crazy stories from when Mollie and I were kids, and she regaled me with similar tales from her youth.

We reached Terminal B with time to spare (Mollie would never believe it when she saw me there on time).

Grabbing a Starbucks, we were waiting in the baggage area, listening for an announcement regarding which carousel would be spitting out luggage from Flight 972 out of Los Angeles, when I saw her bouncing red curls striding our direction.

"Mollie," I yelled across the concourse, waving my arms wildly so that not only she, but every other passenger from Flight 972, was staring in our direction.

As if my first outburst hadn't already drawn enough attention to our little group, Mollie rushed towards me, both of us squealing as we hugged and did a happy dance.

People passed by with smiles plastered on their faces as if to say, 'Oh, look at the long-lost relatives who haven't seen each other in fifty years'. Then, realizing we were not that old, nor did we look anything alike, they more than likely changed their minds and decided we were just a couple of overexcited girls who were ridiculously loud and over-joyous. Shaking their heads, their smiles faded and they rapidly moved on.

But mine and Mollie's smiles refused to diminish. We were too excited that our weekend together had finally begun.

"Mollie this is Kaitlin. Kaitlin, this is Mollie," I said, introducing my two friends.

"Thanks for getting Jess here on time," Mollie said, addressing Kaitlin. "I was worried I'd have to wait a while, but thought if I had to sit around, at least the airport is a fun place to people-watch."

"No problem," Kaitlin said breezily, smiling in my direction. "I kept her on schedule."

"That is so not true," I protested. "I was early to your house. I had to wait for you! I can see how this weekend is going turn out – the two of you ganging up on poor little me."

"Sounds good. What do you think, Kaitlin?" Mollie asked.

"I'm in," Kaitlin replied.

"I'm not," I said in mock disgust. "Maybe Betty and I should just leave and let you two, 'new best friends' hang out together."

"Okay, okay, we'll be nice," Mollie said as she saw her bag circle the carousal past us, just out of reach.

Mollie's suitcase came back around, we nabbed it and exited the airport, ready to begin our girls' adventure.

I had planned Day One as a shopping extravaganza. It had been over three months since I had been to a retail store of any kind (unless you counted the hardware store on Kansas Avenue), and I was ready to spend!

Country Club Plaza, with its beautiful Spanish-style architecture donned in fresco tiles of burnt orange and royal blue, was an outdoor, high-end retail, dining and entertainment mecca located in the heart of Kansas City and was one of the top destinations for visitors to the area. Covering fifteen square blocks, we planned to explore every inch of it before heading back to Marceline.

I found a few new tops and a couple pairs of shorts before we took a break for lunch.

Mollie bought Justin a Kansas City Chiefs' stress ball that he could squeeze to death, as revenge for the team he loved to hate during high-intensity Rams match-ups.

So far, Kaitlin was empty-handed.

We would have to change that after we had a bite to eat and cooled off.

We decide on Mexican, mainly for the basket of tortilla chips and frozen margaritas.

"I love the fountains on every corner," I commented as we waited for our drinks. "I saw a sign that says Kansas City has over 200 fountains … more than any other city in the world besides Rome. Who knew?"

"If it gets any hotter, I might jump in one. Is it always this hot here?" Mollie asked.

She was generally not a complainer, so I was surprised by her bordering-on-whiny comments. Maybe among other things, I was acclimating to the Missouri heat, I thought.

"The temperature probably isn't that different from L.A., but the humidity is what makes it feel so oppressive," Kaitlin informed her. "We only have one more day of this and then a cold front is coming through, and we'll get some relief. I think the farm animals will be as happy as the people."

Mollie and I stared at one another, reading each other's minds, and we burst into giggling as we do so often when we are together. "That is a comment, I am one hundred percent certain, I have never heard in Los Angeles," Mollie said and kept on laughing.

"I guess it's not anything I would have ever heard growing up in St. Louis either," Kaitlin said, joining our laughter.

We had opened the dam of silliness and proceeded to find every topic funny throughout a delicious lunch of authentic Tex-Mex.

Finishing our frozen drinks, we paid the bill and braved the sweltering summer heat to resume our quest for items we couldn't possibly live without.

"How about we duck in here to cool off," I suggested, veering into a trendy boutique that had caught my eye with its sparkly cocktail dresses clinging to headless, window mannequins.

Kaitlin and I were on the hunt for outfits to wear to the premiere, and this shop looked to have a surplus of possibilities.

The two of us chose a handful of garments to try on while Mollie found the store's most hideous formal wear for us to model.

"I am not wearing feathers!" I said to her as she pouted, eyeing a canary yellow dress she had pulled off the rounder.

"I'm just trying to help, you know, get you out of your comfort zone," she said, trying not to laugh.

"Fine, I'll buy it, but only if you let me wear it as your bridesmaid's dress."

"Never mind," she said, quickly putting it back and moving to a different rack with more suitable styles.

In the end, I chose a garnet, high-low cocktail dress with a cinched waist, a hint of lace on the bodice, and flowing satin skirt, while Kaitlin found a sleek, black jumpsuit with a high neckline and peek-a-boo back. Mollie didn't leave empty handed either, finding a stately, diamond (okay ... truth: it was crystal) necklace to perfectly match her wedding gown.

Our last stop was a gourmet food store, where we taste-tested food from across the world. After choosing a couple bottles of wine, some cheese and crackers, and a required box of assorted truffles, we left Kansas City for Marceline, where our afternoon of silliness continued well into the night.

● ● ●

Mollie and I woke to the blazing sun, creeping high into a cloudless sky.

Reenergized after sleeping late, we decided not to waste any more of our day and promptly got ourselves going. I wanted to take her to Main Street and show her our *LeisureTV* projects as well as the other highlights around town.

First stop though, Sunrise Coffee.

"Good morning," I greeted Shelly with a smile and introduced her to Mollie. "We'll both have your famous Café Carmella, medium, please."

"Coming right up," Shelly said as she measured the grounds of her special blend. "I heard rumor of a new store moving next door. You're around the local builders, have you overheard any mention of it?"

"No, but I'll keep my ears open," I said, glad to help. "What type of business, do you know?"

"I've heard it is going to be homemade soaps and candles made locally by someone new in town. They are calling it *Glow Bath and Body Shoppe*, so I've heard."

"Sounds like you've heard a lot more than I'll ever be able find out," I said and chuckled.

"I thought you being so close to Chance Alexander, you might have some inside scoop."

"Chance and I are acquaintances. I'd hardly call us close friends," I said, surprised by her comment.

"Um-hum," I heard Shelly say under her breath.

"I don't think I'm going to be much help getting any more information than you've already 'heard', sorry," I told her honestly.

"Well, you get wind of anything else, you let me know, okay?"

"I'll be happy to."

"Enjoy your day ladies," she said as she handed us our coffees to go. "It's going to be another scorcher. But storms are blowing through tonight, so that should cool things off for the rest of the weekend."

We took our drinks and exited onto Main Street.

"What was that all about, and who is Chance Alexander, this so-called 'acquaintance'?" Mollie immediately asked, taking a sip of her decadent cappuccino.

"I have no idea what that was about, and Chance Alexander is the lead of the local construction crew for our renovation team."

"Tell me more," Mollie pried.

"There is nothing more to tell," I said, for some reason, failing to mention meeting Chance for the first time in the hardware store, or riding in his truck to the Disney farm and Dreaming Tree, or our little inside joke about my various hats.

It just felt private, which was odd, because I typically shared everything with Mollie.

Glancing toward the empty building about to be filled, according to Shelly, with a new specialty shop, I noticed other facelifts occurring on Main Street store fronts as well. Sprinkles had recently installed a candy-colored, striped awning above its entry and, a painter, at that very moment, was applying a fresh coat of paint to the shutters on the Farmers Insurance Office at the end of the block. Across the street, newly placed signs had also appeared in second-story windows, reading 'Coming Soon – For Rent – Call (818)888-LOFT'.

"Let's get out of this heat," I said, grabbing Mollie's arm and dragging her into The Uptown Theater.

In all actuality, my motive for moving indoors was to give Mollie an official tour of the Performing Arts Center. During the *Main Street* watch party at my parents, she had seen the major renovations, but I wanted to show off all of the changes and get her honest opinion about each modification. Her opinions, although not always what I wanted to hear, usually helped me make better decisions, which is why I loved having them in the end.

"This is even more beautiful than on television," she uttered as we walked through the wooden, double doors into the elegant lobby.

"What do you think of the chandelier?" I asked.

"I love it," she said looking up at the red, teardrop-shaped fixture.

"Can you believe it was just hanging, neglected, in a corner of the local antique shop?"

"What a find!" Mollie said in amazement.

"We'll go to Yesterland Treasures later this afternoon, and I'll introduce you to Carol, the owner. It's a fun place to poke around."

I had surprised myself by how much I enjoyed looking for unique pieces when making over these old buildings.

Hearing voices, Erin popped out of her office to see who was visiting the center.

"Hi, Erin," I said. "This is my friend Mollie from Los Angeles. She's staying with me all weekend."

"Nice to meet you," she replied, holding out her hand to greet Mollie. "I don't know what we would have done without Jess. She is a miracle worker," Erin continued in her enthusiastic manner. "The center is thriving! I would have never thought to add an educational wing and that has made all the difference in the amount of traffic we have coming through our doors. And you will have to take a look at the museum. Visitors are loving it!"

"Jess talked about how much she enjoyed working with you and your husband. I can see why," Mollie smiled.

We spent a few more minutes pleasantly chatting with Erin before Mollie and I began our tour of the facility.

I told her step-by-step the designing process used in each room as we walked through the lobby, museum, theater itself, and out the back side of the stage into the multipurpose room.

"Oh," I said, startled at seeing a blond head bent over a laptop, working at one of the tables. "Trevor?"

"Hey," he said, flashing a strained smile.

"I'm surprised to see you," I commented. "What are you doing in here?"

"I'm trying to go over some figures without constant interruptions," he said, a tinge of frustration creeping into his voice.

"Sorry, we didn't mean to disturb you. I didn't realize anyone was using this room."

"You remember Mollie," I said as a way of reintroduction.

"Of course. So, have you planned any more Mickey Mouse parties since we left?" Trevor asked, a touch of sarcasm hinting at his view regarding the *Not Goodbye but See You in Six Months* party I had dragged him to a couple of months back.

"No, that was the only one," Mollie answered, defensively.

I forced a chuckle, but Trevor's joke had fallen flat, and the atmosphere in the room seemed to thicken with tension.

"Anyway, what are you two beautiful ladies doing today?" he asked, obviously trying to recover from his misguided wit.

"After I finish giving Mollie the tour here, I'm going to take her to the Disney Hometown Museum, Farm, and Dreaming Tree. Then, I think we'll grab a meal at the Corner Café, and after that, I plan to show her the nearly-completed Allen Hotel we've been renovating. If we have time, I thought we could scavenger the antique store," I said in one anxious breath.

I, so badly, wanted Trevor and Mollie to like each other, but they just didn't seem to click. *Ugh!*

"You have quite an afternoon planned!" Trevor said, astonishment reverberating through his words. "And how about tomorrow … relaxing?"

"It's supposed to be cooler tomorrow, so I thought we could go to Vista Vineyards and try some of the local wines. Then, it's back to L.A. for Mollie."

Mollie and I looked at each other and frowned at my last comment.

"Well, have fun. It was nice to meet you again, Mollie," Trevor said, using his sweetest voice possible.

"Nice to re-meet you too," Mollie replied politely.

I've known Mollie most of my life and although no one else would pick up on it, her lack of enthusiasm toward Trevor was palpable to me.

Leaving the tension behind, we conquered Marceline in a day, and Mollie loved it all, especially seeing what I was actually doing here and the changes that had occurred, were occurring, and were planned to occur in these old buildings.

CHAPTER 26

Collapsing back at my place, we relaxed after a full day in the hot sun, played with Cooper, and eventually changed clothes, getting ready for our girls' night out. I hadn't told Mollie what we were doing, but I thought she was going to enjoy it. And it was something we had never done before.

"Even though it's a short walk to The Uptown Performing Arts Center, we're driving tonight. Storms are in the forecast and getting caught in a downpour would ruin our evening," I said to Mollie as her next clue.

"That's not much of a clue," Mollie protested, "storms always ruin an evening."

"No, tonight's storms will *literally* ruin our evening," I countered.

"I still can't figure it out. I need another clue," Mollie said, exasperated.

She had been trying to guess our plans all afternoon, but I refused to tell her. It had now turned into a game of wits.

Climbing into Betty, we drove the two blocks to Main Street and our destination.

Kaitlin was standing at the front entrance waiting for us with Mollie's next hint. (I had filled her in on our little game, and she was delighted to help keep Mollie guessing.)

"Many people do it by the numbers, but we are going freehand tonight," she said.

"I have no idea what you two are talking about. Is this some strange Marceline-speak?"

Giggling, we entered the lobby, and each purchased a glass of wine before walking into the center's educational wing.

Upon entering one of the classrooms, we were given lime green aprons and told to find an open seat, by our 'teacher' – a bubbly, youthful looking girl, who was at most in her very-early twenties.

Several groups were already in the room talking animatedly amongst themselves while upbeat music filled the air, giving the room a festive atmosphere.

Kaitlin, Mollie and I found an empty table where a blank canvas and set of paints awaited us.

"I believe that is everyone," Miss I-Am-Still-a-Teenager began. "I'm Riley, and I would like to welcome you to *Painting with a Twist*. Before we begin, did everyone get a glass of wine when they came in?"

"I hope if she grabbed one for herself, she isn't arrested for underage drinking before we finish creating our priceless works of art!" I whispered to Kaitlin.

"I know her family. She's older than she looks," Kaitlin whispered back. "Now pay attention or you will be asking me what to do."

How does Kaitlin know me so well in the short time we've been friends, I wondered. *She must be talking to Mollie behind my back.* Of course, I won't be paying close enough attention, so yes, I'll have to ask her or Mollie what I'm supposed to be doing. That's a given!

"Are we painting that picture?" Mollie questioned, also whispering.

She was pointing to a completed canvas portraying a serene landscape at dusk. A small clump of trees, reaching over the water's edge, gave the sense of a quiet evening along a desolate lake.

"Yes, do you like it?" I asked.

"I love it, but I promise you, mine will never look like that."

"Yes, it will, but you need to pay attention or you will be asking me what to do," I whispered back to Mollie. *It feels good to be able to say that to someone else, for a change.*

Riley began by explaining the process we would be following. First, she would demonstrate, in small intervals, how to paint the beautiful landscape in front of us. Next, we were to recreate what she illustrated on our own canvases. All of our pictures would look slightly different, and she assured us that was to be expected and was actually a good thing. We were all different, so our paintings should also be different. (She must be a Philosophy major!)

I was glad she was open to them all looking different because I was certain mine was going to end up looking like a massive color blob. *Whatever made me believe this was a good idea?*

We began with the sky. It turned out that this sky background was made up of a few, fat strokes of pink, white, and blue in varying degrees of intensity. We watched as Riley added these strokes to the top half of her canvas and *voilà*, she had a beautiful sunset. After showing us the technique, she turned on a portable speaker and *Colors of the Wind* played across the room.

"When the song ends, we move on, so don't get bogged down in one section. Let your brush dance to the music!" Riley directed our group. (Is there a Philosophy of Art major?)

I began tentatively, but upon realizing that we were not required to stay in the lines or create a perfect shade, I started to relax and have fun … until the last chorus of the song came around, and then, I panicked. *Maybe I should lighten the blue in the right-hand corner. Did I miss a spot between the white and pink? I'm running out of time!*

"Brushes down," instructed a chirpy Riley. "If you missed a spot, you can always go back and fix it, but remember, the sky outside isn't one perfect tone, so neither should your canvas look flawless."

"I think my sky is too dark. See how yours has more of a dusky color, and mine almost looks like night?" I whispered to Kaitlin as I deliberated on the best way to decrease the intensity of my shading, particularly the blue section.

"Next, we'll be moving to the setting sun," Riley continued. "I'm going to wash my brush thoroughly, then with a mixture of yellow and orange create a circular motion, like this. Now you try."

Hearing Riley ramble on, I stared at my canvas and decided maybe the shading of my sky was fine the way it was. Looking up, I saw Mollie and Kaitlin pick up their brushes and dab them with yellow paint and realized I hadn't heard a word Riley said.

"What are we supposed to do next?" I asked Kaitlin, smiling at her sheepishly. "I wasn't paying attention."

"We're painting the sun, like this," she showed me on her canvas while shaking her head in an amused I-knew-you-wouldn't-listen-and-would-need-help way.

"That's not too hard," I said, swirling a perfect circle of yellow and orange onto my sky – that I once again concluded was too dark.

Riley demonstrated the next step, and the process of paint, learn, paint, learn, continued until we had rendered a beautiful lakeshore which, surprisingly, looked exactly like a lake waterfront on each of our canvasses.

And as Riley had predicted, all three of our paintings looked slightly different, although it was easy to discern the scene in each one.

When we were approximately halfway through our evening as amateur Picassos, Riley said, "Let's take a five-minute break, stretch our legs, take a look at each other's creations, and get another glass of wine."

"This is fun," Mollie gushed as we got our second glass of wine. "I wasn't sure I'd like it, but I feel like a real artist. And Riley is a great instructor!"

"I think she is going to college to become an art teacher. She'll be terrific. She's really patient and makes it easy to create something beautiful," Kaitlin agreed.

"And she's the first teacher I've ever had who hasn't reprimanded me for not paying attention. I like her!" I added.

We walked around the room and examined the unfinished masterpieces, concluding ours looked as good as any of the others.

Back in our seats, we inserted the rocky shore, a stand of leafy trees, and added the final touches that made each of our paintings even more unique. Riley ended the evening by taking a photo for her website of each group proudly holding their works of art for the world to see.

"I really enjoyed collaborating with you this evening," she said as she passed out a slip of paper delineating dates for different painting experiences she would be leading in the future. "Usually, we stay longer and drink another glass of wine, but a storm is on the way, and I want to get you to your cars before the rain begins and your paintings get soaked. I hope you had fun. I know I did," she said cheerfully and then dismissed us.

Mollie and I hastily told Kaitlin goodnight and hurried ourselves and our creations to our cars.

The wind had picked up significantly, and Betty rocked the entire two blocks home.

"I'm going to pull Betty into the garage," I told Mollie. "Everyone keeps talking about this storm, so I think I'll put her inside for the night."

The detached garage was narrow, smelled musty like damp earth, and was super creepy, so I went in it as little as possible.

Without much room on either side, we squeezed ourselves and our paintings out of the car and dashed to the covered porch before we got drenched and ruined our works of art.

Once inside, I rushed to let Cooper out the back door, but he wanted nothing to do with the high wind and approaching storm. Nudging him forward, I decided a bribe was my only option.

"Come on, big guy, you don't want to have an accident in front of Mollie, do you? I'll give you a treat if you go out!"

Reluctantly, he scampered down the steps and into the backyard, barely finishing his business before a booming clap of thunder scared him right back indoors to the safety of his kennel.

I got a bone for him and opened a bottle of wine for Mollie and me – after all, we were supposed to get a third glass at the painting class. Grabbing some of the cheese and crackers I had purchased, Mollie and I changed into pajamas and settled in for a good, old-fashion slumber party.

We moved from one subject to the next, eventually trying to figure out how we had made it to the earth-shattering topic of "which is the best-flavored Skittle". All the while, the wind had been whipping up a major storm with bright flashes of lightning and thunder explosions that actually shook the house. Commenting on how thankful we were to not be living in the Stone Age as cave women, but instead, had a sound roof over our heads, our conversation moved to a debate over which animal would have been scarier to meet in the wild – an enormous, but sluggish, wooly mammoth or a quick, agile, saber-tooth tiger.

I was defending my stance that the tusk of the mammoth could rip you to shreds in one, easy motion when suddenly, my phone emitted a high-pitched, piercing noise.

Cooper's ears perked, while Mollie and I stared at each other, wondering why a sudden, unfamiliar sound was coming from my phone as sirens began to blare outside as well.

My phone was then buzzing along with a cacophony of other noises surrounding us. I picked it up and saw Ida's name on the screen and immediately answered.

"Hello?"

"This is Ida."

There was an urgency in her voice.

"Grab Cooper and run to your bathroom, right now. Close the door, sit in the tub, and cover your heads. Do you understand? Do not leave until all the sirens go off."

"We're going," I said, rushing to pull Cooper out of the safety of his kennel. "What is going on?" I asked her, almost breathless.

"Hurry, just do as I say. I know you girls aren't from the Midwest and don't understand how serious this is, but a tornado is bearing down on Marceline, as we speak. You need to shelter in the bathroom immediately," she warned and promptly hung up, presumably to take cover herself.

Mollie and I dragged Cooper into the tub and huddled close together.

The bones of the house rattled with each wind gust. Lightening, immediately followed by deafening thunder, was directly on top of us as rain, changing to hail, battered the roof.

Our hearts were pounding so loud, I could hear them over the storm.

Our power flickered, and then went off completely, as the sirens continued to ring through the night air.

Sitting in total darkness, holding tightly to each other's hands, suddenly, everything became quiet and eerily still.

"Do you think it's over?" Mollie asked.

"I don't know, but Ida said to stay here until all the sirens went off, and I trust Ida!"

As the words left my lips, the wind picked up again and a low rumble replaced the sound of rain and thunder.

We continued to sit in the tub for ten, long minutes when the sirens finally ceased, and a light rain was all that was left of the storm.

Flipping on my phone's flashlight, I climbed out of the tub, opened the door and looked around. Everything was in its place, as it should be.

Mollie was right behind me with her light sweeping a path down the hall.

We tip-toed to the porch (I guess we felt the need to be stealth since we were walking through a dark house with only flashlights to guide us) and beamed our lights into the pitch black, front yard.

Limbs were scattered everywhere, but from what we could see, the houses around us seemed to be intact.

I called Ida, and she answered on the first ring.

"Are you alright?" I urgently asked her.

"Yes, I'm fine, dear. We were lucky this time. I just got off the phone with my daughter, Kathy, and she said the tornado touched down and bounced through some open, farm fields a few miles north of us. There will be plenty of clean up waiting for us in the morning, but the severe weather threat is long gone now. I'm sure we won't get any power back until sometime tomorrow, so you girls might as well call it a night and get some rest."

"Thanks for the warning, Ida. You're the best!"

"That's what neighbors do, dear."

Next, I text Trevor who had been watching baseball all evening with Andre and whose biggest concern was the continued interruptions of the coverage due to weather updates. (I guess that meant they survived the storm unscathed!) They had power, which was good, he said, since the Angels and Royals were tied 3 - 3 in the eleventh.

After checking on Kaitlin, Mollie and I were still too wound up to 'call it a night', so we stayed up into the wee hours talking. Eventually, our nerves calmed, and exhaustion took over. We both fell into a restless sleep, where I dreamed of munchkins riding on the backs of wooly mammoths, heading straight into a funnel cloud of swirling, brightly colored Skittles.

• • •

The morning brought to light the extent of the damage from the storm.

Mollie and I each grabbed a cup of cold coffee and sat on the porch (in the, as predicted, much cooler temperatures), surveying the surrounding destruction.

My lawn was so littered with twigs and branches, it was difficult to believe there was patchy, green grass beneath the rubble. Glancing down the street, I saw a neighbor inspecting a giant oak spread across his lawn and blocking the street. Luckily, the tree fell forward, otherwise, he would have a massive crater in his roof and, instead of removing debris from his lawn, he would be decluttering his living room of leaves and limbs. Across the street, I noticed a gutter dangling from the eaves and two houses to the left, a group was already on the roof stretching a blue tarp over, what must be, shingle damage. But overall, the damage appeared to consist mainly of broken trees scattered up and down Mulberry Street.

Deciding to check outside my house, so I could report to the homeowners what, if any damage the wind caused to the exterior, I threw on some old clothes and a baseball cap and dragged myself out the front door.

Looking up to the sound of two pickup trucks turning onto my street, one empty and one with a smattering of people sitting in its bed, I watched with interest as both trucks stopped near the fallen oak. Individuals with chainsaws jumped out of the back bed, and the group began to immediately tackle the tree blocking the road. It was the same group I saw the morning I took Cooper for a walk in Ripley Park. *What did Chance call them – The Beautification Committee?*

Walking the perimeter of my house to the sound of buzzing chainsaws, I didn't observe any major damage, so I then forced myself to enter the side door of the creepy garage to gather some yard waste bags and gardening tools that looked (even though I had no clue as to their real purpose) as if they might be helpful in cutting the branches strewn across my lawn.

Next, I needed to convince Mollie, who was in vacation mode, to help me clean up my disastrous yard. I had convinced her to do many crazy things over the years, so this shouldn't be too hard, I figured.

Eating a leisurely breakfast of boxed blueberry muffins, we took our sweet time before tackling the huge *Jenga* pile in my front yard.

When we did finally make it outside, most of the fallen tree had been cut and removed from the middle of the street. The group had now moved to the large pieces scattered across the lawn. It was then that I noticed a heavily dented car in the driveway that wasn't visible when the entire tree was still intact, and I was so thankful I had parked Betty in the garage.

One of the pickup trucks, full of stumps and limbs, drove by as Mollie and I began gathering, clipping, and placing the debris from the storm into our tall, brown paper bags.

It was a slow process, thanks to it being just the two of us and our inferior tree trimming tools. But, that said, I had brought my Bluetooth speaker outside so we could sing, dance, clip, and try to have as much fun as possible while doing yard work which was not something I was genetically predisposed to enjoy.

Nosily keeping an eye on the activity up the street, I watched the truck return and saw it promptly refill with more debris. This time when it departed, the fallen tree, for the most part, had been removed and the group was beginning to pack up and move on.

That's when I saw Chance throw his chainsaw into the bed of the truck that was hauling the clean-up crew and then walk a couple of houses down the street to Ida's front door, knock, speak to her for a few minutes, then motion the group to join him.

"Hey, Jess, how's it going? Any major damage?" he asked while waiting for his crew to meet him at Ida's.

"No, just an overwhelming amount of limbs, but if that's our biggest problem, I think we were lucky."

"We're going to clean up here first, after that, how about we help you clear the mess from your yard," he offered.

"That would be great, if you have time," I said, more than appreciative.

"That's what we do as the 'Beautification Committee'," he said air quoting in a way that indicated he had nothing to do with naming this group of Good Samaritans.

The pickup truck used for hauling returned, and the 'committee members' started tossing debris from Ida's yard into its bed, clearing her lawn at a much faster rate than Mollie and I could ever achieve using our laborsome technique of clipping and dropping twigs into yard waste bags.

"Who is that?!" Mollie asked with enthusiasm. "He's really cute."

"Now, now, you're an engaged woman," I admonished her.

"Not for me, silly, for you."

"I'm happily dating Trevor!" I exclaimed. "What is it with everybody trying to put Chance and me together?"

"That's the Chance guy the lady at the coffee shop was talking about?"

"Yes, that's the Chance guy," I said, copying her reference and tone.

"And you're not pursuing him, why?"

"Because I am happily dating Trevor, that's why," I said, completely exasperated.

"Too bad," she said under her breath.

I was disappointed, once again, that I was unable to turn Mollie into a Trevor Dorrington fan. (Although … even I had to admit that Chance looked amazing for having spent the morning completing sweaty, physical labor.)

In a surprisingly short amount of time, the loading truck gradually moved in front of my house, and the clean-up crew was in my yard, quickly tossing the bulk of the debris into its bed. They removed more in a shorter period of time than Mollie and I could have dreamed of accomplishing the entire day.

"Where to next?" I asked Chance as the group readied themselves to move on to their next undertaking.

"We drive around looking for large storm damage, elderly folks requiring help with clean-up, or public property needing to be cleared of debris. Want to join us?" he offered.

I thought about the strangers who came to my aid when I fell in the park, of Joanie's help home, of Ida's advice to pay it forward, and of the slight exaggeration I told Trevor when we first met about my commitment to volunteer work – all that in the three seconds it took me to answer, "Yes, we'd love to!"

"Great! We'll get the truck and meet you out front," he said, heading with the rest of the group up the street to the parked pickup.

"I hope you don't mind," I said to Mollie as we grabbed the speaker, moving it and the tools inside. "I feel like I need to repay these people for the kindness they've shown me. Plus, for once, I actually want to help out. Does that make any sense?"

"It's fine," Mollie replied. "Besides, I heard the two ladies saying that half the decking blew off the winery we were going to visit this afternoon, so I don't think we can go there today anyway. They were talking about it as their next clean-up location, but the county dispatched a team to the site instead."

I filled Cooper's bowl, put on sturdier shoes, and ran with Mollie out the front door to the waiting truck. We piled into the back bed with the rest of the crew and drove off to our next destination.

Chance introduced us to the group which included two female teachers, a couple of guys from Alexander Construction, a local farmer and his son (who were luckily not the owners of the land where the twister touched down), the owner of the hardware store, Darryl Smith (yeah! I finally knew his name), Chris Langley from The Uptown Center, plus the drivers of the two trucks who both worked for the highway department. In turn, I introduced Mollie to the committee as we bumped along side streets, combing the neighborhood for damage.

We spent the day clearing truckloads of debris from the streets of Marceline. It was hard, but rewarding, work.

Our last stop was Ripley Park, where we began the arduous task of cleaning the grounds and lake from remnants of the storm.

"Thanks for assisting today," Chance said as we freed the park from nature's litter. "You and Mollie joining us, it made a huge difference in how much we were able to accomplish. You were real lifesavers!"

"I never knew volunteering could be so satisfying," I said. "I felt more reward from helping today than I'm sure anyone actually gained from my hard labor."

"Don't bet on that. Many of the people we helped rely on the young and healthy to give them a hand, just as they cared for the older folks in the neighborhood when they were younger. Believe me, they appreciate every bit of support we can offer. So, are you telling me, you don't participate in any volunteer work in Los Angeles?" Chance asked.

His tone sounded as if he were bewildered that someone didn't do this sort of thing every weekend.

"Not really. I was always too busy," I said meekly. "But I do donate to various charities."

Of course deep down, I know that isn't quite the same as actually lending a helping hand.

"Donating is important, too. An aid organization can't run without funding. They need money and manpower. You do what you can," he added with a shrug. "I just want you to know how much your help is appreciated. And by the way, I like the baseball cap the best."

He gave me his characteristic smirk as he moved on to tackle a large grouping of limbs at the edge of the lake.

I couldn't help but smile to myself. As much as I hated to admit it, I was glad he approved.

With the park soon free of storm damage, Chris announced that a potluck was waiting for us in the multipurpose room at The Uptown.

We had been so busy cleaning that Mollie and I had spent very little time talking, so we chose to walk, just the two of us, the short distance to the center.

"What is a potluck?" she asked.

"I'm not sure. I guess we'll find out in a few minutes. Maybe it's like discovering gold at the end of the rainbow," I said, to which Mollie shook her head.

Mollie may have been laughing at my explanation, but I soon learned that I wasn't too far off.

We entered the multipurpose room and table after table was filled with meats, side dishes and desserts.

Until I saw the mounds of food waiting for our group, I had not realized how ravished I was.

Apparently as a thank you (or as an excuse to socialize), the town comes together bringing platefuls of goodies to share. Our group was instructed to go first through the line, where it was difficult to choose what to eat, each homemade dish looking better than the previous one that I had just loaded onto my plate.

Joining the volunteers, I sat with Mollie on one side and Darryl Smith from the hardware store on the other. Chance joined our group, filling the only empty seat, directly across from Mollie.

"When are you going back to Los Angeles?" Chance asked her, breaking the ice.

"Jess is taking me to Kansas City in the morning to catch my one o'clock flight. At least it's nonstop this time."

And so it went ... we ate, chatted between bites, and then ate some more.

Contrary to my first impression, I found Darryl to be congenial and easy to talk to. He turned out to be your basic 'how to guide' in the flesh and even taught me about a switch on my ceiling fan that I could change to give my porch more of a breeze. *That's handy!*

I also overheard Mollie and Chance laughing and chatting like old friends. They seemed to have hit it off, and I wondered, once again, why she couldn't be like that with Trevor.

After stuffing ourselves, we thanked everyone for the meal and walked home, with full bellies and tired limbs.

"Chance is nice, I don't know why you don't like him," Mollie began not three feet out the door of The Uptown Center.

"Who says I don't like him? I like him fine. I'm just dating someone."

"Where was Trevor today, by the way?"

"I don't know. We left in such a hurry that I forgot my phone sitting on the end table. Surprisingly, it's been nice to be tech free for a day."

When I finally retrieved my phone, Trevor had left a few messages, but not as many as I would have expected. To his credit, he did think we were going to be at the winery all day.

I carried myself, along with my phone, into my bedroom and stretched out on the mattress while Mollie took a quick shower. I text Trevor, filling him in on our eventful day.

Suddenly, realizing how exhausted I was beginning to feel, I cut my conversation with him short and went to look for Mollie so we could spend the last few hours of her visit together.

To my dismay, I found her, with a towel wrapped around her wet head, already sound asleep on the couch.

● ● ●

"It was a great visit," Mollie said as we neared the exit for Kansas City International Airport.

"Thanks for inviting me. I wasn't sure what to expect, but it was really fun … except the part where we had to cram into the bathtub with a dog," Mollie said and laughed. "I can see how you fell in love with Cooper, though. He's pretty special, and it makes me feel better knowing you have a dog in the house, since you live there alone."

"I'm not alone! Did you see how many people would be around to help me if I needed anything?" I said, pulling into a drop-off slot.

Mollie grabbed her carry-on and her protectively wrapped painting as she climbed out of Betty.

Putting the car in park, I popped the trunk, removed her piece of check-in luggage, and went to where she was waiting on the curb for me to hug her goodbye.

"You know, Jess," she said as she turned to enter the airport.

(I could hear one of her brutally honest opinions coming – which I'm sure I've mentioned that I love and hate about her.)

"I haven't seen you this happy in a long time. This place suits you."

"What are you talking about?! I'm an L.A. girl."

"Just making an observation," she said and chuckled, waving one last time.

"I'll see you in less than three months," I yelled out to her.

And for the first time, it occurred to me that leaving Marceline might be harder than I thought it would be.

CHAPTER 27

It was hard to believe we had already reached the end of August. With our second renovation complete (and on schedule – which continued to please Cassandra!), we were ready for the official unveiling to the owners of Allen Hotel, Charles and Jazelle Victor.

Lucy was bringing the Victors to the site, following the same protocol used in the reveal of The Uptown Performing Arts Center, the only difference being that Taylor would be joining me for the shoot. Since the Victors came across more stoic and less animated than the Langleys (or to be precise, Erin Langley) and appeared slightly aloof on camera, I had brought Taylor in to liven up the walk-through. She was such a natural at adding energy to her surroundings.

Intentionally coordinated, Taylor, in a surprisingly tame aqua and pink flowered sundress, and I, in a classic solid tee (today's shade – fuchsia) and white skinny jeans, we met Lucy, with the Victors, in front of the hotel, where filming began.

On the sidelines, once again, ready to critique Episode 2 of *Main Street* were Trevor, Andre, and Mr. Biggs, along with his daughter Samantha, who looked sophisticated in a sleek, light gray cropped pant suit with sky-high heels stretching her already long legs into oblivion. (*No, I'm not intimidated!*).

"Are you ready to see the new Allen Hotel?" I asked as the cameras rolled.

"Yes, we are anxious to assess the new design," Jazelle replied.

Could she get any stiffer in her delivery, I wondered. *Ugh!*

"Alright then, remove your masks!" I announced, trying to pump excitement into the reveal.

For fun, we had provided them with sleep masks to cover their eyes, rather than standard blindfolds, embellished with the hotel's signature cursive 'A' logo.

"It looks lovely," Jazelle stated, her tone one of being sincerely awestruck.

"The bricks were so dirty and dull before," added Charles. "It looks as if the building was erected yesterday rather than having been constructed over one hundred years ago. Now, the architectural accents and keystone brickwork catch a person's eye, as they should."

"Obviously, the classic awning and those stunning wood and glass doors are what makes the entrance so attractive. Although the bricks are nice too, darling," Jazelle said to her husband, pointing out the more prominent improvements.

"Only a man would notice the bricks over the beautiful exterior motif," she whispered to me.

I smiled at her dry humor, which was totally uncharacteristic from what I knew of her. *Maybe this will go better than I anticipated.*

"And those side lamps are exquisite," she continued, aloud.

"They look as old as the building … the way the brass diamond pattern surrounds the golden globe, don't you agree?" Taylor interjected.

"Yes, I would have thought they were antiques. I hope the rest of the hotel maintains the combination of vintage and modern in the same manner as this front entrance," Jazelle replied.

"Oh, we think you're going to love it! Are you ready to see inside then?" Taylor asked enthusiastically.

It was Taylor's suggestion to have the Victors' initial impression of the hotel lobby be seen through the eyes of a guest. So, the film crew moved upstairs to position their camera equipment and Taylor, going with them, prepared to greet us from behind the richly polished reception desk made of exquisite, Brazilian mahogany.

Giving the team a chance to get in place, I slowly accompanied the Victors up the elevator to the second floor.

As the doors opened, Jazelle and Charles gasped in unison.

"Charles, can you believe this?! These doors used to open to a dimly lit hallway that led to battered wood doors of small office spaces. Now, it is an airy room for guests to enjoy and feel welcome. I can't get over the change!"

"It is not possible that this is the same space," Charles responded. "I would have bet a million dollars this was an entirely different building."

"Welcome!" Taylor called out from behind the check-in station.

We moved forward as the Victors took in the changes.

Mahogany paneled walls paired with an ecru arabesque flooring kept the area from being too dark while also giving the room a timeless appearance. Off to the right, a small anteroom held two love seats, facing each other, separated by a rectangular (also mahogany) coffee table and in the corner were a pair of matching wingback chairs.

"I would have never chosen paneling, assuing it would appear old and stuffy, but instead, it gives the lobby an elegant feel, particularly with the added pillars and the beautiful diamond millwork on the front desk," critiqued Jazelle.

"I'm glad you like the pillars where they are. They are load bearing, so we had to work around their existence, but I agree, they give the room character. If you'll notice, the sconces on the pillars match the gorgeous crystal chandelier hanging in the center of the lobby. And we wanted the guests to feel welcome as soon as they got off the elevator, so we added the round table beneath the light fixture and placed that large vase of fresh flowers in the center to brighten the room."

"Do you have a reservation for this evening?" Taylor asked, continuing her role as reception clerk.

Jazelle paused to smell the locally grown flowers, artfully arranged on the center table, as I walked her and her husband to the check-in desk.

Providing us with a key for Room 201, Taylor cheerfully directed us to our accommodations. "Your suite is through the hallway to the left of the elevator, and will be the first door on the right," she said, using her hands to motion us along in case we didn't understand her verbal instructions.

As we waited for the camera crew to set up inside the guest room, I described some of the standard amenities that allowed the suite to qualify as tech-friendly.

"Inclusion of high-speed internet access, multiple USB ports scattered throughout the room, and a voice assistant smart speaker are a few of the features available for your guests. Once we are inside the suite, I will point each of these items out for the camera," I explained.

We were told the camera crew was ready, so the Victors passed the key card in front of the electronic pad and slowly opened the door.

Peeking inside, they were greeted by a small sitting area furnished with a sleek modular loveseat, doubling as sleeper sofa, which allowed each room to increase its occupancy capacity.

"Just as I hoped," Jazelle stated as she walked into the larger, open bedroom. "A classic lobby yet contemporary living space for our guests."

"The white oak flooring, made of engineered hardwood, matched with the gray and black patterned area rug, give a warm, but stylish look to the room," I said, beginning my narrative.

"And easy for upkeep," added Charles, making it apparent, once again, that aesthetics were not his first priority.

With the curtains pulled back, plenty of light illuminated the room, showing off its chic furnishings. Against the charcoal gray wall was a black panel positioned directly behind a king size bed topped with a dove gray duvet and copious amounts of fluffy pillows; a mounted flat screen television hung over a black lacquered six-drawer dresser; and a licorice black rounded armchair sat in the corner, beckoning a tired guest to pick up a book or relax while watching a movie.

"I would absolutely stay here," Jazelle said approvingly. "It feels very elegant yet comfortable."

"All the furnishings in this room are from USAMade," I said, seeing a big smile come across Mr. Biggs' face as he nodded his head. "Since we were decorating multiple suites, we wanted to use well-crafted, yet stylish designs that could be purchased within a modest budget. Redecorating and exorbitant costs don't have to be synonymous."

The Victors spent time exploring the room's comforts and attached bathroom with its tiled walls, glass shower stall, rain shower head, and bowl sink.

Similar to the Langleys' reveal, it was my job to keep Charles and Jazelle moving, since we were only allowed eleven minutes for this segment of the show.

"Our last stop will be the roof! Shall we check it out?" I suggested, eager to show them my favorite part of the entire renovation.

"Welcome to the Rooftop Garden," I said as our group exited the elevator leading to a terraced bar.

High-top tables were scattered around the perimeter with more outdoor seating surrounding elongated, glass fire pits. A covered cocktail bar was open for service, and decorating the entire space were strings of fairy lights and well-positioned planters.

"We were most excited about this change to the hotel," Charles exclaimed.

"And it doesn't disappoint," Jazelle added. "It's a perfect addition, literally the cherry on top!"

Although confident in our remodel, I was still relieved that the Victors were as pleased with the rooftop venue as they were with the rest of the hotel.

Taylor, now positioned behind the bar, offered us each a glass of champagne, and we toasted to the success of the Allen Hotel.

• • •

After the cameras stopped rolling and the champagne had long been consumed, I sat at a high-top table in the Rooftop Garden and learned from the Victors how they came to own the hotel and their active participation with the local government in the development of marketing strategies to encourage Kansas City residents to consider Marceline as a weekend retreat.

I thoroughly enjoyed the conversation. It turned out the Victors were more interesting and at times, funnier, then I had realized. I wished them a pleasant afternoon and informed them that I would see them again the next morning at the ribbon cutting.

Since the transformation of the Allen Hotel was a reopening rather than a renovation, the mayor had scheduled a ribbon cutting ceremony with community leaders for early the next morning. A reception, open to the public, would follow in the hotel lobby, giving Marceline residents a chance to see the newest addition to Main Street. What a perfect way to spend a Saturday, I thought.

Looking for Trevor, I found him with Mr. Biggs, and Samantha Biggs, seated on the anteroom's couches in deep discussion regarding our third, and final, project – a convenience store/deli turned farm-to-table food mart and mini bistro.

I decided not to interrupt and instead elected to hear the overview from Trevor at our customary, Saturday night dinner date. Maybe I would suggest we start with drinks at the Allen Hotel – since a rooftop bar was where our story began.

● ● ●

Standing at the edge of Ripley Park, directly across from the freshly washed bricks of the Allen Hotel, I melded into the crowd of onlookers gathered for the ribbon cutting ceremony.

Although not openly involved in the scheduled festivities, I was required to make an appearance as a member of the *LeisureTV* team, and I had to admit it was a relief to be on the viewing end of a production, for a change.

Jonathon, the only cameraman needed for the shoot, was taking unscripted footage of the event, which would be edited into the final cut of *Main Street's* second episode.

As I watched from the sidelines, Mayor Knowell, standing with Charles and Jazelle Victor and members of the Marceline

City Council, made a short speech and, with grand formality, cut the large red ribbon stretched across the front of the hotel entrance.

The surrounding crowd cheered – because that's what one was supposed to do when a grown man using giant scissors (where does one even find such an item?) cuts a ribbon (too wide to ever be placed on a wrapped package) in half – but it was tradition!

People began to mill about, some going inside for a peek at the lobby, guest rooms, and rooftop bar, while others headed to the park to shop for locally grown fruits, vegetables, and handmade crafts. It was the last Saturday of August, and Ripley Park was full of vendors, there for the Farmer's Market held monthly from May through September.

I found Jonathon and suggested he take some footage of the crowded market for our third, and final, episode of *Main Street - Marceline.*

Jonathon agreed that adding candid shots of the Farmer's Market into the next segment would add a human-interest touch, and so he began moving 'inconspicuously' into the crowd with a bulky camera sitting atop his right shoulder.

Rumor had it that if the ratings for the second episode were as strong as the first, we would be moving to a new location for *Main Street – New Small Town to be Announced at a Later Date.* Adding these kinds of scenes should make our show resonate with people across America whose town might be chosen as our next possible locale.

Located on the opposite end of Main Street, Express Market had temporarily closed its doors, ready for renovation to begin on Monday. It would reopen again in six weeks as Fresh Express Market. The idea was to expand the summer Farmer's Market by bringing it indoors, making fresh, farm-to-table, organic food available every day, year-round. We had already filmed the walk-through, so all that was left was one more renovation and reveal.

Since Trevor was busy all day with the hotel's reception, I decided to grab some fresh produce for our dinner and to stock up for the week ahead.

Stalls of broccoli, cauliflower, kale, spinach, onions, carrots, potatoes, and peas lined one side of the park, while various berries, grapes, apricots, plums, peaches, and pears were for sale in stalls located on the opposite side of the lake.

I leisurely strolled through all the choices, filling my reusable grocery sack with a variety of nutritious foods. It was a beautiful, sunny morning and having skipped breakfast, I decided to take a seat on one of the empty park benches, enjoying the sparkling sunlight and one of the sweet, juicy peaches laying on top of my stash.

"You look lonely, want some company?"

"Sure," I said as Chance came around the bench and sat next to me.

"Want a peach?" I asked, trying to discretely swipe away the excess juice dribbling down the side of my face before he noticed.

"No thanks, but it looks like you got a ripe one," he said and chuckled.

Once again, I had given him a reason to smile (according to Chance) or smirk (according to me).

"You're out early this morning," he said.

"I had to attend the ribbon cutting, so I thought I'd buy some fresh fruits and veggies while I was out. How about you?"

"As a committee member, I help set up and break down the stalls for the Farmer's Market, so I'm actually working. I thought I'd take a break and watch the ceremony. By the way, you did another nice job on the hotel. I'm impressed!"

"I just hope they get enough visitors to keep it running," he added.

"Why wouldn't they? The City Council is making a big push to market Marceline as a quaint get-away. I think it will do great!"

There was an odd pause in our conversation before Chance said, "So you don't know about the hotel's colorful past and why it eventually closed?"

"No," I said warily, "but you have me intrigued. What happened?"

"Prior to prohibition," he began, "Marceline was a thriving railroad town. It was what was known as a crew change stop. One set of workers would exit the train, having traveled from as far as New York, and a new set of workers would board, headed for California. Men would receive their pay at the local bank and, with money in their pockets, would set out for a good time. When prohibition was enacted, however, that good time vanished. So, the owners of the Allen Hotel, always looking for a new opportunity, decided to turn the lower-level restaurant into a speakeasy for after-hours customers. This, as you can imagine, brought quite a diverse crowd to Marceline. A bellhop, named George Cast, who was by all accounts a religious man, didn't approve of the illegal activity occurring on the premises and threatened to go to the authorities to have it stopped. By then, the Allen family was making too much money on their illegal operation and couldn't let that happen, at any cost. Legend says that Old Mr. Allen, himself, lured George upstairs when he knew no one would be around and pushed him from the upper-level, breaking George's neck as he tumbled from the height of the top stair. After George's death, accounts of his spirit roaming the halls late at night, loudly warning visitors to repent and leave the premises, flourished among the visitors. After years of complaints, the hotel eventually closed as no guests would stay more than one night. In the end, George won the battle. The Allen's, destitute, sold the hotel and left Marceline for good, but folks say if you are near the building after midnight, you can still hear the warning voice of George Cast coming from inside the building."

"That is not true," I said skeptically.

"Believe me or don't, it's up to you. But remember, I've lived in Marceline my whole life, and you have been here only a few months, so I'm sure you know the truth more than I do," he said and shrugged.

"Why didn't we ever see his ghost when we were working on the property?"

"Because it was daylight, and he doesn't come out until after midnight when the speakeasy would have been roaring with inebriated patrons and loud music," Chance replied.

"I've talked with the Victors and they never mentioned George Cast," I said, still trying to catch him in a lie.

"Would you repeat the story if you were trying to open a new establishment? Not a great way to start a business," he countered.

"Hey, Joe," Chance called out to a worker I recognized from the job site. "I was just telling Jess the story of George Cast, and she doesn't believe me."

"Everybody knows the story of Old George, quite a tale," he said as he continued walking toward a group of local farmers who were discussing the effects the current weather was having on their crops.

"What can I say, ask anyone who's lived here their whole life, and they will tell you that George Cast haunts the Allen Hotel," Chance said, matter-of-factly.

"I will," I said, knowing the exact person to ask – Ida – and I would quiz her the minute I got home.

She would tell me the truth.

"Hey, Chance."

We both looked in the direction of the main park activity where Darryl Smith, my new friend from the Main Street Hardware Store, was walking in our direction.

"We've got a late-arriving vendor, any chance you can help me raise another stall?"

"Oh, hi Jess, I didn't see you sitting there. Hope I'm not interrupting," he added.

"No, I was taking a break and testing one of my purchases. I just had a peach, and it was delicious!"

"Best produce for miles around," Darryl announced proudly.

"Come on, Darryl, let's set up that tent. See you around, Jess."

Chance and Darryl moved toward the far end of the park as I left my comfortable spot on the bench, stopped at a couple more stalls to fill a few smaller bags with an assortment of fruits and vegetables, and made my way home, dragging heavy, overfilled bags of produce in my wake.

● ● ●

Following our typical routine, Cooper and I bound up the battered stairs of Ida's porch on the way home from our afternoon walk through the neighborhood. I had something to give her … and … something to ask her.

Happy to see her sitting outside, lazily rocking in her customary chair, she, as usual, seemed to be waiting for our visit. (*I'm sure her sixth sense told her we were coming!*)

"How was your walk, dear?" she questioned as I wrapped Cooper's lead around the porch railing.

"Great! Have you been sitting here very long?" I asked, trying to be as nonchalant as possible.

"No, I just decided to come out, enjoy some fresh air, and take a rest on the porch."

I knew it! She was definitely waiting on us!

"And now, I have some lovely company to join me."

"Do you mind watching Cooper?" I asked, purposely being vague. "I need to run home and grab something."

"You know I never mind watching Cooper, but don't be too long, or we might start talking about you," she teased. "Right, Cooper?"

At the sound of his name, Cooper raised his head, but immediately laid it back down on the cool planks, ready for a nap.

I quickly returned with two of the smaller bags I had lugged home from Ripley Park – one full of various fruits and the other packed with fresh vegetables.

"I picked up some produce from the Farmer's Market for you to enjoy," I said, nodding at the two bags in my hands. "I wasn't sure what were your favorites, so I got a little of everything."

"How thoughtful! I used to love to go to the Farmer's Market when these old legs worked better. Nothing says summer like stalls full of ripe tomatoes or blackberry stains that won't leave your fingertips."

Or peach juice, embarrassingly running down the side of your mouth while sitting on a park bench, I thought to myself.

"Well, I purchased both of those items, so I guess it's still officially summer," I smiled.

"Would you mind setting the bags on the kitchen counter? I'll wash everything later and prepare me a summertime feast. Oh, and pour yourself a cold drink while you are inside," she added.

"I will, thank you. Can I get you a refill?" I offered as I opened the screen door.

"No, I'm fine for now."

I returned with a glass of fresh, pulpy lemonade. (I would never admit it to Ida, but I only had a can of powdered lemon drink in my pantry.)

"Nothing tastes as refreshing as your lemonade," I told her.

"So much better than those processed sugar drinks they sell at the grocers," she replied.

(I don't care what she says, she has the mind-reading gift, no doubt about it!)

"I took pictures of the new Allen Hotel to send to my mom and my friend Mollie. Would you like to see them?" I asked.

"I'd love to," she said.

I handed her my phone and demonstrated how to scroll though the photos.

"I remember when that place was bustling with guests," she said.

"It's a shame what happened. I just recently heard the story of George Cast and why the hotel closed," I commiserated.

"Who is George Cast?" she asked, perplexed.

"The ghost who haunts the Allen Hotel," I retorted.

"Now, who told you a fancy tale like that?" Ida inquired, staring at me over the rim of her glasses.

"Chance Alexander," I answered sheepishly.

Ida began laughing so hard I thought she might fall right out of her chair.

"You know that boy is pulling your leg, don't you? There are no ghosts in that hotel."

"But Joe, a guy we work with, walked by and verified Chance's story," I said, unconvinced.

"Did said Joe happen to be about Chance's age, similar in build and height, and have dark, curly hair?"

"Yes."

Ida continued chuckling. "That's Joe Harper, Chance's best friend since they were kids. He'll agree with anything Chance says."

I started to ask how she knew this, but remembered I was talking to Ida. The same Ida who had knowledge of all-things Marceline and beyond!

"These photos are delightful," she commented after finally composing herself and taking another look at the pictures on my phone. "I'm particularly fond of the way you refurbished the lobby. It reminds me of the original Allen Hotel. Such a beautiful place! Takes me back to when I was a young girl. We were little hellions back then, daring each other to run inside and ring the bell on the check-in desk. If the person didn't get caught, the rest of us would take turns buying the brave soul a piece of penny candy from the drugstore down the street," she reminisced. "But time and people move on, and a new hotel reopens, looking as lovely as the old one, only with a lot more fancy gadgets, I imagine."

"You're right, there are plenty of those. We tried to appeal to the young professional looking for a relaxing retreat," I said.

"Well, from the looks of these pictures, it appears you met your goal," she said, her compliment sincere. "Now tell me about your next project."

Excited that Ida liked our updates to the Allen Hotel, I happily recounted for her the plans for our next renovation.

"We start on Monday reimagining the Express Market and changing the appearance of the store to match its new name – Fresh Express Market. It will still carry staples people want to pick up, without going to the larger grocery store, but these items, for the most part, will be organic or plant-based. The current deli located inside the market is going to be transformed into a small, farm-to-table bistro with a few tables in the front of the store, plus a limited amount of sidewalk seating. It will be like making the Farmer's Market available every day, all year long."

"That sounds very interesting. I can't wait for the pictures when it is completed."

"Don't worry, I'll keep you up-to-date on the store's progress, whether you want me to or not," I grinned.

Thanking Ida for the lemonade, I woke up Cooper for our short trip home. It was time for lunch, and I knew how much Cooper couldn't wait for his scoop of dry dog food and a bowl of water. For me, it was a delicious ham sandwich and a tumbler of processed sugar drink. Cooper and I, we definitely knew how to feast!

CHAPTER 28

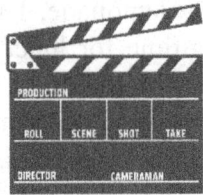

After our Saturday 'date night' dinner, Trevor and I decided to join the inaugural festivities at the Rooftop Garden. The reception in the lobby from earlier that day had moved to a party on the roof with live entertainment and drink specials.

We grabbed a drink from the bar. I chose the special, which was aptly named *The Main Street* – a mixture of vodka, St. Germain, pineapple juice, and club soda, garnished with a cinnamon stick, and Trevor went for a more traditional, Jack and Coke.

Snagging the last empty table looking down Main Street with its row of Victorian, cast-iron streetlamps glowing amber in the night, we noticed a group of people gathered below The Uptown Theater's brightly lit marquee buying tickets for the late show. On the opposite side of the street, a couple ambled down the sidewalk, out for an evening stroll.

It was a vastly different setting from The Roofstop's view in Los Angeles, but it was just as pleasant and relaxing.

I looked around at the crowd and was disappointed not to recognize anyone except the Langleys, who were sitting in the far corner with a small group of friends and, of course, the Victors, who greeted us as we exited the elevator.

"There are a lot of unfamiliar faces here tonight," I commented.

"I am sure there are plenty of people in Marceline you haven't met ... yet," Trevor replied.

"Is that such a bad thing? Getting to know the people here," I retorted, feeling a small knot tighten in the pit of my stomach. *Here we go again ... that one topic we just can't seem to agree on.*

"No, but as I've mentioned before, I don't see the point in getting involved when we are here for such a short time," Trevor countered. "Anyway, you are right, I don't recognize many of these people, either."

"When I was talking with the Victors yesterday, Jazelle mentioned they had invited a multitude of friends from out of town to help them celebrate the hotel's grand opening. They are completely on board with marketing Marceline to the Kansas City population as a hidden get-away and decided to start with their own family, friends, and acquaintances."

"It looks like they were successful, this place is packed," Trevor commented, looking around at the completely filled tables.

"Imagine how busy it will be on the weekend of the *Peter and Wendy* premiere," I remarked. "I can't believe the show's opening is only four weeks away. Time has really flown."

"It has gone faster than I thought it would," he admitted. "I was planning on visiting my brother in Denver a couple of times while we were on location here, and I haven't even made it out of this town. Although, I am going the week after next to see my nephew play in his state championship soccer tournament. I'm told, as goalie, he is like a brick wall. My brother says his team is favored to win, but that he needs his 'Lucky Uncle Trevor' in the stands to guarantee they clinch the title."

"Note to self, lonely weekend in two weeks," I pouted.

I would have loved to meet Trevor's adored niece and nephew, but he didn't seem to pick up on my mild hint, and I didn't want to be the stereotypical, pushy girlfriend.

"I'm sure you will find something to do with one of your new friends," he said as Charles Victor stopped by our table, checking to see if we were enjoying our drinks.

We chatted briefly about the size of the crowd, the lovely view, and the success of the day's activities. Like an expert party host, Charles left our table and deftly moved on to the next group, amicably greeting each guest as if they were the most important person in the bar.

"Do you know how the Victors came to own this building?" I asked Trevor.

"I have no idea," he replied.

"Like I said, I was talking to them yesterday after filming the walk-through, and they told me they actually inherited the hotel from her reclusive uncle."

"Seriously?"

"Apparently, Jazelle's Uncle Leo, a long-standing resident of Marceline and owner of this building, was known for enjoying a good party and a stiff drink. Years ago, on the way home from a night of celebration, Jazelle's aunt and uncle passed over a set of railroad tracks they had crossed a thousand times, only this time, they were met by an oncoming train and wound up in a horrific accident. Jazelle's Aunt Margret did not survive, but her Uncle Leo, although no one could explain how, was found unscathed, only without any recollection of the accident. Even though the night was stormy with rain pouring from the sky and zero visibility, her cousins blamed their father for their mother's untimely death and refused to have anything to do with him after the accident. Falling into a deep depression, her Uncle Leo lived the rest of his life as a recluse, never leaving his home. Only a neighbor who brought him groceries, a doctor who made house calls, and Jazelle's mother, her Uncle Leo's favorite sister, were admitted in to see him. The tenants in the street-level shops ran themselves, paying their rents on time, but the upstairs rooms of the building that he once so proudly owned became vacant and neglected. Jazelle's mother would drive from Kansas City every month to check on her brother and try to coax him out of the house, but to no avail. After years of routinely driving to Marceline, Jazelle's mother was diagnosed with breast cancer. When she succumbed to the disease, Jazelle followed in her mother's footsteps, driving from Kansas City to Marceline once a month to check on her Uncle Leo. She never minded the trip because she was quite fond of her unassuming uncle. Five years ago, Uncle Leo passed away and, in his will, he left all his property to Jazelle. Her and Charles hadn't known what to do with this old building and were considering putting it on the market when they were approached about joining the venture to renovate and reopen the hotel as part of the *Main Street* series and decided to move forward and give operating a hotel a try."

"You amaze me, Jess! You've met these people, what five times, and you know their life story. I can barely remember their names. No wonder everyone becomes your friend," Trevor said, not hiding his awe.

"Thank you," I whispered, touched by his compliment.

"It must be nice to inherit a chunk of property," Trevor remarked after a moment of comfortable silence. "I wouldn't mind having that kind of long, lost uncle."

"Me either," I agreed. "My only uncle is a mail carrier whose children adore him, so I don't believe I'll have any luck there."

"Why would you need to inherit anything? Aren't your parents loaded?"

"What made you think I come from money," I said, laughing out loud.

"I don't know, just different hints you've dropped from time to time."

"Really, like what?" I asked, truly surprised.

"I've heard you talk about the villa your family owns and the expensive wine you drink when you are with them."

I had forgotten how Trevor used to eavesdrop over the partition in our L.A. office. And that's the only place he could have heard such nonsense.

"My mother has always jokingly referred to our house as 'The Villa'. My parent's home is the exact opposite. It's comfortable, full of love, and a place where all are welcome, but it is no mansion. It's a simple, three-bedroom ranch with a crappy yard and absolutely no view. And I hate to disappoint you, but they often drink wine out of the box. How is that for loaded?" I said, setting him straight.

"Come on, Jess. Who gives their daughter a diamond bracelet just because they are leaving for six months?"

"Mine," I said defensively. "They wanted something to remind me of them when I was miles away, so they gave me this bracelet to wear on my wrist at all times, keeping them close by my side, day or night. I found the gesture to be thoughtful, kind and touching."

"So, are there any other 'hints' you would like me to clear up, since we are on the subject?" I ask sarcastically, not liking the direction this was heading, at all.

"Don't get offended, Jess. I guess I misinterpreted a couple things you've said over the past few months, but when you mention you have been all over the world, or you put yourself through college to prove you didn't need Daddy to take care of you, or you pay Cassandra to find you the best place to stay in Marceline, what am I supposed to think?"

"Okay, none of that is true. I've hardly been off the West Coast except to Florida, once," I said, when it dawned on me why he thought I was a world traveler. "You heard me talking to Taylor, didn't you?"

"I honestly don't remember who you were talking to," he replied.

"I told her about seeing Hidden Mickey's all over the world because I was in Epcot! In Disney World! Secondly, I paid my own way through college, so I could prove to myself that I was mature enough to take care of me – not because I stubbornly didn't want Daddy's money. And lastly, the idea that I would pay off Cassandra – that, I will not even dignify with an answer."

"Jess, you asked, and so I'm just telling you what I saw. It doesn't matter how much money your family has. I'm sorry I've gotten you upset. I was only making a comment about how it would be nice to have a rich uncle, that's all," he explained, setting down his empty drink glass and reaching for my hand.

"I'm sorry, too, I guess I overreacted."

"How about we go back to your place and make up?" he suggested, smiling sheepishly.

And it was that look of his that I just couldn't resist, even if I wanted to.

Trying to shake off our last conversation and return to what had started out to be a pleasant evening, I replied, "Now that's a good idea!"

CHAPTER 29

Finishing my meeting with Darryl Smith, I looked at the clock on my phone and was relieved to see I was just in time to give Trevor a quick good-bye before he left for Denver and his three-day weekend of official Uncle Trevor duties. I could not believe how fast time was flying. It was already September, and I could feel my time in Marceline beginning to wind down.

Darryl, Taylor and I had spent the afternoon looking through copious numbers of catalogs, choosing the perfect glass front for the new Fresh Express Market. Our final design included white colonial style grids on the full-length windows, which would wrap around the front and sides of the Market's inset entrance. A full-glass door with a dark charcoal frame, for contrast, would lead customers into the airy shop and bistro.

Pieces were gradually falling into place for our third and final renovation.

I text Trevor and we agreed to meet behind The Uptown Center, where his already-packed motorcycle was parked and ready to ride. He was anxious to be on his way, so he could reach Denver before nightfall.

"Thanks for waiting," I said breathlessly, having run across the street to find him sitting on his bike grinning at a text on his phone, probably from his brother.

Stepping forward, I wrapped my arms around his neck.

He promptly returned his phone to the pocket of his leather jacket.

"I'm glad I'm not too late to give you a proper good-bye. Another minute and you would have had your helmet on, and I wouldn't have been able to do this," I said, leaning in and giving him a long, deep kiss, the kind that I hoped would make him regret not asking me to tag along.

"I'll miss you," I said as we slowly moved apart.

"You won't either," he said and laughed. "You and Kaitlin will be so busy, you will forget all about me."

"Not going to happen," I countered. "Unfortunately, Kaitlin's not planning for us to return home until late Sunday, so I guess I won't see you until Monday morning at work, which seems like a long time from now."

"Mondays always come quickly. It will be here before you know it."

"I guess you're right," I reluctantly agreed. "Have fun with your family. And no matter what you think, I'm still going to miss you."

I gave him one final kiss and watched as he put on his helmet, started up his motorcycle and sped out of town.

• • •

I was still disappointed at not being asked to travel with Trevor to Denver, but at least I wouldn't be sitting home alone all weekend. Kaitlin suggested I accompany her home, to St. Louis, for a college sorority sister's low-key bachelorette party.

The Wonderful World of Marceline

Even if it wasn't my first choice, it should be a fun weekend. Kaitlin and I always had a good time together. It was to be a short trip, leaving Saturday morning and returning Sunday night, which meant I only had to arrange dog sitting for two days.

Arriving earlier than I am out of bed on a typical Saturday, Kaitlin let herself in, knowing I would still be frantically packing some last-minute items.

"Are you ready?" she called down the hall.

Rushing out of my bedroom with wet hair and a half-open Kate Spade overnight bag, I saw her bend down and offer Cooper a small treat.

"You spoil him, you know," I said, cramming my belongings into the overstuffed bag and making it possible, but not easy, to finally close the zipper. "My vet advises me to limit the number of treats I give him, if I want to keep him healthy."

"Your vet is very wise, but I'm not your vet right now. I'm Cooper's self-appointed Godmother, and I can give him treats if I want."

"You better not say that too loud or he'll expect birthday and Christmas presents too," I remarked over my shoulder as I ran into the kitchen to make sure all of the appliances were off and the back door was locked.

"I'm ready," I announced, returning to the front room.

"You be a good boy for Emily and Olivia," I said in doggie speak, hugging and squeezing Cooper until he wiggled out of my arms.

The twins down the street loved Cooper, so I was comfortable that he was in capable hands for the next two days. That their mom was a registered nurse was an added bonus. *How much difference can there be between dogs and humans?*

Kaitlin filled me in on her friends as we made the three-hour trip from Marceline to St. Louis. Brianna, the bride-to-be, was divorced a couple of years ago from Ryan, a guy they all despised and could never understand her attraction to in the first place. When she married Ryan, they threw her a big – rent a party bus and stay out past the time the bars close – celebration. This time, the events, including her and Nathan's (hubby No. 2) destination wedding, were much more restrained. The bachelorette party was actually more of an excuse to get a group of sorority sisters together than to celebrate Brianna's upcoming nuptials.

"So, you know, someone at the party will probably ask you where you went to high school."

"Why would they ask me that? I'm sure they have never heard of my high school in Los Angeles."

"True, but I may have failed to mention that you're from out-of-town. It's an unofficial St. Louis thing, an icebreaker of sorts. People from outside the area find it odd, but locals use it as a way to make a common connection. St. Louis is like a small town wrapped in a big city. It's sort of like the six degrees of Kevin Bacon, only in St. Louis, it is more like three degrees. A lot of people live their entire lives in the St. Louis area, so when someone learns where you grew up or which high school you attended, they often realize you know some of the same people and voilà, now you're friends for life."

"I've never visited St. Louis. I hope I get a glimpse of The Gateway Arch," I said, a not-so-subtle hint. "You never see a picture of the city without that monument in the background, and it looks so big and shiny. Is it truly as awesome as it appears?"

"I've grown up around it, so I guess I take it for granted. When people from outside the city visit, they seem to think it is, so yes, I guess The Arch is as awesome as it appears. Unfortunately, we don't have time on this trip to go inside and to the top, but I'll make sure we drive through downtown before we leave so you can at least see its shiny silver legs rising up from the waterfront. But you do know what that means, don't you?"

"No," I answered warily.

"It means that since we don't have time to properly explore The Arch on this trip, you'll have to come back and visit us in Missouri, after you return to California. You know, we have tons of great attractions besides The Arch. We have a world-renowned botanical garden, one of the top zoos in the country located in historic Forest Park, a New Cathedral filled with more mosaics than anywhere else in the world, The Wheel which gives a different view of the cityscape. I could go on and on with things to do, and I haven't even mentioned the great food, some of which you will get to sample tonight," she paused for a breath. "Am I convincing you to not be a stranger and visit us, from time to time?"

"Why, yes, Miss Tour Guide, I believe you have," I said and laughed. "I must admit, even though it is very different from home and there are definitely things I miss about living in L.A., I've liked Missouri much better than I would have ever thought possible."

"Well, having you around has been a real boost for Marceline, and I guarantee you, I'm not the only person who believes that."

"Stop it! You're going to make me sad to leave," I replied.

"It's amazing how a small town like Marceline can seep into your soul and actually change you as person. At least, it did for me," Kaitlin reflected.

"I know what you mean," I murmured as we exited the highway and entered the stomping grounds of Kaitlin's youth.

Astonished, as we drove down side streets and eventually pulled into her family's driveway, I was struck by how similar Kaitlin's neighborhood was to my parents'.

"We're here," Kaitlin announced, unfastening her seatbelt and hopping out of the driver's seat.

We grabbed our bags, and I followed her to a brightly painted yellow front door, where she inserted her key and let us inside.

"Anybody home?" she yelled, wiping her feet on the entryway rug and comfortably slipping off her sneakers.

Kaitlin's mom appeared around the corner, drying her hands on a dish towel, with a smile the size of the Grand Canyon spread across her face.

"You made it! I just finished baking cookies. Come get some while they are still warm."

I had not eaten anything that morning, and the aroma of the fresh baked cookies was making my stomach growl.

"Mom, this is Jess. Jess, this is my mom, Michelle." Kaitlin introduced us.

"Nice to meet you." I lifted my hand to shake hers and decided the gesture was too formal, so I turned it into a small wave. *Now, I just look goofy.*

"Thanks for having me this weekend," I said, trying to recover and appear somewhat normal.

"It's our pleasure. Anything to get Kaitlin home for a few days."

Before tackling the warm cookies waiting for us in the kitchen, we took our bags to our bedrooms. Looking around my room, I surmised that little redecorating had been done since Kaitlin moved away years ago. Painted a pale pink, the room was filled with white French provincial furniture, a chintz patterned bedspread and ruffled curtains. I knew Kaitlin had an older sister and assumed this must have been her room, at some point. According to Kaitlin, her niece, who visits from Philadelphia, would not let them touch her 'princess room'. And although I felt I had stepped back in time, I also felt the warmth of the happy family living in this house. I reached for my bracelet, missing my own mom and dad.

The Wonderful World of Marceline

We ate some delicious chocolate chip cookies while visiting with Kaitlin's parents. Her dad, having come in from working outside, joined us for our snack. They were interested in learning about my transition from Los Angeles to Marceline and shared with me how much they enjoyed Episode 1 of *Main Street* and wanted to hear all about Episode 2, set to air next week.

After giving ourselves a sugar high from too many cookies, Kaitlin's dad went back to his weed whacking, and the three of us moved into the dining room where Kaitlin's mom had littered the entire table with family photos. She was tackling the monumental task of transitioning all their old family pictures from prints to digital photos.

No one would be eating dinner in this room any time soon, I thought to myself.

We started rooting through the stacks and couldn't stop laughing as we flipped through pictures of Kaitlin from baby to awkward tween, completely rearranging Michelle's organized piles, to her mock displeasure. I was having so much fun with Kaitlin and her mom that the afternoon flew by in a flash and, before we knew it, it was time to primp for our evening out with Kaitlin's college friends.

We made our way to a small Italian neighborhood affectionately called 'The Hill' (although the area appeared pretty flat to me). The streets were narrow, and there were no empty parking spaces anywhere near the restaurant. Circling the same blocks a few times, we finally grabbed a spot from a customer leaving and wound up, luckily, parking only a few blocks away.

Walking to the restaurant, I discovered we were in the middle of an older neighborhood with a smattering of homes, corner restaurants and bars, Italian grocers and bakeries. The scent of baked goods escaping from one doorway to the next made my mouth water. Obviously, food was important in this part of town.

Wanting to meet in a location where they could talk, it was decided to have dinner first, then proceed to the bars to toast Bride-To-Be Brianna, and listen to live music. At a long table, set up in a small room off the main dining area, we found twelve of Kaitlin's college friends already chatting away with drinks in their hands and appetizers on the way.

I was a little nervous that I wouldn't fit in, but everyone was warm and welcoming, and I quickly began to relax and enjoy myself.

Once they found out I had never been there, they immediately took over my dinner selection, making me try the toasted ravioli (a St. Louis original – amazing) and recommending I order the Italian salad (homemade fresh dressing – amazing), warm bread (with crispy edges – amazing), and the *Vitello con Gamberetti* (with a side of Pasta Carbonara – amazing).

This had to be the best Italian food I had ever tasted and that included my mom's lasagna!

I was so full I could hardly breathe, but after a satisfying meal, we were on the move to the Soulard area for more of a party atmosphere and to start the real celebration.

"I hope you had a good time, even though you didn't know anyone," Kaitlin said as we walked the three blocks to our car.

"I did," I answered. "Your friends made me feel like I was one of them. It was nice."

"Did anyone ask you where you went to high school?" she chuckled.

"No, but Janie told me she has some big shot aunt who lives in L.A. and wondered if I'd ever heard of her. I told her, politely, that Los Angeles is a big place and regrettably I didn't know her aunt. She laughed it off remarking that it was probably a silly question and then started telling me about a trip she took to California last summer and how much she loved the sun and the beach."

"That's Janie. One of the nicest people you would ever want to meet. She's super book-smart, but unfortunately, it doesn't always transfer to commonsense."

"So, in a second, I need you to look off to your left," Kaitlin abruptly changed the subject as we drove toward our next rendezvous point.

Coasting over the crest of a hill, the shining curved light of The Gateway Arch stretched into view, rising into the blue-black sky like a silver talisman guarding the city.

"It is as awesome as it appears in pictures!" I gushed. "I can't believe how tall it looks."

"You really get a sense of how towering the structure is when you stand at the base of one of the legs and look straight up. It makes a person feel truly small."

I stared at the monument for the rest of our short drive as it popped in and out of view. I don't know if it was the engineering feat, or the way it shined in the night sky, or that it was such an American icon, but something about it fascinated me, and I couldn't seem to look away.

By the time we arrived at our destination, the bar was packed, and the music was blaring. Weaving our way through the crowd, we somehow found our group without too much difficulty, gathered directly in front of the band.

I was glad we had met for a quiet dinner first because the only way for us to converse in this space was by yelling over the excessive noise. You could almost hear a collective sigh throughout the room when the band finally took a break between sets.

We stayed for a few hours and agreed that not being in our early twenties anymore, the bar scene had lost some of its luster, and when the band resumed its deafening tirade, we decided to leave.

• • •

After sleeping in and devouring an enormous brunch (*I may never eat again!*), Kaitlin and I hit the road for our return trip to Marceline.

We had to make a stop in Columbia, at the University of Missouri Veterinary Health Center, to restock supplies and medicines Kaitlin dispensed in her clinic for pets and livestock alike. The VHC was a required stop for Kaitlin anytime she went home.

Having completed our errand, we left Interstate 70 for Missouri Route 5, the smaller state highway which led directly into the heart of Marceline. Lush pastures full of livestock, ripe cornfields ready for harvest, and framed farmhouses on acres of land moved past my passenger window. I had such a new appreciation for their simple beauty.

"I've been there," I pointed in the direction of a large warehouse-style building coming up on our right.

I had not realized until then that I had been on this particular road. "Taylor and I had fun picking flooring and other items for The Uptown Performing Arts Center in that store. I couldn't believe all the interesting choices they had in their showroom, not to mention the décor options. It's funny, I think over time, our roles have reversed. I earned a degree in television, but I have fallen in love with decorating, and Taylor has an interior design degree, but she has fallen in love with the filming portion of our assignment."

"Life does seem to take us in directions we could never plan, but the unexpected is what makes it fun, don't you agree?" Kaitlin asked.

I had never really thought about it, but Kaitlin had a point.

"You're right. For instance, I would have never dreamed while sitting in my little cubical in L.A. that I would be sent to film in a remote location, with a guy I had been lusting after for months, that said guy and I would become deeply involved, that I would love a job for which I was only semi-qualified; and I would make a new friend for life!"

"Deeply involved?" Kaitlin repeated me verbatim. "So, I take it you and Trevor are in a good place?"

"I haven't shared this with anyone, because Mollie, my usual confidant, for some reason doesn't seem to like Trevor, but I think once we're back in Los Angeles, Trevor and I have a real future. I know it's early, but I feel like we click ... like this relationship is different from others I've experienced. We're completely comfortable in each other's company. If we have a small disagreement, it doesn't last and we make up, which is blissful, I might add. He is so thoughtful, the way he took care of me when I hurt my ankle, and besides, I'm crazy about him."

"I'm happy for you, Jess, and I hope Trevor turns out to be everything you wish for. You deserve it," Kaitlin said sincerely.

"Now tell me about this doctor from the Brookfield Animal Hospital you are taking to the premiere in two weeks," I pried.

Kaitlin filled me in on Rory, her new love interest, and the rest of the drive sped by. Reaching Marceline in record time, we arrived as the autumnal sun was setting in the west, saturating the sky with the most spectacular hues of pinks, reds, and oranges.

On a whim, we decided to end our weekend with a drink atop the Rooftop Garden, enjoying one of the last beautiful evenings before sweater weather took hold.

Exiting the elevator, it was obvious we were not the only people who had chosen to spend this pleasant evening outdoors. Stopping at the bar to order our drinks, I scanned the empty tables looking for the best view of the still vibrant sunset.

I caught the back of a sun-bleached blond head talking intimately to a raven-haired beauty sitting off in a corner, as if in their own little world.

"Trevor?!" I exclaimed, striding in their direction.

"Jess," he looked up startled. "I thought you were in St. Louis," he responded, sitting back in his chair and releasing his hand from Samantha Biggs' hand.

"I thought you were in Denver," I countered.

"I was, but I got home earlier this afternoon, so Samantha and I decided to get a quick drink and discuss some future projects we're developing. Sam, you remember Jess, from our firm."

"Hello, Jess, nice to see you again."

Samantha Biggs greeted me with a voice as smooth as her perfectly tailored, silk shirt.

I couldn't believe how calmly the two of them were sitting together, smiling at me like this was a perfectly normal scene when my heart was racing, at what had to be, an unhealthy rate.

"I can see what type of projects you two are developing," I said to Trevor and quickly turned away from him so he couldn't see the tears brimming in my eyes.

Then, I practically sprinted to the exit.

Kaitlin instantly met me at the elevator where I was frantically jabbing the down button, wondering why, when there were only two other floors, it was taking so long.

"Let's get out of here," she said and grabbed my arm as the door finally opened to take us back to ground level.

"I feel so foolish," I said as we got into her car. "Wasn't I just saying how I thought I had a future with that jerk?"

Tears began to stream uncontrollably down my cheeks. "How I could have been so wrong?"

I felt as if I'd fallen, hit my head, and finally jolted my mind into seeing what people close to me had been hinting at for a while. "At least now Mollie can say 'I told you so'."

"First of all, Mollie is not going to say, 'I told you so'. She is going to wish your heart wasn't breaking and that she could be with you right now. And who knows, maybe there is a perfectly good explanation for Trevor being out with the snooty Ms. Biggs tonight."

"He was holding her hand and practically sitting in her lap," I argued. "He referred to me as 'Jess, from our firm'. I think the explanation is pretty clear."

Pulling in my driveway, Kaitlin, like the good friend she had become, suggested coming inside with me and keeping me company for a while. I thanked her for the offer and the lovely weekend, but I told her I actually preferred to be alone, if she didn't mind.

I let myself into the quiet house, dropped my keys on the side table, and bent down to pet Cooper, who was patiently waiting to greet me at the door. Clearly, the girls had completely spoiled him while I was gone, because although he was happy to see me, he was not jumping on me ecstatically, as if he had been neglected for the past two days.

After unpacking my overnight bag, I changed into my most comfortable, I-feel-sorry-for-myself lounge pants with an oversized T-shirt. And then I went for the carton of Rocky Road I had stashed in the back of the freezer. Spoon and tub in hand, I made for the couch to indulge my sorrows with chocolate, marshmallow, and almond pieces, all swirled into creamy decadence.

"I guess it's just us again." I said to Mona, whose leaves had listened to my sob stories before. "I don't think you ever liked Trevor either, since he refused to sit next to you when we watched television. That alone should have told me he wasn't 'the one'. So, tell me, how is it everyone, except me, saw Trevor for what he truly was? Even Cooper never warmed up to him, and he loves everybody! But you want to know what the real problem is Mona? The real problem is that I really, really liked him," I said as my phone, lying next to the lid of my half-eaten container of ice cream, unexpectedly rang.

"It's Trevor. Should I answer it or let him sweat?" I asked the ever-pragmatic Mona. "If he's calling rather than texting me tonight, he must be feeling bad."

Letting the phone ring several times was about as much sweating as I made him experience. I never had been good at playing games.

"Hello," I answered, trying my best to sound unaffected by the evening's events.

"Hey, Jess. Sorry about tonight. I planned on telling you the next time we were together, but I just don't think it's working out between us. I didn't mean for you to find out this way, honestly."

"I didn't realize you felt that way. It didn't appear that you were having any doubts last weekend when we came back to my place."

"We've had some good times while we've been stuck in Marceline, but it's not like we made any commitments to each other, and I think it's time for us both to move on."

"You are the one always preaching about not making friends with people in the area when we are leaving here in a few weeks, so why all of the sudden are you hooking up with someone outside of L.A.? Is it because she has money, and I don't?" I asked and then laughed at the absurdity.

There was nothing but silence on the other end of the line.

Seriously?! I couldn't believe I had just guessed his true motives. I wasn't rich, so I was out. Samantha Biggs was loaded, so she was in.

"You're kidding me," I admonished. "You are so shallow! You are actually admitting that you're chasing her money! She'll figure you out much quicker than I did, I promise you."

"No, you've got it all wrong," he stumbled, trying to cover his guilt-by-omission. "The show's ratings have been high enough that USAMade is setting up our next *Main Street* location, and Sam and I are going to be working closely on this next production. We see eye-to-eye on how we fit into these small towns and the difference the show can make for their communities. We've made a real connection."

"Well, I'm happy for you. I hope you and *Sam* get what you deserve. Good luck Trevor," I said and promptly ended the call.

CHAPTER 30

I spent the next week following my new routine: going to work, avoiding Trevor, coming home, preparing dinner, and watching documentaries on Nat Geo. I saw no one and text little. Cooper kept giving me the 'It's not raining, why won't you take me for a walk?' look, but for once, it wasn't working.

By Sunday, I decided it was time for the pity party to end and so, I took a long, hot shower – not the jump in, jump out version I had called a shower all week – and put on a light sweater and jeans. The weather had cooled, and it felt like fall in the crisp outside air.

Grabbing a pair of casual boots from the closet, I saw my beautiful, deep red dress, on its hanger, waiting for next weekend's premiere. The town was in a mad frenzy preparing Main Street for its special guests, but unlike the town, I had lost all sense of enthusiasm for the event. Since I wouldn't be wearing the dress any time soon, having firmly decided not to attend the premiere, I pushed it to the back of the closet. I had no desire to see Trevor and Samantha together and, although Kaitlin had practically begged me to go with her and Rory, I had been the third wheel enough times with Mollie and Justin to know how uncomfortable that could be.

Walking around in a fog for the past week, I had forgotten to empty the junk mail out of my mailbox and therefore was served a sticky note, on my screen door, letting me know I would not receive any more valuable flyers and advertisements until I emptied the mailbox standing on the curb of my driveway.

Going outside to complete my civic duty, I heard my named called by Ida, who was rocking, as usual, on her porch.

I could never resist her invitations, so I climbed the steps and plopped down in my rocker.

"I haven't seen you all week. I was starting to get worried about you."

"It's been a long week," I admitted. "I know you visit with your daughter on Sundays and will be leaving soon, so I won't bother you with the details."

"You are never a bother, dear. Besides, they won't be here for a while yet. Why don't you tell me what's bothering you."

I filled her in on Trevor – from where I thought our relationship was headed, to his betrayal, and my desire for the premiere and frankly, this job, to be over. Surprisingly, it felt good to share with someone who was impartial and wise.

She listened without interruption. And just as I finished my long narrative, Chance pulled up in front of her house. Not seeing any downed tree limbs or 'beautification' needs, I wondered if he was here to fix something inside her house. I hadn't talked to her all week and now, I felt guilty because she probably needed help with a repair, and I had been holed up in my own little world, moping about, when my neighbor needed help.

"Hi, Jess," Chance said, walking past me and straight to Ida.

He leaned down and gave Ida a kiss on the cheek and uttered, "Hi, Grandma."

I about fell out of my rocker.

CHAPTER 31

"Chance is your grandson?" I asked, astonished, looking from Ida to Chance and back to Ida again.

"Why yes, dear," she answered, as if it was the most obvious statement she had ever made.

"Ida is your grandmother?" I repeated. "But your last name is Alexander and Ida's last name is Jenkins."

I was so confused.

"My middle name is Jenkins, and my mom's maiden name is Jenkins, if that helps," he said.

And then he gave me that silly smile, which aggravated me to the core.

"You mean Kathy is your mom?" I asked, trying to put it altogether. "How did I never know this, living next to your grandmother for the past five months?"

I then turned to Ida. "And you let me sit in this rocker, multiple times a week, sharing my stories, including one about the Allen Hotel's infamous ghost, which your grandson made up at my expense, and you never said a word!"

As if to make matters worse, she promptly began divulging my private rant from this afternoon to an unwitting Chance. "Jess was filling me on that scoundrel she's been dating. Caught him lusting after that fancy girl who lives up in the Biggs' mansion. Now, she says she's not going to the premiere. Have you ever heard of such rubbish?"

"I'm not going to the premiere," I said indignantly. "I'm staying in my little house until it's time to move back to California and forget this whole disastrous experience!"

"You don't mean that, Jess," Chance calmly responded, taking his grandmother's side. "If you hadn't come to Marceline, you wouldn't have Cooper, you wouldn't have met Kaitlin, and you wouldn't have made a difference for a whole lot of people from a small town in the middle of Missouri."

"Like who?" I questioned. "I'm sure you're not referring to people who don't tell me they are related to my next-door neighbor or my next-door neighbor who doesn't tell me she is the grandmother to a guy I work with, who magically appears out of nowhere to repeatedly laugh at me."

"Jess, you know that's not true. I don't know how many times I have to tell you, I'm never laughing at you. What you do is make me smile from the inside, out. Every time I happen to run into you, it makes my day. You are warm, funny and, apart from today, the most optimistic person I have ever met. You know, I would be honored to escort you to the premiere," he offered sincerely.

"Thanks for the offer. And I appreciate the pity invite, but I'm not going."

"Will you at least thing about it?" Ida implored.

"No!" I answered emphatically.

And without saying good-bye, I took myself back home to continue sulking.

● ● ●

I should have never fallen for the letter carrier's subpoena to empty my mailbox, I thought the next day. Not only would I have never shared my plight with Ida, but now, when I got home from work, I wouldn't have any mail, either.

Today's post contained not only the usual ads and flyers, but an actual piece of real mail. A lone card, tucked inside the circulars, fell to the floor as I went to throw the junk mail into the recycle bin. Addressed to me, the card contained no stamp or return address.

Curious, I slowly opened the envelope and before reading the sentiment, flipped to the inside to see who had sent me the mysterious greeting.

The blank page was filled with a singular sentence:

Please be my date on Saturday, Chance.

Ugh! Flipping to the front of the card, I saw the caricature of an old-fashioned typewriter, pictured with the text, *I know I push your buttons sometimes*, and the single word, *Sorry*, typed on a sheet of paper scrolling from the top of the machine.

Date. On Saturday. *Not a chance in hell*! I dumped the card straight into the trash.

Not only was he a man, and I had decided to swear off the male species for the rest of my life (I even looked into a Franciscan convent in L.A. that allowed you to have a pet – although I think they also preferred you were Catholic, but I could work on that. I grew up Methodist. How different could they be?), but also, Chance had deceived me – just like Trevor. *Okay, maybe not exactly like Trevor.* Chance didn't two-time me right in front of my face after he realized I wasn't an heiress to some imaginary fortune, but he wasn't completely honest either and that's important to me. To be fair, I guess the subject of him being Ida's grandson never really came up, but Ida could have told me. *I'm beginning to think she was hoping to match-make us all along and was just waiting for the perfect moment.*

Tuesday didn't get much better.

Pulling in my driveway, I noticed the dead flowers had been removed from my window boxes and replaced with deep purple miniature mums. Although I was happy to see that the landlord was tiding up the house for the next renter, I found it odd that he had inserted a large red bow in the middle of the vibrant annuals.

On closer inspection, I spotted a card peeking out from within the buds of the new plants with the word *Jess* printed across the envelope. This card, with a bouquet of beautiful flowers gracing its front, was void of text. Written on the inside was the following:

> *Purple flowers symbolize grace and charm. That's you! Please will you be my date Saturday, Chance.*

I went to throw this card in the recycle bin with the one from yesterday, but then I saw the card, with the picture of the typewriter, lying on the floor next to the bin.

Odd. I must have missed the trash when I hastily disposed of it.

I picked up yesterday's card and set it, with today's note, on the counter. Smiling to myself, I decided that maybe it was a sign that I shouldn't so easily discard (no pun intended) Chance's kind gestures.

By Wednesday, when I arrived home from work, I looked for a sign that Chance had been by my house and left me another message. When I didn't locate any trace of a card or note, I was surprisingly disappointed.

Still in my moping routine, I prepared some frozen chicken strips and a fresh salad and sat down with my fancy cuisine to watch a rerun of *Great Migrations* on Nat Geo. (It seemed like a perfect choice since that was what I would be doing in a couple of weeks, migrating southwest. Except in my case, it was for the rest of my life. I had no intention of migrating north again, ever. I was done with adventures!)

The red crabs were making their way to the beach for breeding season when my phone pinged. I picked it up and noticed an unfamiliar number displayed on my screen. Even though I didn't recognize a number, I'm not the sort of person who can ignore a call or text, so I clicked open the message, which said:

> *Hope you don't mind, my Grandma gave me your number. Now you have mine, so if you change your mind about going with me Saturday, shoot me a text day or night.*

(The text was followed by a GIF of Gene Wilder as Willie Wonka screaming, *"The suspense is terrible!"*, which played over and over.)

This time, I actually laughed out loud.

Chance's attempts at persuasion had become a game, and I was looking forward to his next move, although I still had no intention of going to the premiere.

So, when I arrived home from work Thursday, it was no surprise when I saw a package on my front step.

I jumped out of the car, anxious to see what was inside. I read the note first:

> *I remember you telling me, when you need advice, you and your houseplant have a heart to heart and before you know it, all your problems are solved. A little gift for your plant (sorry, I can't remember its name) in hopes that if I can't persuade you to go with me Saturday, your trusted, therapist plant can!*

I peeked inside the bag and found a giant canister of plant food.

I had to give it to the guy, he was creative!

Anxious for Chance's next hidden message, I left work Friday afternoon in the best mood I had been in for weeks. I had managed to operate from various remote locations and had therefore spent little time at the actual Fresh Express Market renovation site. Happily, that had allowed me to avoid both Trevor and Chance all week.

As I approached Betty, I saw a note waiting for me on my windshield, tucked under the driver side wiper blade. I unfolded it and immediately recognized Chance's strong, masculine handwriting scrolling across the page. It was fairly long, so I decided to wait until I got home and was relaxed on my porch to read it.

I may have driven home much quicker than normal and practically pushed Cooper out the back door, but soon I was enjoying the cool breeze blowing through the screens of my porch, and with a 'start to the weekend' cocktail (okay, beer) in my hand, I began to read:

Dear Jess,

This is the last time I will bother you, but I want you to understand how honored I would be to escort you to tomorrow night's premiere. This is not a 'pity invite' as you so eloquently called it, it is a sincere wish that you will grace this simple, country boy with your beautiful presence.

Since your arrival last May, you've affected this town in ways you can't even imagine. Every person you've met has become a new friend; acquaintances are always greeted with your contagious smile; and old, empty buildings have turned into beautiful, thriving businesses. Marceline will not shine as brightly, in its finest hour, without you.

Tomorrow night is great publicity for Marceline, but it is also a tribute to you! You made this happen! Please don't watch from the sidelines. Let me show you all that you have accomplished and all the good you have achieved. You are a caring, smart, but most of all, strong woman. My wish is for you to hold you head high, enter that theater tomorrow night and show the world the Jess I get to see every day.

I will be on your porch steps, gently knocking on your screen door, at 8 o'clock sharp. If you answer, you will make me the happiest man alive. If you don't, I will understand, and not bother you again. Please think about it. I hope, with all of my heart, you answer that door and allow me to escort the most amazing girl in Marceline down that timeless red carpet.

Chance

Why is he so nice?! I was mad. I was hurting. And I didn't want to go to the premiere! But who was heartless enough to ignore a letter like the one I had just read?

I had twenty-four hours to make up my mind. I would usually have text Mollie or called Kaitlin, but I knew what they would both say. Besides, I needed to make this decision on my own.

Really, what was the point? I was leaving in a couple of weeks, but on the other hand, it was only one date.

● ● ●

I awoke on Saturday morning as confused as I was when I went to bed the night before. After weighing all the pros and cons of attending the premiere – and unfortunately, the pluses and minuses were equaling out to an even fifty-fifty – I spent the day running and rerunning over different scenes from the past six months.

Before I knew it, it was seven o'clock, and I needed to make my final decision.

If I was going, it was time to get ready. If I wasn't going, it was time to climb into my comfy clothes, grab my newest sulking flavor, Cookies and Cream, and hide under a blanket.

CHAPTER 32

I heard a light knock at exactly eight o'clock, covered my ears, and shook away the doubt of my decision.

Taking one last look in the mirror, I quickly moved to answer the door before I lost my nerve and changed my mind.

Standing before me was Chance, looking like I had never seen him before. Dressed in a black, slim-fitted suit with a burgundy and black striped tie extending from his starched white shirt, he literally took my breath away.

A matching handkerchief peeked out from his breast pocket, and stylish cuff links were visible as he stretched out his hand, like a complete gentleman would, to help me down the front steps.

"You look stunning," he gushed as he reached for my other hand and then took two steps back to get a better look.

My garnet, high-low, asymmetrical evening dress matched perfectly with his ensemble, as if we had purposely coordinated our attire. I had decided to wear my hair in a sleek chignon, to emphasize the tiny sequins on the lace bodice, and I had added small diamonds to my ears to compliment the bracelet gleaming on my wrist.

Standing in front of Chance in my four-inch, silver, open toe-stilettos, I looked up at him and smiled.

Even I had to admit, we looked pretty good together.

"Thanks for being persistent," I conceded.

"Thanks for answering the door," he replied.

"This is the one time I wish I owned a car," he admitted as we walked to his truck, and he attentively opened the passenger door and offered me a hand up into the cab. "You are too lovely to be climbing into a pickup truck."

"Thank you, but I don't mind," I said as I slid into the passenger seat.

Turning my head, I saw Ida standing on her front porch, smiling broadly. She raised her hand in a brief wave, and I returned her gesture. She really was an amazing lady, who had, I was discovering, an equally amazing grandson.

We reached the premiere after most of the fanfare had taken place. My guess was Chance planned it that way, knowing my skepticism about attending.

Walking the red carpet into the freshly decorated lobby, we headed straight to our designated seats.

Jude Law and other cast members were sitting in a sectioned off part of the theater and, as always, I wasn't even remotely star struck. Apparently, though, I was in the minority, because I noticed people discreetly pointing to the group as if they were caged animals in the city zoo.

Suddenly, the lights dimmed, the stars overhead illuminated, and for dramatic effect, the screen lowered from its hidden location in the ceiling. The long-awaited movie premiere had begun.

As it turned out, I enjoyed the film immensely. It was full of action and humor, yet stuck to the time-tested tale of *Peter Pan*. Everyone filed out of the theater praising the film, but instead of congregating in the lobby, the crowd left promptly for the reception at the Biggs' Mansion.

This being only the second time I had been to the estate, and the first at night, the mansion seemed have an aura surrounding it. With lights glowing through its tall, arched windows, it felt even more imposing than it had a few months prior when we had recently arrived in Marceline and were being introduced at the formal garden party.

Leaving the truck with a hired valet, I took Chance's arm as we made our way through the impressive entrance. A large crowd had gathered in what I was confident was once referred to as the Grand Ballroom. The space seemed to glimmer with its ornate gold leaf ceiling, opulent crystal chandelier, and stately gold columns adorned with intricate Corinthian capitals. A grand piano sat on a raised platform, emitting soft music in the corner.

Tuxedoed waiters were passing through the crowd, offering guests champagne and hors d'oeuvres from silver platters. Chance found us each a glass of champagne as I spied Kaitlin, looking stunning in her chic, black jumpsuit, with an attractive gentleman who must be the infamous Doctor Rory Ferguson.

"Do you mind if we mingle over by Kaitlin? I'm anxious to meet her date. I've heard all about him, but we've never met."

"Are you kidding? It would be my honor to walk the most beautiful girl here across the room."

He then offered me his arm.

I rolled my eyes at his compliment (although deep down, I admit, I was thrilled by his comment). He flashed me that irresistible crooked smile of his, and linking my arm in his, we strolled over the highly-polished, marble flooring toward Kaitlin and Dr. Ferguson.

Don't fall. Don't fall, don't fall.

Introductions were made all around, and we casually chatted as a group until Rory and Chance began passionately armchair quarterbacking about the Chiefs' defense and what improvements needed to occur, even though the team was predicted to be on the road to an outstanding season and perhaps a Super Bowl appearance.

"I'm so glad you decided to come to the premiere," Kaitlin said, squeezing my arm.

"I am, too. I don't know why I was being so stubborn."

"It would have been a shame to leave that dress hanging in the closet. You look incredible."

"Why, thank you, Ms. Andrews. You look rather elegant in your choice of evening attire as well," I replied in my best sophisticated voice.

"By the way, I haven't told you how much I appreciate you listening to me go on and on and on over the past couple of weeks. Thank you. To good friends," I said, tipping my champagne flute toward Kaitlin's.

"To great friends," she replied back, clinking my glass.

"I wish we could take a picture for Mollie, since she wouldn't let us purchase these gorgeous outfits without her approval. But unfortunately, I don't believe this is the venue for selfies," I said and chuckled.

"I know, I was looking for the photo booth with all the props when I came through those massive front doors, but I couldn't find one," Kaitlin said and then giggled.

"I also need to sneak a picture of Taylor, have you seen her?" I asked.

"No. What crazy design is she wearing tonight?"

"Remember that yellow dress with the feathers Mollie jokingly wanted me to buy when we were at The Plaza?"

"Noooo," Kaitlin replied, obviously remembering the hideous, faux canary outfit I threatened to wear as a bridesmaid's dress.

"Yes, but it's a little different, and it's absolutely stunning," I exclaimed, nodding my head in Taylor's direction.

Judging from Kaitlin's expression as she took in Taylor's bright yellow dress with flared skirt and one shoulder, feather-accented bodice, she agreed with me.

"How does she do it?" Katlin stared in amazement. "People would think I killed a bird in my care and turned it into a dress if I wore something like that, but instead, she looks like she belongs on the cover of a fashion magazine."

I started to reply when we were interrupted by Mr. Biggs' voice filling the large ballroom.

"Good evening, I would like to welcome each of you, especially our honored guests who thoroughly entertained us this evening in their latest hit, *Peter and Wendy*."

There was a brief round of applause before he continued.

Suddenly consumed by the view before me, I didn't hear anything beyond the intro of his speech.

On the platform, positioned in front of the grand piano, was Larry Biggs, flanked by his wife on one side and his glamourous daughter, Samantha, on the other, with her arm linked through a black-tied Trevor.

This is why I didn't want to leave my house tonight! My stomach was in a knot, and all I wanted to do was go home.

His address was short and to the point. But staring at the happy group in front of me, it felt as if it lasted for hours.

"How about we get out of here," I heard a male voice whisper in my ear as Mr. Biggs' speech ended and people returned to their private conversations.

Turning, I saw Chance looking sympathetically into my eyes.

"That is an outstanding idea," I said, feeling tears coming.

After saying a quick good-bye to Kaitlin and Rory, and with Chance's hand resting on the small of my back, we snaked through the crowd to the front doors, retrieved the truck from an idle valet attendant, and happily left the glowing mansion on the hill.

"It's still early. If you want me to take you home I will, but if you're up for it, I'd like to show you how one is supposed to spend a crisp, fall, Saturday night in the country. Not a staged event with pretentious stars and fancy speeches, but a night with real stars and genuine conversation."

"I'd like that very much," I said, realizing the last place I wanted to be was home alone.

We pulled into the nearest gas station with an attached convenience store.

"I know we're not dressed for it, but is beer okay?" Chance asked as he pulled into one of the empty parking spaces.

"I would actually love a beer. I'd choose beer over champagne anytime, how's that for sophisticated?" I laughed, and it felt so good to do so.

He opened the rear sliding window to let in some fresh air as he ran into the minimart and quickly returned with a six-pack of Bud Light bottles.

Leaving the gas station, we made our way back down the dark, two-lane country road. It was so empty it made me feel as if we were the only two people left in Marceline.

After a couple of miles, he turned onto an even more desolate roadway and then onto something that could only be described as a dirt path, where he eventually parked the truck.

Turning on the truck's radio, he found a mix of soft country and adjusted the volume so we would be able to hear it though the rear window. Opening his driver door, he hopped out and came around to my side of the truck, offering his hand as I climbed down from the cab. We walked to the back of the truck, where he lowered the tailgate. He sat on its edge and patted the area off to his right, suggesting I should join him.

"You've got to do what I say, okay?" he said as I sat next to him on the open tailgate. "You'll love it, trust me."

"You know that sounds like a line that should make me run for my life, don't you?"

"I'm not that kind of guy, I promise."

"I'm pretty sure that's what they all say," I said and laughed nervously.

"Okay, close your eyes and lay back in the truck bed. I get it, it sounds bad, but believe me, you won't be sorry."

I did as he said, partly because if he got out of line, he knew I would tell his grandmother, and I was pretty sure that was one person he never wanted to disappoint. I closed my eyes and slowly leaned back until my head rested on the bed of his truck.

"Okay, open your eyes," he directed.

I slowly opened my eyes and was staring at a kazillion stars in varying degrees of brightness shining down on me. From my vantage point, it was as if I was completely surrounded in a color deeper than black with gleaming lights making tiny pinpricks in the inky canvas. It made me feel ethereal. And here I thought the stars in my backyard, when I first arrived in Marceline, were spectacular, but compared to this, they were mediocre, at best.

Chance laid down beside me.

"You are right, I've never seen anything so beautiful!"

"Welcome to God's country," he said.

I chuckled to myself, remembering Trevor describing this area as 'godforsaken country'.

We lay in comfortable silence, listening to the song of the cicadas mixed with music drifting from the truck speakers, and stared at the vast universe stretching above us. After a few minutes, Chance sat up and removed the cap from one of the cold beers.

"Want one?"

"Thanks, that would be great," I said, reluctantly rising from my view of the night sky.

I took a sip of the refreshing cold beer as I adjusted my position on his tailgate, my silver stilettos dangling above a patch of uncut field grass. "Where are we anyway?"

"I own fifteen acres out here. We're on the back portion of my land," he told me as he removed his jacket and placed it over my shoulder.

"You were shaking," he added as he loosened his tie.

"You live out here?" I asked. "Doesn't it get lonely?"

"Not at all. I'm only ten minutes from town, and I prefer to call it peaceful rather than lonely."

"Wow, so where's your house?"

"On the other side of the hill that is impossible to see in the dark," he said and laughed. "It's what I like to call 'a work in progress'."

"What do you mean?"

"I've designed it so I can build it in stages. Right now, it's pretty small...a couple of bedrooms, kitchen, and living area. But the design is such that I can add on as I need or want. I'm actually really proud of it."

"You designed and built your own house?" I asked in awe.

"I am a carpenter from a family of carpenters – on my dad's side," he quickly added. "It's what we do."

"This town and its people never fail to surprise me," I announced, shaking my head. "I can't imagine someone back home building their own house. Instead, in Los Angeles, you would hire an agent to find you a sustainable architect, who would assign his assistants the task of drawing up eco-friendly plans, who would pass it on to a developer, who would have to acquire permits from the zoning commission, who in turn would have to procure the go-ahead from the city council. Then the developer would hire a construction team and would have to wait to start building until the project made it on the union docket, but of course that wouldn't happen until the construction workers ended their strike ... and so on and so on."

I sighed and said, "Everything here seems so much simpler."

"I'm not sure life has to be so complicated," he replied.

"I'm beginning to see that. Before I came to Marceline, I used to literally run to all my appointments, and I still wouldn't make it on time. I was always in a hurry, worried about being late. But living here, I've learned my life doesn't have to be in a constant whirlwind to accomplish all of my goals. I can relax on a porch, without feeling guilty, and enjoy watching the birds or reading a book and still be productive."

"And there's another difference," I continued, suddenly wanting to share all of my thoughts with him. "I used to need to be informed about all the latest fashion trends and how to advance in my career, or perform better in bed, from the all-knowing writers at *Cosmo*. Now I read books, with actual chapters! Granted most of them are fluffy chick lit, but some are historical fiction," I asserted. "Besides, I never said I wasn't a work in progress."

I briefly paused to catch my breath, but now that I was on a roll I couldn't seem to stop babbling.

"When I first moved here," I continued, "instead of telling you I enjoyed bird watching, I would have told you that I recently learned the names of all the bird species inhabiting this region from my current literary choice, *The Encyclopedia of Northern Missouri Birds*. I don't know why I used to feel the need to exaggerate every (okay, not every, but most) life events, funny stories, or even my skills and abilities. It never got me anything but trouble. My over-exaggeration is the catalyst that actually brought me here."

"Then maybe over-exaggerating isn't so bad after all," Chance said, stopping me mid-ramble.

"I can't see your expression right now, but I know you are smirking at me, Chance Alexander."

"You caught me! Yes, I am *smiling*, just like I smiled at you when you were looking for that silly mouse trap, or rescuing a lost dog, or talking about your therapist plant, or wearing an oversized hard hat and yes, even when you were angry at me and my grandmother. And I'm most definitely smiling now, as every thought in that beautiful head spews out of your sensuous mouth."

He pulled me to my feet and into his arms as we began to slow dance to the soft music filling the night air.

"You know what else I'd like to do?"

"No, what else would you like to do?" I asked, feeling my pulse quicken and my entire body tingle with anticipation.

"What I've been wanting to do since the first day I met you," he whispered in my ear as his warm breath trailed down my neck to my waiting lips, and he gently kissed me under the canopy of stars.

CHAPTER 33

Early the next week, I had stopped in at the Fresh Express Market to link up with Andre and pass along measurements for a giant blackboard to be hung on the wall directly behind the cash register. Its purpose was to advertise specials and seasonal offerings. Not having seen him lately, we spent a few minutes catching up, discussing the final touches needed before the reveal, and sharing rumors regarding future projects in the works.

At the conclusion of our conversation, I felt the phone in my pocket vibrate signaling an incoming call, and I excused myself. Even though I didn't recognize the number, I answered it, out of curiosity. It was Mr. Biggs' office requesting my presence at a meeting scheduled for Friday, one o'clock, in the USAMade Distribution Headquarters.

So here I sat, waiting for what? I had no idea.

"Ms. James," announced a smartly dressed woman from behind a combined teakwood and white laminate, curved reception desk (product No. 604999-7483 available on the USAMade website). "Mr. Biggs will see you now."

She ushered me into an office, not unlike Cassandra's, only missing the view.

"Have a seat, Jess," Mr. Biggs offered, pointing to a blue fabric captain's chair facing his solid oak executive desk.

"Nice to see you again, Mr. Biggs," I stated as I offered my hand in a formal greeting.

"Nice to see you also. And please, call me Larry," he said, shaking my hand. "I'm sure you've been wondering why I wanted to meet with you."

"It has crossed my mind," I said, practically choking on my nervous laughter.

"I have a proposition for you, young lady. You see, I have a new project in the works, and I feel you would be an excellent addition to the team."

My insides began to churn. It seemed that I had heard this exact same speech six months ago, and I began to grow uncomfortable with where this might be headed.

"I've been impressed with the designs you created at the three renovation sites, and I would like to hire you, not as an employee, but as a consultant, for my next venture. I need someone who can think beyond the standard."

Larry explained the project and the commitment that would be required. I would have access to USAMade's lawyers and accountants in setting up my own design business. Once the business was registered, USAMade would pay me a consultant fee (an amount beyond my wildest expectations) to make this new undertaking a reality. He would like me to join him with unlimited resources at my disposal, but also with a single catch – I must commit to staying in Marceline for a minimum of one year.

I was in love with the project, just not with the catch.

Cassandra had already made us aware that we would be moving, with USAMade, to Abilene, Kansas, where they had begun construction of their newest fulfillment center. Filming the next episodes of *Main Street* began right after the New Year, and I was already experiencing trepidation about continuing on with the show and working with Trevor as my boss. Larry had added to my discomfort by informing me that Samantha would be overseeing the construction of the new center in Abilene, so he could stay behind and coordinate his newest undertaking. So, if I stayed on as part of the *LeisureTV* crew, it would be both Trevor and Samantha I would have to answer to and, although I knew how to put on my big girl pants, I just didn't know if I wanted to.

Even though it was up to me to make the final decision, I decided to enlist the opinions of the people who mattered most in my life.

Calling Mom and Dad first, I got their reaction which, of course, included Granny's take on the proposal. Next, I text Mollie to hear her brutally honest thoughts, I discussed the plan with Kaitlin over dinner at Corner Café, consulted Cassandra, shared the proposal with Taylor and also had a deep discussion with Chance about staying another year in Marceline.

After entertaining each person's sentiments, I was still totally conflicted.

"I don't know, Mona," I lamented while sitting on the end of my couch, scratching behind Cooper's ears. "Everyone is encouraging me and agreeing about what a great opportunity I'm being afforded, but I've been mentally preparing to go back to Los Angeles. Staying in Missouri wasn't my plan. I have to give Larry Biggs my decision by tomorrow, and I'm just not sure."

For the first time, it didn't work. Mona was not helping me solve my dilemma. Actually, the only vibe I got from her was, 'I'm thirsty, can you please get me some water?'

I decided my only move was to call on the big dog!

I grabbed my keys and drove Betty to the one place I could think clearly – The Dreaming Tree.

I leaned against the base of the tree, as Walt Disney did so many years ago, and reflected on how far I had come and where I was going. I scanned through my life, from growing up in L.A. with Mollie and my family always by my side, to the best night of my life with Chance Alexander, sitting in sequins and silver heels on the tailgate of his truck while drinking cold beer, gazing at the stars, talking about our hopes and dreams, and ending with a kiss the likes I've never experienced, to … and that's where I got stuck.

I deliberated with myself for an hour as I listened to the birds chirp high in the trees that were turning shades of crimson, amber, and vibrant orange. I watched a squirrel search for a place to hide the walnut he would recover in the dead of winter and laughed at bunnies chasing each other across the open field.

And … I finally came to my decision.

• • •

It was the morning of the third, and final, reveal before *Main Street* moved to Kansas and began the process all over again. Taylor and I had arrived early to add some last-minute touches before owner, Omar Stanfield, with his son Winston and daughter Stella, were led down Kansas Avenue to be wowed (fingers crossed) by their new Fresh Express Market.

Out front, setting up his team, Jonathon signaled to Trevor that they were ready to roll.

As with the other two properties, Trevor, Andre, Larry and Samantha were on the sidelines, ready to give their critique at the end of taping. I text Lucy, and she started the process of leading the Stanfields in our direction.

Seeing the three of them walking down the street with what appeared to be large apples covering their eyes, I laughed to myself. We had decided to customize all the masks, now and in the future, to match the theme of the renovated establishment.

"Are you ready to see the new Fresh Express Market?" I asked as the foursome reached our small group waiting on the sidewalk.

"We're ready," they replied in unison.

"Alright then, remove your masks!" I announced.

As with the other two renovations, there was an excited gasp as they got their first look at the business' updated exterior.

"Dad, it's gorgeous," Stella said excitedly, grabbing her father's arm.

"I'm speechless," Omar replied, his eyes sparkling in the sunlight.

"We wanted the exterior to feel as fresh as the food within the market," I began with the formal reveal for the cameras, "that's why we've set two planter boxes containing citrus trees, one on each side of the entrance, to draw in patrons. These trees can survive in temperatures as low as five degrees Fahrenheit, so they only need to be moved indoors during a deep freeze. We will show you some ideas as to where they can be placed as decorations once we move inside."

I continued my narrative pointing out the most prominent changes. The brick façade had been altered into a glass, wrap-around front, where four bistro tables, two on each side of the entrance, could be seen through the full-length, gridded windows. Covering the inset entrance, a gray and white striped, concave awning had been added for a touch of color. Lastly, a custom, coir doormat, with *Fresh Express Market* stamped on it in black, sprung from a coarse tan background, providing a friendly greeting as customers entered the farm-to-table, organic food store.

The Stanfields seemed inordinately pleased with each enhancement and appeared equally excited to continue the tour and see what awaited them inside.

"Before we move to the interior of the market, I have an announcement I would like to share. I wanted to let you know that this will be my final episode hosting *Main Street*. It has been a pleasure and dream come true to be part of the transformations that have occurred up and down Marceline, Missouri's Main Street. I have enjoyed every minute of the experience."

Out of the corner of my eye, I caught the look of surprise on Lucy, Andre and especially Trevor's faces. Next to Trevor, Larry Biggs stood, broadly smiling, and gave me a brief nod of approval.

"I would also like to introduce you to Taylor Lubouski, *Main Street's* newest Rehab Design Specialist, who will be taking you on a journey through our next edition of *Main Street* from Abilene, Kansas."

I had passed the torch, or in this case, the microphone, to Taylor as she, and her boundless energy, guided the Stanfields inside their newly renovated market.

Standing alone on the sidewalk, I looked down Kansas Avenue with satisfaction, smiled, and turned toward home.

EPILOGUE
Nine Months Later

Chance tenderly grabbed my hand as we walked with other local residents out of the well-attended, monthly, City Council meeting. The town was abuzz over the evening's agenda for addressing the tourist explosion that had rocked Marceline in the last six months. Our favorite proposal – the addition of a versatile town trolley. The weekend trolley would loop down Main Street, provide transportation to Vista Vineyards, as well as offer hop on, hop off, stops at each Disney site along the way. Suggestions also included adding a local guide who could share stories and antidotes unknown to the average traveler or renting it out for evening events held at the winery – a kind of *Uber* trolley.

Reflecting over the numerous developments occurring in Marceline, I realized how closely my life had mirrored the town's, changing in ways I could have never imagined.

After agonizing over my decision to stay in Missouri, I had decided to take Larry Biggs up on his offer and form my own design company – *Dreaming Tree Designs*. And it had been a huge success, thanks to Larry and the fruition of his idea that included me as part of his team.

Larry had been working with a national organization to offer veterans, injured in the line of duty, an opportunity to work at

USAMade. Inside the fulfillment center, a section of the facility was to be refitted to accommodate wheelchairs, adjustable workstations, and voice recognition tools. The second part of the program was where Chance and I came in.

Unbeknownst to me, Jim Alexander had planned to retire after completion of the last Main Street renovation project, handing over the bulk of his business to Chance. (Truth: it was more of a semi-retirement since he was still on the Board and liberally gave Chance advice, whether he asked for it or not.) Larry had also contacted Chance, as the new head of Alexander Construction, to determine the feasibility of his idea. After much discussion, a plan was set in motion, and I was brought on board.

For the last nine months, Chance and I had the privilege to design, build, and decorate smart homes for veterans and their families employed by USAMade, allowing them to become the independent citizens they were prior to their injuries. It had been the most rewarding experience of my life! And what made it even better – the opportunity to work closely with Chance.

After our magical night under the stars, Chance had become the main fixture of my life, although Cooper still ran a close second. I had no idea how true love could fill every aspect of one's life with joy. I always saw it reflected in Mollie and Justin's happiness, but I never fully understood...until now.

Chance and I flew home for their wedding, where he met my friends and family, this time at an elegant reception rather than a Mickey Mouse-themed party. I had the feeling, by the time we left, they all liked Chance better than me. Not surprising, he also hit it off particularly well with Granny.

Mollie had text me last week to tell me she was doing well and that, the ultrasound showed it was a girl. I couldn't wait to spoil my future Goddaughter! Ida had already informed me that it was going to be a girl, but I didn't tell Mollie. I had asked Ida how she could possibly know an unborn baby's gender, from a thousand miles away, and she told me about some fancy means of predicting a baby's sex based on the placement of the moon, but I was confident she really had a vision or saw it in her crystal ball.

I couldn't wait for my parents to meet Ida. They were going to love her. Coming next month to visit me for the first time, they had decided to turn the trip into a long overdue vacation, slowly taking the same route I traveled over a year ago. *Just a year ago!*

It was hard to believe that I had not known the people, surrounding me now in this parking lot, my entire life. They treated me like family. As Ida always told me, 'Honey, we're a family in Marceline. When one person hurts, we all hurt, when one person's happy, we're all happy', and she couldn't have been more accurate.

Chance and I disentangled ourselves from the group outside the City Hall, quickly climbed into the cab of his truck and drove to Mulberry Street. I was lucky enough to make a deal with the owners of my cute little *Airbnb* and was now their official, long-term renter.

After letting Cooper out, I threw some popcorn in the microwave, grabbed a couple of drinks to take to Chance in the living room (where he had already turned the television to the correct station and was lounging comfortably on the couch in his usual spot, right next to Mona).

"Thanks," he said as I handed him his drink.

"Popcorn is still popping. Do you need anything else?" I asked.

"Just you," he said, pulling me into his lap and wrapping his strong arms around me.

"Miss it?" he asked.

We were watching the last episode of *Main Street–Abilene, Kansas*, hosted by the one and only, Taylor Lubouski.

"Not at all," I replied. "I love what I do. Besides, if I were there, I wouldn't be with you and that would have been the worst mistake I ever made. I love my life, but more importantly, I love you!"

"I love you too," he said, bringing his lips to mine for one of his intoxicatingly passionate kisses.

Unfortunately, at that same moment, not only did the microwave ding, but Cooper began incessantly barking to be let inside – apparently, he didn't want to miss the show, either.

"I guess that will have to wait for later," I said and laughed.

"Promise?"

"It's definitely a promise!" I replied, giving him my best seductive glance.

I retrieved Cooper, filled the popcorn bowls, and returned to the living room to find Cooper settled into his preferred spot – between his two favorite people.

The intro music signaled the opening of *Main Street*. We turned our attention to the screen in time to see Lucy escorting a masked couple to the front of a luxury hair salon.

"Are you ready to see the new *Transformations Hair Boutique*?" asked a buoyant Taylor.

The enthusiastic couple agreed in unison.

"Alright then, remove your masks!"

In front of the couple stood a classically designed entrance containing freshly painted, extra-tall, antique double doors with brass accents. They saw, for the first time, what had been staring at them all along – a treasure, that with a little love, shined in ways they never dreamed possible.

I could relate to that.

FROM THE DESK OF DIANE MANLEY

I hope you enjoyed my debut novel *The Wonderful World of Marceline* and that it made you smile and dream about what if … in the same way Walt Disney dreamed big ideas as a child in his small, rural town of Marceline.

Word-of-mouth is vital for an author to continue to grow readership. If you enjoyed the book, please leave a review on Amazon.com, even if it's just a sentence or two. That's how other readers find my books! Your reviews make a ton of difference!

Also, I love to connect with my readers, so join me on or at:
Facebook
Goodreads

Happy reading and Thank You for choosing my book.

Diane
July 2021

P.S. If you love "feel good" books (like I do!), I hope you'll add my next story, *The Key to Friendship: A Novel*, to your reading list. It's coming soon!

ACKNOWLEDGEMENTS

How does one recognize all of the people that cross their path and impact their life experiences both big and small? So many parts of this book are snippets taken from time spent with family, close friends and even acquaintances; be it from a memorable trip, a kid's sporting event, a night out with friends or a simple conversation. I have listened, laughed, and learned from so many people that it is impossible to thank all of you. But if you see yourself in part of this book, know you were in my heart, and I was broadly smiling as I shared with readers our time together.

First, I want to thank my dad. For several years he wanted to visit Marceline, Missouri, and see the town that shaped Walt Disney. Less than a three-hour drive from St. Louis, sadly few in our area had heard of the rural community, much less knew its story. I, regretfully, was one of those people. So, one sunny day, I packed up my parents and we headed northwest for the short trip. I love all things Disney (although would not consider myself a fanatic) and here was an opportunity to see where it all began. The museum, corner café, family home, barn, and especially the dreaming tree are truly inspiring and well worth visiting. In contrast, the actual city of Marceline, like so many small towns across the country, left me feeling melancholy. As the city's population in the region had declined so had the opportunities and businesses along Main Street. It made me wish there was a way to revitalize not just Marceline, but all the small towns where, years ago, trains stopped or riverboats anchored. And so, Jess, Mr. Biggs, and *LeisureTV* were born. The road trip that spring afternoon was much more moving than I could have ever imagined. For that, I would also like to thank the people of

Marceline who work tirelessly to preserve and improve their town's treasures and for sharing them with the rest of us!

A huge thanks to my family, especially my husband and kids, Greg, Ben and Brad, who teach me daily what is most important in life. To my immediate family, thank you for initially reading my manuscript and encouraging me to turn it into a book. To my in-laws' crew, thank you for the past and future Disney World memories. What adventures they have been!

I also want to thank Donna, Joan, Kathy, Linda, Nancy, Sherry, Tracy … (you know who you are) … for your contributions, big and small. If you look closely, you should see yourself in one of the characters or as part of their experiences.

Lastly, I would like to thank D. D., my editor, whose constructive criticism was always encouraging and positive and who has made this journey such a fun experience!

ABOUT THE AUTHOR

Diane Manley lives with her husband in the Greater St. Louis area. She enjoys traveling to different locations all over the country, but is always happy to return home to her beloved Missouri where she is currently at work on her second novel…

BOOKS BY THE AUTHOR

THE WONDERFUL WORLD OF MARCELINE

THE KEY TO FRIENDSHIP: A Novel

SANTA SATURDAY – An Ashwood Christmas Novella

EXCERPT FROM THE NEXT DIANE MANLEY NOVEL:

THE KEY TO FRIENDSHIP: A Novel

MEGYN

Hobbling around my apartment, looking for my other designer shoe, I wonder how it's possible for the same individual to be one personality at work and a completely different persona in her personal life? And to be successful at both!

Well, welcome to my world – the world of Megyn Ross! It's like I have a split personality where Professional Megyn and Personal Megyn are fighting for equal time inside my twenty-nine-year-old body.

There's Professional Megyn – neat to a fault with an organized workspace and alphabetized client folders, perfectly arranged on her computer's desktop, meeting each deadline on time or earlier than requested, climbing the corporate ladder, and earning the fat paycheck.

And then there's Personal Megyn – messy, with clothes strewn on every piece of furniture in her apartment, unable to find her phone or handbag as she rushes out the door, procrastinator extraordinaire never finishing a task or project, bargain hunter searching for 'too good to be true' deals in a game she must win ... and the list of contradictions goes on.

Over the years, this has made me a great employee, but the world's worst roommate. Which is why I currently live alone in an upscale, one-bedroom apartment overlooking the Power and Light District in Downtown Kansas City.

My two best friends, Claire and Paige, will reluctantly admit that surviving the experience of living with me has turned them into better people. Although, they are both happy it is a memory to laugh at rather than their current state of affairs.

Claire, now the mother of two little boys, says she can handle any at-home disaster after living with "Mayhem Megyn" for four years. And Paige claims, after rooming with me, she has mastered the art of patience and tolerance. *So, I figure, why change when my chaotic lifestyle has helped others?* Although, spending my morning looking for my missing taupe, Chloé mule is causing me to reevaluate that thought!

Tonight is our girls' night out, which is why Claire and Paige are on my mind as I search for my other shoe. No matter what happens during the month or how many times we've seen each other during the most recent thirty-day period, the last Friday of each month is set aside for the three of us – and just the three of us! We even made Claire plan her wedding and honeymoon so that they didn't land on the last weekend of the month. It's a pact we pinky-sweared to when moving to our own places, and one we plan to keep until we're old (like in our sixties and seventies).

Aha! – there it is peeking out from behind the trash can. This time, even I am baffled at how my shoe ended up in that spot!

I slip it on, grab my bag, dash out of my apartment and hurry for the elevator. I despise being late to work and looking for my shoe has put me behind. Now, rather than being an hour early, I'll only beat my co-workers by forty-five minutes. (Really, I don't go in early to impress anyone. I just accomplish more, uninterrupted in that first hour, than I do the rest of the morning.) For me, not being early, is being late ... and Professional Megyn detests being late to her job!

As the elevator dings to let me know it has reached my floor, I remember my leftovers are sitting on the refrigerator shelf in my kitchen. Sprinting back to my apartment, I quickly unlock the door, snag my lunch, jog back to the elevator, and am finally on my way downtown to my desk at Hanover Advertising.

Entering the newly-renovated Town Pavilion Building, I leave Personal Megyn outside in the early morning sunshine and immediately turn into Professional Megyn as I walk through the revolving doors into the spacious lobby with its polished concrete floors and bright white walls adorned with natural wood accents and video murals.

After making my way to the eighth floor, I pour a cup of coffee (*three sugars and one cream*) and head back to my desk to answer a few emails, review my schedule for the day and start my main task of analyzing the report data outlining current branding trends for our group's latest client.

To most people, scrutinizing data sounds incredibly boring (*and why I need copious amounts of sugar in my coffee*), but I find it fascinating. Digging into what entices people to buy products or determining the role images, logos, theme music and messaging play in maximizing sales are some of my favorite tasks as a Branding Specialist at Hanover.

The group's individual findings are being compiled today in preparation for next week's presentation by our team leader to *Bongo,* a new video game developer looking to break into a very tight market. I decide to scan my report one last time, before handing it in, verifying the research backs my conclusions on how to best reach *Bongo's* target market.

"Hey, Megyn, is that report almost ready?"

So engrossed in proofing the final copy, I nearly jump out of my chair at the sound of Brandon's voice booming in my right ear.

"How many times do I have to tell you not to sneak up on me?" I say, swiveling my chair to face the source of my agitation.

"When do you think the last time was that I could sneak up on someone?" Brandon, my 6'4" colleague, asks, followed by one of his famous belly laughs.

"About ten seconds ago," I say, catching my breath.

"I've never met anyone as laser focused as you, Megyn. Didn't your mother teach you to be aware of your surroundings?"

"Yes, when I'm alone in a parking lot, not when I'm trying to work at my desk!"

"You can never be too careful. Maybe I'm really a bad guy you need to keep an eye on."

"You are a bad guy ... you're keeping me from finishing this report," I say, giving him a playfully evil stare. "If you let me get back to work, I'll have it for you in about fifteen minutes."

"Perfect!"

• • •

After filing my report, I spend the remainder of the morning cleaning up the *Bongo* files, reviewing a couple of new leads, and readying myself for the afternoon meeting I've willed myself not to dwell on since waking up this morning.

Today marks my five-year review with Bob Gottinger, my immediate supervisor. At Hanover, employees typically either move up or out at the five-year mark. I've never had a bad review, but this is a big one! And I am *NERVOUS!*

I barely eat two bites of the leftover grilled chicken I retrieved from my apartment this morning and nod in the appropriate places as Brandon tells me a story about ... *hmmm* ... and I realize I have no idea what he's been saying throughout our entire lunchbreak.

Returning to my desk, I gather my tablet to take notes during the dreaded meeting, although I'm not sure what notes I could possibly need to take unless it's steps for clearing out my desk and visiting HR one last time.

STOP IT!

Taking, what seems like the longest walk of my life down the office corridor, I inhale a deep breath and knock lightly on Mr. Gottinger's open door.

"Come in, Megyn…"

• • •

"Sorry I'm late," I say, rushing to our usual high-top table at Tres Amigos on the Plaza.

It's after 5 o'clock, which means Personal Megyn has returned in full force for Girls' Night Out.

It also means – Happy Hour! Not only does Tres Amigos have the best margaritas in the city, but the festive-colored stucco walls, arched niches filled with authentic pottery and artwork, and vibrant hand-painted chairs can make even the toughest week ease from my mind and bring me to my happy place. My personal *la silla* ('chair' being one of the few words I still remember from high school Spanish), designed with two toucans enjoying life in a garden of vibrant flowers on its back panel, and a fishbowl margarita are waiting for me.

Claire and Paige take a break from their conversation as I plop into my seat, place a small shopping bag next to my chair, and sip the 'Margarita on the Rocks – No Salt'.

"I got stuck in William Sonoma."

"What were you doing in William Sonoma?' asks Claire. "You don't cook."

"They're having a drawing for this top-of-the-line knife set, and I needed to put my name in to win," I say, taking another sip of my drink. "This margarita is really good!"

"Double shot," adds Paige. "But once again, need we remind you, you don't cook!"

"So why do you need a knife set? Don't you still get those organic meals delivered?" asks Claire, who left dinner cooking in the oven with explicit instructions for Carson about meal, bath and bedtime for their two boys.

"Yes, but sometimes they make you cut the carrots and cauliflower sent with the meals."

"And you need a top-of-the-line knife set to cut a few vegetables?" she asks, apparently not ready to let me off the hook.

"It doesn't matter, you know I never win! Anyway, I felt guilty about filling out the slip for the free knives and then walking out the door, so I nosed around for a few minutes. Look at these cute, holiday, cast-iron cookies stamps I found on clearance," I say, proudly pulling a package out of the shopping bag next to my chair and showing them a box covered in pictures of beautiful reindeer, ornaments, and snowflake cookies.

Looking at each other, then looking at me, my two best friends loudly chime in unison, "But, you...don't...cook!"

"I know, I know, but this year I'm going to make Christmas cookies. Really," I say to the two skeptical faces staring back at me.

Rapidly changing the subject (because deep down, I know they are right), I thank them for securing my unofficially reserved chair. "Did you have to steal it from someone like last month?"

"No, luckily it was available. Although I'm surprised they let us back in here after the scene you made retrieving your 'signature *la silla*' from that cute guy who was sitting in it."

"It was not a scene, Claire. That is what's called flirting, and it worked because we went out last weekend."

"That's who you went out with Saturday night?" Claire asks, astonished.

"Where did you go, and how did I not know about this before now?" Paige probes, sounding slightly offended that Claire knew about my date and she was just now being informed of an event on my social calendar.

I love Claire and Paige like sisters, but Claire is married, and Paige is engaged so, when they aren't living vicariously through my social life, they are hounding me to find 'Mr. Right', which can get a little annoying since I'm in no way looking to settle down.

"It was no big deal. We went to the Royals game, that's all. He ordered nachos for me as a joke and then offered to switch with someone in another row if my seat wasn't acceptable," I say, rolling my eyes.

"Sounds like he has a sense of humor. Sooo?" Paige inquires in that 'give us all the details' voice of hers.

"It was ok. He wasn't really my type."

"He was gorgeous," Claire counters. "How could he not be your type? Your problem, Megyn, is you're afraid of commitment."

"We have been through this a million times ... I am not afraid of commitment."

"You're not afraid of commitment, because that would mean seeing someone more than once. You know what you have, you have relationshipphobia. No, actually you have seconddatephobia."

Paige, Queen of the Google Search, grabs her phone and starts frantically typing.

"I found it," she announces in record time. "Philophobia, the fear of falling in love – that's what you have!"

"I do not have 'Phillyphobia' or whatever it is you said. I like being single! I'm having fun and concentrating on my career. Is that so bad?"

"You've got to hear some of these other phobias," Paige says and chuckles, completely ignoring me since I am not sharing any juicy date details.

"Who knew that metrophobia is the fear of poetry. I mean, are there really people who are afraid of rhyming words?" She giggles. "Okay, guess what this one is, omphalophobia."

"The fear of *Charlie and the Chocolate Factory* workers?" I venture, taking what I believe is a reasonable guess.

"Those weren't Omphalos they were Oompa-Loompas," Claire says and laughs, punching my arm like we're kids watching the movie, and I'm not paying close enough attention.

"Give up?"

Claire and I nod our heads, encouraging Paige to continue.

"It's the fear of belly buttons."

The three of us roar with laughter and, as typically happens when we get together, the silliness begins.

"So, what's it called if I'm afraid of someone reading a poem about innies and outies?" I ask, taking a large sip of my drink.

"Normal," Claire replies.

Her dry sense of humor makes me nearly choke as I attempt to swallow another gulp of my drink.

"How about a-ra-chi ... bu-ty-ro phobia," Paige says, phonetically sounding out the word.

"Fear of the alphabet?" Claire speculates.

"Now that's just ridiculous, Claire. Who would be afraid of letters?" Paige chuckles. "It's the fear of peanut butter sticking to the roof of your mouth, which is so much more rational!"

"Who makes up this stuff?" she exclaims while she continues reading. "Here's a good one, *optophobia is the fear of opening one's eyes, which can be extremely debilitating.* You think?! Or how about ablutophobia the fear of bathing, and plutophobia, the fear of money. Do you think these are for real?"

"I don't know, but I can tell you I don't have plutophobia. I had my five-year review today, and I'm definitely not afraid of the possible promotion and raise they offered," I announce, changing the subject from the absurd back to real life.

"I can't believe I forgot to ask! I know you were stressing about meeting with your boss. I guess if they are offering you a promotion, it went great," Claire surmises.

"Yeah, really great! Mr. Gottinger has been impressed with my research and David, our team leader, even gave me credit for the theme we're pitching to *Bongo,* the new video game company I told you about. Since *Bongo* is the company's name, I suggested we use Todd Rundgren's song *Bang on the Drum* and alter the lyrics slightly to 'I don't want to work, I want to play on my games all day'. It gives a fun vibe gamers can relate to."

"No wonder he liked it, it's really clever," Paige says admiringly.

"I researched the copyright issues as well as what effect the song has on our brains. Did you know studies show listening to exciting music increases our heart and breathing rates, and causes adrenaline to enter the bloodstream? That's why we use music in advertising, to entice customers to buy a product. The consumer wants to feel the way they do when they hear the song and subconsciously think if they buy the product, the feeling will continue."

"You used to be fun, Megyn, now you're just getting boring," Claire teases.

"Well, Mr. Gottinger didn't deem it boring because, based on my performance lately, he offered me a chance to direct my own team. Which means a possible promotion and raise! I've been made Lead on our next pitch and, if it goes well, I'm movin' up!"

Once again, we revert to our younger days as Paige and Claire scream with excitement, like tweens seeing their favorite pop star.

"So, what do you have to pitch to earn this big promotion and therefore start picking up the tab for our nights out?" Paige inquires.

"I lucked out. It's Glitz Cosmetic Company who wants to rebrand their entire line."

"That's perfect for you!" agrees Claire as she and Paige begin throwing out ideas that become more outrageous with each concept.

When their campaign slogan becomes 'Glitz Cosmetics – beauty solutions for homemakers to hos', I finally stop them, at which point I inform them that they are not welcome on my team, thank you very much!

We order some food and another margarita (single shot) and spend the rest of the evening talking nonstop, as always. Claire about her boys. Paige *not* about her wedding (which keeps getting pushed off – I've quit asking why), and me about work.

"You know, in a few months, we'll practically be able to order off the senior menu," declares Claire sarcastically. "I can't believe we are about to turn THIRTY! What happened to our youth?"

"I know," Paige agrees. "I try not to think about it, but this birthday is really bothering me. THIRTY, it sounds so old."

"It is old! You can't do something irresponsible and blame it on being young anymore," I add. "We should do something exotic to celebrate the passing of our youth. I know, let's each of us come up with an idea and, next month, we'll pick the best plan for a big celebration."

We all agree to conjure up an exciting suggestion for ushering in a new decade as we gather our individual bills and move to the checkout counter.

We're going home at the exact time we used to head out for the evening! We are getting old, I decide, as I try to determine if I'm tired and want to go back to my apartment and curl up with a good book or meet up with some other friends at a bar closer to home.

As we walk out the door, I drop my business card into the large, hand-painted glass jar sitting next to the cash register.

"You do that every month, and have you ever won the free dinner?" asks Paige.

"Nope. I keep trying, but sadly, I never win anything."

"Oh wait! My package," I say and rush back to retrieve the William Sonoma bag (containing the cookie stamps I'll more than likely never use), which was still sitting next to my 'signature *la silla'*.

I walk with Claire and Paige to our cars, give them each a hug goodnight, and decide to head back to my apartment.

Made in the USA
Monee, IL
19 July 2025

21456929R00184